WHAT READERS ARE SAYING...

ABOUT JOSLYN CHASE

"Author Joslyn Chase has now confirmed my first impressions of her being a formidable suspense writer bound to make readers sit up and take notice." ~ **Amazon reader**

"Joslyn Chase's storytelling prowess transcends mere excitement; it ventures into the realm of inspiration, reminding us of the power of narrative artistry." ~ **Conrad Bux, author of *Killer Witness***

"Author Joslyn Chase expertly weaves high-stakes action with complex character development to please readers who want a fully-rounded novel." ~ **Reader's Favorite**

"As always in her writing, the settings and action scenes are vividly portrayed and the relationships between the characters are seamless and authentic. Ms Chase has a talent for bringing characters to life." ~ **ReadnGrow**

"There is a reason Chase is an award-winning author. Highly recommended." ~ **Justin Boote, author of *Badass***

"The author is a great storyteller." ~ **AstraDaemon**

"Joslyn Chase skillfully connects subplots, then injects a few surprises, then connects things again in an interesting cycle; weave, disassemble, repeat." ~ **Ron Keeler, Read 4 Fun**

"In the movie Field of Dreams, there is a now famous line, "If you build it, they will come." Apply this sentiment to Joslyn Chase—if she writes it, we will come and read it." ~ **William DeProspo, author of *Unlikely Outcome***

"Joslyn Chase paints intriguing pictures with vivid, colorful descriptions...you feel like you have a front row seat from which to watch as everything unfolds." ~ **Amazon reader**

Get your next Joslyn Chase book free!

But catch up on your sleep now.

Once you start reading, it'll be *No Rest* for you!

Get the book free when you join the growing group of readers who've

discovered the thrill of Chase!

Get started now at joslynchase.com

OR

simply scan the QR code below

ALSO BY JOSLYN CHASE

Nocturne in Ashes

Staccato Passage

Cincher's Waltz

Steadman's Blind

The Steadman Mysteries series

The Tal Bannerman Thriller series

The Cathryn Harcourt Mystery Shorts

The Historic Suspense series

Rapid Pursuit

The Tower

The Devil's Trumpet

Falling For The Lost Dutchman

No Rest

What Leads a Man to Murder

Death of a Muse

Crimes Upon a Midnight Clear

Christmas Crime Stories to Bring You Home for the Holidays

Joslyn Chase

Paraquel Press

CRIMES UPON A MIDNIGHT CLEAR

CHRISTMAS CRIME STORIES TO BRING YOU HOME FOR THE HOLIDAYS

Paraquel Press paperback edition, published by Paraquel Press, 2025

https://paraquelpress.mailerpage.com

ISBN: 978-1-952647-42-0 (softcover)   978-1-952647-41-3 (ebook)
978-1-952647-47-5 (audiobook)

Library of Congress Control Number: 2025917163

Excerpt from *Steadman's Blind*, copyright © 2019 by Joslyn Chase

"Mall Cop Christmas Parade" was first published in *Alfred Hitchcock's Mystery Magazine*, Jan/Feb 2024

"Santa's Eyes" was first published in *Alfred Hitchcock's Mystery Magazine*, Jan/Feb 2025

"Green Storm Rising" was first published in *Breakneck*, Paraquel Press, 2022

"Incredible Christmas Capers" was first published in *Pulphouse Fiction Issue #36*, December 2024

CRIMES UPON A MIDNIGHT CLEAR

Publisher's Cataloging-in-PublicationData

Names: Chase, Joslyn.

Title: Crimes upon a midnight clear : Christmas crime stories to bring you home for the holidays / Joslyn Chase.

Description:University Place, WA : ParaquelPress, 2025.

Identifiers: LCCN 2025917163 | ISBN9781952647420 (pbk.) | ISBN 9781952647413(ebook) | ISBN 9781952647475 (audiobook)

Subjects: LCSH:Crime – Fiction. | Christmas stories. | BISAC: FICTION / Crime. | FICTION / Thrillers / Crime. | FICTION / Holidays.

Classification: LCC PS3603.H37 C75 2025| DDC 813 C--dc23

LC record available at https://lccn.loc.gov/2025917163

CONTENTS

Introduction — 1

Mall Cop Christmas Parade — 4

Santa's Eyes — 20

Green Storm Rising — 41

Incredible Christmas Capers — 77

And To All A Good Night — 88

A Very Krampus Christmas — 127

Silver Secrets, Crimson Ties — 146

Duet For Piano & Chisel — 180

Cold Busted — 217

Solution — 220

Bowling in the New Year — 221

Sample from Steadman's Blind — 234

About the Author — 250

INTRODUCTION

Home for the holidays.

It reaches across cultural differences and religious diversity. It transcends feuds and family vendettas. It stands independent of demographics or personal circumstances. I speak of the primal drive within each of us to be home—meaning among loved ones—at special times.

It's the comfort food of companionship.

Life, however, doesn't always arrange things to conveniently accommodate the human longing to be home for the holidays. I didn't watch a lot of television growing up, but one of my sharpest childhood TV memories is the scene from *Happy Days* when Fonzie heats a can of ravioli over a hotplate and dines alone on Christmas Eve.

Any number of factors can interfere with the desire to be home and among loved ones for Christmas. Job demands might figure into it. Geographical and economic challenges might get in the way. War, disease, death, divorce, or family discord may play a part.

In this book, the common factor is crime.

Sheriff's Deputy Randall Steadman is the hero of the full-length thriller, *Steadman's Blind*. He also features in two of the short stories in this collection.

"And To All a Good Night," takes Steadman and his wife, Vivi, to a friend's mountain retreat for Christmas. Vivi's fear that it will be a busman's holiday is justified when a murderer strikes, calling Steadman to work outside his jurisdiction to solve the crime.

With Vivi by his side, Steadman considers himself home for the holidays. But someone else at the retreat has come home to kill.

The other Steadman story, "Silver Secrets, Crimson Ties," keeps Steadman busy over the holidays with a murder to solve and a Christmas festival on hold until he does.

In "Santa's Eyes," a recently divorced young woman faces Christmas alone, with only her suspicions about a rogue department store Santa to keep her company. In this case, crime may be the key to bringing her home for the holiday.

"Mall Cop Christmas Parade" is all about one man's quest to get home for Christmas. He's just got one tiny thing to pick up at the mall first.

"Incredible Christmas Capers" takes you right up close for a unique and unpredictable home invasion experience you won't soon forget.

In a very special collaboration mystery, "Duet for Piano and Chisel" brings my series characters Riley Forte and David Peeler together, pooling their skills to crack a case that will keep you guessing to the end.

"A Very Krampus Christmas" brings Homeland Security agent, Tal Bannerman, into the action when he and his partner attempt to pull off a wacky heist during a crime boss's Christmas party.

And Tal Bannerman is back for more off-the-wall and high-stakes action in "Green Storm Rising," a zany little thriller set near the town of North Pole, Alaska—very far from home and family.

But someone's got to keep the world safe so others can enjoy Christmas at home.

And in the spirit of the season, I've got a couple extra gifts for you. I included a mini-mystery for you to solve. Have fun with it but don't peek at the answer until you've given it your best shot!

And to round off the holiday season, there's a bonus story for the New Year, inspired by actual events because truth really can be stranger than fiction.

Get ready to kick back and settle in for these stories full of Christmas treats and surprises. You'll feel right at home for the holidays.

Joslyn Chase

Bavaria, Germany

Mall Cop Christmas Parade

The boisterous noise of a reveling crowd broke over Bradford Hines like a smashing wave on the surf as he left the mall restroom and turned toward the fountain at the heart of the shopping superstructure. The buzz of excited patrons with their armfuls of rustling bags rose and fell like the murmuring sea. An occasional shout of glee floated overhead, reminding Brad of a seagull's call, and above it all, the holiday carol soundtrack played in imitation of a constant ocean breeze.

Christmas in California.

In the river flow of mall traffic, Brad got caught behind a family of six. Mom pushed a stroller laden with purchases and holding a small screaming bundle wearing a red knit hat with antlers. The three older children shouted jubilantly along to *Rudolph the Red-Nosed Reindeer,* erupting with "Like a light bulb!" at random intervals.

Brad felt a pang. His own three little ones were in Maryland, waiting for him to come home for Christmas. He did not intend to disappoint them.

He passed a shop styled like a Swiss chalet and the tempting aroma of roasting sugared nuts made his stomach growl. He thought about stopping, but wanted to finish his business here and get to the airport on time. Pressing on toward the crossroads, he made his way to the busiest part of the mall, adjacent to the food court and packed with a swarm of people.

An enormous Christmas tree rose majestic beside the fountain, trimmed with red velvet bows, pine cones, and gold beads. Tiny lights twinkled from its evergreen branches like merry points of starlight and a myriad of elves beneath it handed out coupons and invitations to sales events.

Brad stopped beside a pillar and let the crowd surge past him. Pulling a phone from his jeans pocket, he pretended interest in it while surreptitiously studying the hoard of shoppers. In this mass of humanity it was almost too easy to find what he wanted. Slipping back into the stream, he navigated toward an Asian gentleman browsing a jewelry kiosk. The man's jacket gaped open as he leaned over to examine pieces that caught his eye.

His wallet was ripe for the picking.

Joggling into the Asian man, Brad apologized and let the crowd carry him away in its momentum. He had the wallet, and it felt fat with goodies. Strolling casually through the food court, he stopped as if considering his choice between pizza and fried chicken. He thumbed quickly through the brown leather wallet, noting the wad of cash, the row of credit cards.

And something else interesting. It appeared to be a postage stamp but felt stiffer and looked a little off-color. Like an LSD blotter. Brad tucked the tiny bit of paper away for later and pocketed the wallet.

As he neared the exit, he wondered how quickly he could summon an Uber to take him to the airport. Three steps before he reached the glass doors edged with silver-frosted snowflakes, a hand grasped his shoulder and he turned to see a woman, her red hair pulled into a no-nonsense bun at the back of her head.

"Stop right there, sir," she said, without a trace of holiday cheer. "You need to come with me."

Brad's heart did a little double-thump in his chest. He hadn't seen this woman when he'd surveyed the crowd. But clearly, she'd seen him.

"I don't think so," he told her, shifting his weight toward the exit. "I have a plane to catch."

Her grip on his shoulder tightened and she tilted her head, drawing his gaze to the blouse beneath her jacket where he caught a glimpse of a shoulder holster.

She was armed. He wasn't.

"Mall security," she said, flashing an ID card. "We need to talk."

Brad weighed his options and decided to go with the woman, avoid a scene, a chase, the empty threat of a bullet in the back. Mall cops don't shoot pickpockets, do they?

She led him to a table at the edge of the food court and motioned him into a chair.

"If you're straight with me," she said, "we can handle this nice and easy. Here and now."

She sat very upright in her chair, glaring at him with narrowed eyes. Brad judged her to be about thirty, pale skin, no freckles. She had a pointy nose that combined with her reddish hair to create the impression of a fox, and her green eyes, too close together, gave the otherwise pretty face a feral look.

She crossed her arms over her chest. "You need to work on your technique."

Brad mirrored her body language. "I don't know what you mean."

"Come off it," she snorted. "I saw you take the wallet from that Asian man at the jewelry counter. There's no point denying it."

The look she gave him was a challenge to do exactly that, but he didn't oblige. After a moment, she laid one hand on the table, palm up, inviting him to hand over the wallet.

Briefly, Brad mulled over possible courses of action. Sighing, he pulled the wallet from his jacket and placed it in her open hand.

"You're right. I'm sorry. In the spirit of the season, can we consider the matter closed?" he pleaded. "I have a family to get home to—my wife, three small children. Please don't ruin Christmas for them."

Pursing her lips, the woman stared at Brad for almost a full minute. She peeked into the wallet, making sure he hadn't swiped the money and credit cards.

"I suppose—in the spirit of the season—I can return the wallet to the owner and let you off with a warning. But if I ever see you in this mall again, you're toast," she warned, giving him a nasty look with her green close-set eyes.

"Of course," Brad promised. "You won't see me here again." He rose from the table. "Thank you."

The woman stood also, giving him a tight smile. They stepped away from each other and once more Brad started toward the exit doors. He hadn't gone three steps when two men in mall cop uniforms closed in, blocking the way.

"We got 'em," one of the men said into his radio.

Brad's head reeled a little but he didn't put up a fight. His path to the airport was getting bumpier by the second.

The Little Drummer Boy played in the background as static burst over the security man's radio, followed by something Brad couldn't make out.

The larger of the two mall cops, whose badge identified him as Ronald Moore, nodded as if the man on the receiving end could see him. "We're bringing them in now."

"All right," said the other security officer, Duncan Samuels. "Let's take a walk. Whatever the two of you are trying to pull, it stops now."

Moore, a man with the color and build of a brick wall, placed a firm hand on Brad's arm while the smaller man gripped the red-haired woman by the elbow.

"Don't give us any trouble," he warned. "Let's go down to the office and see if we can clear this up."

As they pressed through the holiday crowd, Brad reached for his phone and hit a number on speed dial. He started to speak, but Moore removed the phone from his hand and ended the call, sliding the phone into his own pocket.

"I'll pass this on to the police and they can decide whether to let you use it."

They crossed in front of the Swiss chalet again but now the smell of roasting nuts made Brad's stomach do a slow turn in his gut, all appetite erased. He thought of Bonnie, his wife, and the kids at home. He thought of the 747 that would be leaving without him.

Turning down a corridor, they passed through a thick metal door that closed behind them, instantly dampening the cheery noise of the masses. The room was dim, light kept low to facilitate viewing on the bank of monitors stretching the length of one wall. Two additional men in uniform sat in swivel chairs, ignoring their arrival, eyes glued to the screens.

"Have a seat." Moore's words were an order rather than in invitation. Brad sat. The woman hesitated, her chin jutting out in silent protest before she sank slowly into one of the molded plastic chairs against the wall. A row of paper snowflakes taped to the cinder block fluttered a little in the breeze of a ceiling ventilator.

"First, let's have the wallet," Samuels said. He held out a hand toward the woman.

"I don't know what you're talking about," she said, her tone glacial.

"You don't know what we're talking about?" Moore turned to one of the men at the monitors. "Cue up that video, Al. Let's have another look."

Brad watched himself on the grainy playback, moving toward the Asian man, slipping the wallet from his jacket and disappearing into the crowd. He shuddered. The woman was right—he needed to work on his technique.

"Al catches that on the video," Samuels said, "and gives us a shout-out on the radio. But before we can work our way through the crowd, he sees *this* on a different monitor."

The view switched to the food court, Brad and the woman at a table, the wallet changing hands.

"And that's what we're talking about," Moore said. "The wallet, please."

Brad cleared his throat. "She's carrying," he warned. "You might want to make that your priority."

Instant tension filled the room. Moore's face went from brick to stone. Hard and gray.

The woman raised her arms above her head. "I don't have a weapon," she said, giving Brad a poisonous look. Samuels moved forward, flicking open the woman's jacket to reveal the shoulder holster. Empty.

But the wallet was there too, in an inner pocket, and Samuels took it. He poked through it, nodding when he saw the money and plastic still in place.

"Okay," Moore said, "we're shutting down your little duo act. I suggest you each get your own lawyer and stay the hell apart."

The woman leaned back in her chair and crossed her arms, staring at the ceiling as if cursing the moon. "We are not a duo."

"Damn right we're not," Brad agreed. "I don't know who she is and I wish we'd never met."

A metallic click sounded and the door opened. A blonde woman in uniform entered, laden with bags from the food court.

"Lunch is served," she announced.

As the security team gathered around the bags to collect their lunch items, Brad leaned over to the red-haired woman, giving her a hard glare.

"Why'd you tell me you were security?"

She glared back. "This is my turf. Find your own mall."

Moore and Samuels sat at a table with the blonde, eating lunch. Al and his partner kept their places at the bank of monitors, watching while they munched. Brad sneaked a peek at his watch.

Samuels saw the gesture. "You in a hurry?" he asked.

"I got a plane to catch."

The group at the table laughed. Moore pointed a burrito at Brad. "No plane for you, son."

"Soon as we're done eating," Samuels said, "we're calling the cops. Maybe they'll be kind enough to drop you at the airport."

Amid snickers, the door clicked open again and two men entered. The security team jumped to their feet, clearly surprised.

One of the men, a distinguished-looking Asian in a custom-tailored dark blue suit, held a gun. He turned it in Brad's direction, motioning him and the redhead to their feet.

"We'll take it from here," he told the room.

"Who are you?" Moore asked. "And how did you get in here?"

The Asian turned an expressionless face to Moore and his team. "We're from corporate," he said. "We got word you apprehended two members of the Kaplin gang."

His companion, a burly man with a blond ponytail and muscles barely contained within the strained seams of his gray suit jacket, rounded on Brad and his supposed accomplice like a sheep dog driving his flock.

The Asian smiled approvingly. "This is above your pay grade, gentlemen. And lady." He bowed to the female member of the security team. "No need to call the police. We'll deal with this internally. The wallet, please."

He held out his hand and Samuels promptly handed off the wallet.

"And now," said the Asian, 'we'll take our leave. Merry Christmas."

He gave another small bow and gestured with the gun for Brad and the redhead to exit the room. The burly man wrapped a hand the size of a baseball glove around Brad's upper arm as if the gun was not enough encouragement to keep him moving.

Deeper into the bowels of the mall they went, taking a narrow flight of stairs downward. Brad didn't know who these new players were, but he felt sure about one thing—they weren't from corporate. A chill feathered down his back.

"How did you do that?" he asked the Asian. "Just get them to hand over the wallet and turn us out?"

"Ancient Chinese secret," said the blond man. "I get a kick out of it every single time."

The Asian pressed his lips together in a prim, self-satisfied smile. "I used a simple pattern interrupt. Surprise creates suggestibility, allowing authoritative demeanor to carry the day."

"They'll be second-guessing themselves now," Brad said.

"Yes," the Asian agreed. "But the chickens have flown the coop. You are now in our hands."

The ponytailed blond stopped at a service door, pushing it open to reveal an underground loading area. He prodded Brad toward a waiting panel van with a dry cleaning logo on the side. The engine started as they approached and Brad caught a glimpse of another Asian, young with a pencil mustache, behind the wheel.

Ponytail rolled open the side door of the van. "Get in," he said, giving Brad a shove.

Brad and the redhead climbed in and sat down on the bare metal floor. She scowled at him as if this was his fault. He scowled back. If she hadn't stepped in, he'd be boarding a plane to Baltimore right about now.

Instead, he had no idea where he'd be by the end of the day.

The van pulled forward, moving fast, and Brad's heart revved, keeping time with the engine. They headed up a slope and breached daylight, making a left turn into busy Christmas traffic. Ponytail sat on the floor, too. He'd pulled a gun from somewhere on his person and sat holding it almost casually in his lap, a bemused smile on his lips.

They drove for roughly twenty minutes in what Brad thought was a northerly direction. The road thrummed away beneath them, sending vibrations up through the metal floor into every nerve-ending in Brad's body. The pounding of his heart had gone from overdrive to somewhere around fourth gear when he looked toward the front passenger seat and saw the Asian searching through the wallet.

Brad guessed he was looking for something more than money and credit cards. He watched the man pull the wallet apart, then bark an order at the driver. The van pulled to an abrupt stop.

Apparently he hadn't found what he was looking for.

The door rolled open and Brad caught a peek at a strip of forest land, pines and maples. He smelled piles of damp, dead leaves, dissolving into the loamy earth. He saw the Asian's face, grim and determined.

"Where is it?"

And that's when Brad accepted he might not make it home for Christmas.

Might not make it home at all.

"I don't know what you're talking about," the woman said.

Ponytail pulled on her bun, sending her hair tumbling to her shoulders. He took a handful and yanked.

"I don't know what you want!" she shrieked, her eyes going wide with pain and fear.

The Asian turned his gaze to Brad.

"I don't know either," Brad said. "I clearly picked the wrong man to pickpocket. It was a random choice, a bad one."

"You don't know how bad," the Asian told him. He gestured to his goon and Ponytail shoved the woman aside and focused his attentions on Brad, grabbing his right hand in a bone-breaking grip.

"I can see the wallet is very important to you," Brad managed to say through gritted teeth. "But I really have no idea why."

The Asian nodded and Ponytail applied pressure to Brad's middle finger, snapping it like a pencil. He groaned, felt sweat break out on his forehead.

"We're not members of the gang you're looking for," he said. "You have to believe me."

Ponytail laughed. The Asian said, "I do believe you. We know you are not members of a gang. You spy for the FBI."

"What!" Brad sputtered, shaking his head. "I'm a carpet cleaner. That's all." He hesitated. "And a part-time pickpocket."

"Enough!" The Asian slammed his fist against the side of the van. "The man you stole the wallet from is Kang Bolin."

Brad stifled a moan. His finger throbbed like a son of a gun. "The name means nothing to me."

"He works for Chinese Intelligence," the Asian said. "For the Ministry of State Security. He's been leaking Chinese national secrets to you."

"No! You're mistaken," Brad said. He fought down a wave of nausea. "Boy, am I having a bad day."

"Your day is about to get much worse."

The Asian tipped his head and Ponytail grasped another finger. Brad tensed, preparing for another jolt of searing pain, but before the breaking pressure was applied, he heard the *blat-blat* of helicopter blades and swirls of dust danced up from the ground.

A voice came through the chopper's loudspeaker.

"This is the FBI."

"Surrender your weapons immediately and exit the vehicle with your hands up," the voice commanded.

Ponytail dropped Brad's hand but kept a firm grip on his shoulder. The helicopter dropped lower and Brad felt the force of the wind generated by its whirring blades. The sound bouncing off his eardrums rocked him—an auditory assault, but a welcome one.

And then another sound pierced through the barrage. Sharper. Louder.

Gunfire.

The young Asian driver ran for the woods, firing skyward at the helicopter as he went. A series of shots rang out from the chopper and the man fell, sprawling to the earth. He didn't move.

Three black SUVs squealed to a stop behind the white panel van. Their doors flew open and six FBI agents emerged, taking cover behind the open doors.

"Drop your weapons! Step away from the vehicle and keep your hands where I can see them," ordered one of the agents, a man with a deep raspy voice. Brad squinted through the glaring light and swirling dust. He saw the Asian in the dark blue suit standing with his hands raised, a gun at his feet.

The woman jumped out of the van, presenting her empty hands like a game show hostess displaying a prize. Brad took a step forward. Ponytail's hands dropped to his center of gravity and shoved hard, catapulting Brad from the van.

He hit the dirt and rolled to a stop. The white panel van roared to life, tearing down the road with Ponytail at the wheel. The helicopter followed, spewing bullets.

Brad watched the van fishtail, swerving off the road. It dipped and crashed into a stand of pines, coming to an abrupt standstill with one of its wheels suspended above the surface soil, spinning.

"You, on the ground!" the deep-voiced agent shouted. "Put your hands where I can see them."

Brad, on his belly in the dirt, raised his hands, showing them empty. Immediately, an agent was on him, securing his hands, shackling his wrists.

"Watch it!" Brad shouted, wincing. "That thug broke my finger."

The agent yanked him to his feet, ignoring the plea for gentleness. Brad stood, shaking with adrenaline, finger throbbing, flanked by the FBI.

A female agent held the red-head by one arm. The hair Ponytail had loosed fell across her face, veiling it from Brad's view, but he figured she was giving him the stink-eye. She was cuffed like him, hands behind her, enclosed by clanking hardware.

Three agents surrounded the Asian who stood with expressionless face, wrists similarly cuffed. With the helicopter's noise fading into the distance, Brad was able to pick out pieces of the conversation.

"...got Gong Wei at last."

"...commendation for this one, no doubt."

"...for interrogation, but what about the other two?"

"...Christmas in county lockup."

Brad watched agents load the Asian, presumably Gong Wei, into the back of one of the SUVs. Red-head climbed into another, and agents on either side of him led Brad to the third.

"I'm innocent," he told them. "I had nothing to do with this. Those guys took me hostage."

The car door opened and a hand atop his head guided Brad into the back seat of the SUV.

"Tell it to the judge," said the agent.

"I was just trying to get home for Christmas," Brad said.

"Yeah, aren't we all."

The car door slammed and the convoy of black SUVs pulled onto the road, passing the smashed white panel van already swarming with crime scene personnel.

Brad watched it grow small in the rearview mirror.

The faint odor of burning oil hung in the air and Brad, straining his eyes at the dashboard, saw the Check Engine indicator glowing red. The SUV's powerful motor hummed and he found it somehow soothing, relaxing the claw of tension that had been squeezing his gut. He drew a full breath for the first time in what seemed like weeks.

The SUV bumped over railroad tracks, joggling Brad, making the cuffs dig into his wrists and waking the pain in his broken finger. Brad thought they'd been fastened unnecessarily tight.

"Hey," he called to the passenger agent up front. "I'm pretty uncomfortable back here."

The agent turned his head, grinning. He tossed Brad a key.

"Give you a chance to work on your skills, Hines."

Brad caught the key in his lap and let it fall to the seat between his legs.

"There you go, Carter," he said. "Always thinking about the welfare of your agents."

The man up front laughed, watching while Brad scooted and stretched, wriggling until he had the key in his hand. His broken finger screamed in protest but Brad didn't want to look like a wimp so he swallowed the pain.

Finally, he managed to fit the key into the cuffs and release his wrists. He rubbed them to restore full circulation, taking care not to knock his aching finger.

Carter nodded approvingly. "Not bad, under the circumstances." He paused, his eyes going hard in a piercing gaze. "Did you get it?"

Brad gave him a thumbs up. "I got it."

"How'd he hide it?"

"He put it in an A-bomb, acid blotter. Looks like a postage stamp."

"Microdot, you think?"

"Yeah, lab technicians will break it loose and the analysts will crack it," Brad said. "One more leg up on the Chinese."

"Well done, Hines. And good job maintaining your cover."

"What can I say? I'm just a simple carpet cleaner caught in the wrong place at the wrong time."

The agent's face softened. "I'm afraid you missed your flight and won't be able to catch another one tonight. Debriefing will take a while and you'll have to get that finger splinted."

Brad sighed. He'd expected nothing more. Or less. All part of the job. He was looking at a long night ahead.

But tomorrow?

Tomorrow was Christmas Eve, and he'd be on a plane by midday. Home in time to kiss his wife, tuck the kids in their beds, and play Santa.

Home for Christmas.

He couldn't ask for better than that.

SANTA'S EYES

S anta's eyes froze me midstride.

The store was crowded—just three days left on everyone's advent calendar—and impatient customers pushed past where I stood rooted to the faux wooden floor. Sleigh bells jingled, ring-ting-tingled, and an announcement came over the store's intercom system.

"Customer needs gift-wrap service in the houseware department. Gift wrap to housewares."

I pulled in a deep breath laced with the scent of popcorn balls and fudge. I'd frozen next to the candy counter and the heady fragrance helped snap me out of my trance. Stepping clear of the flow of traffic, I turned to watch Santa's retreating figure.

One department store Santa looks very much like every other department store Santa. It's in their job description. But above the standard white beard, the eyes remain uncovered, windows to the soul.

And I'd just glimpsed a dark soul.

I was convinced of it.

I'd recognize those ice blue orbs anywhere. Floyd Rickles had worn a Santa suit and listened to the demands and desires of lined-up boys and girls when I'd worked at Macy's four years ago. I'd often heard his hearty "Ho, ho, ho!" and seen children's faces light up during my rounds as assistant manager.

He'd done a good job. Most of the employees agreed that he was a superior Santa, though perhaps a little standoffish as a person. Sales in the toy department had flourished under Floyd's reign as St. Nick. Pleased parents had unleashed credit cards and indulged their offspring at an unprecedented rate that Christmas season. All had seemed well.

Until Santa hauled away the jewelry department in his big red bag.

And now, that same Santa was here, using his time and handy disguise to case the jewelry display at Hardison's, where I was now employed as Head Clerk.

I plunged back into the stream of shoppers and let it carry me to the escalators. Joggling my way onto the rising metal staircase I gnawed at my lip, crammed between a woman laden with shopping bags and a man holding a coat covered with wiry hairs and smelling of dog.

The giant support pillars were festooned with gold-colored garlands and scarlet Christmas stockings twined with tiny twinkling lights. The air hummed with the expectant noise and antsy movement of a crowd intent on crossing every item off their gift lists. As we ascended, the heavy smell of clashing colognes let me know we'd be met at the top by the perfume sprayer from Cosmetics.

I dodged her and made my way to Mr. Beckham's office.

"He's busy, Ms. Sattler," his secretary said when she saw me.

"This is urgent," I assured her.

Sighing, she lifted her handset and motioned me in.

Gerald Beckham, General Manager of Hardison's Department Store, sat behind a desk littered with papers and envelopes. His scalp, a mottled shade of purple, shone through a layer of thinning hair and each of his double chins bore a dimple dead center. He shuffled through the papers with a distracted manner and waved his hand at me as if shooing away a pesky fly.

"I really don't have time, Molly."

"Would you say that if you knew a thief was robbing the jewelry department?"

He stood, startled, his chins quivering. "What!"

"Not at this very moment," I said, sitting down and drawing the chair closer to his desk. "But very soon, Mr. Beckham."

He sat too, and regarded me with narrowed eyes. "As I think I mentioned, I'm busy. Explain yourself, and make it snappy."

"The Santa you hired is Floyd Rickles. The man who carried away the entire stock of Macy's jewelry in his red velvet bag."

Beckham's mottled purple grew a shade deeper. "He most certainly is not. The man's name is Joseph Dilber, and I had him thoroughly vetted. What's more," he said, letting his gaze return to the stacks of paper on his desk, "the toy department is thriving and Joe Dilber is a big part of that."

"I'm telling you, Mr. Beckham, it's in the eyes. That Santa is Floyd Rickles."

"You're mistaken, Molly. Now please—you stick with your duties and let me attend to mine."

I'd been dismissed.

No matter. I happened to know that Warren Woolrich, the store's owner, was on the premises this very moment, buying gifts and creating photo ops for his personal assistant to post on social media. I tracked him down and managed to pull him aside while the PA passed out candy canes to a gaggle of children.

I told him what I knew about Floyd Rickles.

"But my dear Ms. Sattler," he said, patting at his mustache. "It's not the same man. This one is Joe Something-or-Other, and Gerald tells me he's doing a splendid job. Receipts from the toy department are rolling in."

"Yes, he's an excellent Santa," I agreed, "but that's how he distracts us from his true purpose in the store. Everyone's so impressed with his ho, ho, ho, that they don't notice him casing the joint."

"Casing the joint?" He chuckled. "This is no gangster film, Ms. Sattler. Besides," he added, taking her hand and patting it, tilting his head for a smile at the camera, "the man you're talking about was tried in a court of law and acquitted."

"I saw that on TV, just like everyone else, Mr. Woolrich. But Macy's surveillance video clearly showed Santa emptying trays of jewelry into his bag and leaving the store."

"Of course it did. And as Rickles's defense attorney pointed out, anyone could have put on a Santa suit to rob the store. It's the perfect Christmas disguise. The police searched Rickles's house. Not a trace of the jewelry, or anything else to tie him to the crime."

He dropped my hand and straightened his necktie. "I'm sure you're worrying without cause, Ms. Sattler. Please don't let it ruin your Christmas."

He lifted a hand, as if waving to an adoring crowd, and the PA snapped a few more shots. They left me standing in Men's Wear, a candy cane in my hand and no idea what to do next.

I went to my own office and closed the door, shutting out the piped-in strains of chestnuts roasting on an open fire and the chatter of shoppers in line for customer service. Kicking off my high heels, I let my toes bunch into the deep pile of the Turkish rug I'd brought from home on the day I started this job.

Pouring a cup of coffee, I let the vapor tickle my nose as I typed "Floyd Rickles" into my search engine. There was work I should be doing, but I couldn't settle my mind on it with the image of Santa's arctic blues taunting me.

My concerns had been given no credence by those who should have cared the most. Was I overreacting? Imagining a bogey man in a Santa suit?

The pictures and news items that popped up on the screen were as I remembered them. It's true the man had been acquitted, but I'd never doubted his guilt.

And wouldn't getting away with it once make him all the more likely to try it again?

Next, I entered the name Joe Dilber into the search box and discovered something very interesting. Old Joe and Mrs. Dilber are characters from the Charles Dickens story, *A Christmas Carol.*

Both of them thieves.

Mr. Rickles, it appeared, liked to play games. When choosing a new identity for himself, he'd taken a blending of names from a Christmas story, names of thieves. A secret source of amusement, I suppose.

More sure of myself than ever, I turned to my tasks and worked until closing time. The growing sense of stillness, rather than the clock, let me know the day was ending. With a sigh, I opened my door and prepared to receive each department's receipts as their managers reported to my desk.

Three days to Christmas, and I was in no hurry to get home to my lonely apartment. I had put my signature on the divorce agreement less than three months ago and I still felt raw, severed, and bewildered. I'd worked hard to be a caring and attentive wife to Felix, a conscientious companion, a good person.

I couldn't figure out where it had all gone wrong.

No one in the office had switched off the music and the cheery holiday tones now acted like a depressant on my spirits. I forced a smile onto my face as the receipts started coming in and by the time the last department reported, the muscles behind my ears were taut and strained and I felt a headache coming on.

Locking away the cash and bundled receipts in a safe set into the wall of my office, I glowered at the sparkly ornaments set on a shelf above, placed there by my friend Kayla from the Women's Clothing department. A tiny stuffed elf sat in the center of the display and some grinchy part of me wanted to smack the smile off its elfin face.

Enough.

I needed to do something about this growing Scrooge-on. Taking my cell phone from my purse, I activated the screen and flicked through my contacts until I found what I was looking for. Sucking in a deep breath, I held it and hit the call button.

"I've reconsidered your offer," I said when Detective Mark Adams answered. "I would love to have a drink with you. Are you free tonight?"

"I can meet you in an hour."

"Perfect. I'm at work but I should be finished here soon. Where should we meet up?"

"I'm hungry. Can we make it a dinner date?"

"Sounds great."

We arranged to meet at a Mexican restaurant not too far from my apartment. I ended the call and went out for my evening rounds, walking through each department to make sure the registers were properly cleared and all was in order.

As I finished, I ran into Victor Tatum, one of the night guards.

"I'm ready to make the deposit run, if now's a good time," I told him.

He nodded, accompanying me to my office where I retrieved the large pouch I'd prepared. Together, we took the elevator down to the service entrance and walked the block to the night deposit box at a nearby bank.

Forty minutes later, the hostess seated me at a table where Mark waited, perusing a menu.

"I'm a chimichanga kind of guy," he said as I slid into the booth. "With the works, guacamole, sour cream, pico de gallo. What'll you have to drink?"

I gave my drink order to the hostess and she left. "Chimichanga sounds good to me." I set the menu aside and concentrated on mustering engaging chit chat, putting off what I really wanted to talk about.

Halfway through our chimichangas, I set my fork down and wiped my mouth on a napkin. "Mark, I saw something today that really disturbed me. Can I tell you about it?"

He swallowed and took a swig from his glass of Dos Equis. "I might have known you wanted something out of me besides my scintillating company."

I suddenly found myself fighting down a lump in my throat. Squeezing my hands together hard under the table, I said, "First and foremost, I really am interested in your company. That's why I called. I promise. But..."

"Molly." He caught my eye and held my gaze, his expression solemn. "You can tell me anything."

I let it pour out—the robbery four years ago at Macy's, the trial and acquittal, my persisting suspicion, and today's encounter with those eyes above a snow white beard. The eyes I recognized.

"He's planning it again," I finished. "I just know it."

"You're certain it's the same man?"

"Positive. I went to the store manager, but he doesn't believe me. And the owner is too caught up in promoting his public image to pay any attention to what I had to say. What can I do?"

Mark took another bite of chimichanga and chewed thoughtfully. "I don't know that there's anything you can do proactively. You can't prove he's up to anything illegal. Even if he's changed his name and picked up another job as Santa, he was found not guilty in a court of law."

I gulped some water. "There must be something."

"Well," he hesitated. "I could give you a tracker to place in the merchandise. That way, if he does take it, we can find him. Provided he doesn't find the tracker first."

"What about catching him red-handed?"

Mark's eyes narrowed, skewering me with a disapproving gaze. "That would be dangerous, Molly."

"He likes to be clever about the Christmas holiday. Last time, he made his move on Christmas Eve and I've no doubt he'll do it again. I could hide and watch. Call 911."

"Don't even think about it."

"Okay."

I ate some chimichanga while he watched.

"I can see you thinking about it," he said.

"I can't do *nothing*," I protested. "You expect me to just go home Christmas Eve and sit around by the tree, waiting for the news? Besides, there's no one to care if something happens to me."

Mark reached out and caught my hand, gripping it tight. "It so happens you're wrong about that," he said.

We finished our meal and strolled a bit among the light-bestrewn shops before I kissed him lightly on the cheek and said I better be getting home.

I still didn't relish the thought of my empty apartment. But inviting him up seemed too rushed, too soon.

Too desperate.

The next morning, a big bunch of Christmas roses arrived for me at the office. I put them on the corner of my desk and stared. Fragrant and gorgeous, they filled the room with more hope and cheer than I'd been able to wring from Kayla's elf and company.

I opened the card and a little shiver of pleasure ran through me. The flowers were from Mark. Included in the envelope was a small disk, about a half inch square. Thoughtfully, I placed it in my desk.

After my morning routine, I stopped by the jewelry department and browsed the display cases. It was busy and several customers had arrived in front of me. The sales associate, a pretty woman in her mid-thirties with red hair and a delicate nose ring, helped meet their shopping needs. When she'd finished with them, she turned to me.

"Is there something I can help you find?" she asked.

"Hi, I'm Molly, from Administration."

"Right. I've seen you around and Mr. Orkins told me who you were."

"Oh, good." I gave her my best smile. "I was thinking about getting my mother a necklace for Christmas. Something simple."

As she pointed out various possibilities, I scrambled for some way to solicit information without sounding creepy or stupid. Couldn't come up with anything.

"Do you see much of Santa Claus in here," I tried, "or does he spend all his time in the toy department?"

She gave me a sharp look. "Actually, I've been seeing quite a bit of Santa. We've been dating for six weeks."

This surprised me, but it only made sense. A way for Rickles to cull information and a plausible excuse for hanging around during closing time, observing the procedures.

"Oh! Well, lucky you. I guess you'll be getting a little something extra in your stocking."

She rolled her eyes. "That's really original."

I left the jewelry counter without buying anything and wandered over to the toy department. Santa's big chair rested on a raised platform draped by a crimson velvet skirt. A line of children wound around the front of the platform, tended by two pert elves in green tunics and candy-striped tights.

I skulked around to the back of the platform and saw a bit of fabric poking from beneath the skirt. A different shade of red, more like Santa's costume. I crouched down and pulled at it.

It was Santa's bag, and it contained something heavy.

I tugged it farther into the light and hefted it, hearing metallic objects clank inside. Heavy objects. Like a wrench for smashing glass cases. Or wire cutters for snipping through protective mesh.

Or a gun.

Before I could loosen the drawstring and look inside, two shiny black boots entered my field of vision and Floyd Rickles cleared his throat.

"That's Santa's bag, little girl," he said, his jolly tone edged with menace. "It's wrong to poke into things that don't belong to you. If you're naughty, you won't get any presents for Christmas."

A few onlookers laughed. I felt heat rising in my face, but I stepped close to St. Nick's billowing beard and kept my voice low.

"I know who you are, and I know what you did, Floyd Rickles. You won't get away with it a second time."

"Ho, ho, ho! I have no idea what you're talking about."

Snatching the bag from my hands, he clanked away.

I headed back to Jewelry and asked to speak with Mr. Orkins, the department manager.

"Is there something wrong?" asked the woman behind the counter.

"Not at all," I assured her. "Just a bit of business I need to discuss with him."

She gave me a hassled look but went to summon her supervisor. *We Wish You a Merry Christmas* piped gaily through the sound system and I thought I detected the faint aroma of chocolate chip cookies. Probably a scented candle burning in housewares to encourage cookware sales.

Mr. Orkins arrived at the counter and invited me into the back room.

"Tomorrow is Christmas Eve, Ms. Sattler," he scolded. "As you can imagine, we're rather busy. What is it we need to discuss?"

"Mr. Orkins, you are a conscientious manager. You do a superb job in Jewelry. If you knew someone was going to rob your department, what would you do to stop them?"

He scowled. "Really, Ms. Sattler. Can't this kind of theoretical crisis management wait until after the holidays?"

"I'm not speaking theoretically, Mr. Orkins. And after the holidays will be too late."

He gawped at me. "What are you saying?"

"I'm saying that I believe a thief will rob your jewelry department after closing on Christmas Eve."

"If that's true, we should call the police."

"And tell them what? That I have a hunch?"

"Well, what *do* you have, Ms. Sattler, that leads you to this incredible notion?"

I told him about my experience with Floyd Rickles four years ago and that the same man now wore a Santa suit in our very own toy department.

"I just examined his bag and I believe it contains tools for breaking in and maybe even a gun."

"You believe? I thought you examined the bag."

"I lifted it up and felt something heavy inside and heard metallic items shifting around. Before I had a chance to open it, Santa intervened and took it away. I warned him that I was onto him, but the man is arrogant. He probably took it as a challenge."

"What do you propose we do about it?"

"I propose we lay in wait on Christmas Eve. I have a tracking device I can hide among the merchandise and a policeman friend who's agreed to stay on alert. If Santa shows up, you call 911 and I call my friend."

He pulled at his lower lip as he stared at me, considering. "My wife won't like it. She's made plans for us to attend a party on Christmas Eve."

"Think how pleased your wife will be when you're the hero who saved Christmas."

He snorted. "That's a bit dramatic, don't you think? It's only jewelry."

"Yes, but when you save the store from the crushing blow of a robbery, Mr. Woolrich and Mr. Beckham will be grateful and impressed. Not to mention your wife."

He let a long breath of air sigh through his lips. "All right," he agreed. "I was dreading the party anyway. But we're staying strictly out of sight and calling the police. No interacting with the criminal."

"Absolutely."

I went back to my office and got to work on my clerical duties. For lunch, I ate a bowl of microwaved soup at my desk. Tomato-scented vapor rose as I crumbled a couple packets of crackers into the soup, singing along to *We Three Kings*. I didn't know the proper words, so I sang the version about an exploding cigar.

There was a knock on my open door as I finished the soup. I looked up to see Floyd Rickles entering my office. He closed the door behind him.

And he was carrying his bag.

I scrambled for something to say that wouldn't reveal my sudden panic. "If you're here to collect your paycheck, it's not ready yet. We'll send it to the address we have on file."

"I'm not here for my paycheck."

He advanced to my desk and dropped into a chair beside it.

"I'm here because you're right. I am Floyd Rickles."

He spoke with a dejected air and a contrite expression. "Or at least, I *was* Floyd Rickles. I changed my name because I've changed myself. I'm not the man I used to be."

I stared, struggling again for something to say. Before I came up with anything, he continued.

"I don't mind admitting—since I can't be tried again for the same crime—that I did take that jewelry." A pained look crossed his face. "And I've been sorry ever since. I sold it to a fence for a fraction of what it was worth and blew the money in about two months. They say crime doesn't pay, and I've found that to be true."

He clasped his white-gloved hands in front of his red velvet chest and looked at me earnestly. "I decided to turn over a new leaf, put my past behind me and start fresh. The one thing from my old self I kept was my love of Christmas, my desire to be Santa and delight the kiddies."

Suspicion swirled through me and I wasn't willing to let it go. "What's in your bag, then?" I asked. "Children don't usually ask for hardware as a Christmas wish."

He lifted his bag to my desk with a clank.

"I was taking these home for my neighbor, a ten-year old named Tommy. I paid for them. Receipt's in the bag."

Leaving me to examine the bag's contents, Rickles rose and paced the floor of my office. He seemed genuinely humbled and worried that I might not accept his penitent claim. With good reason.

I didn't.

The bag contained a set of horseshoes, along with rules for how to play. The band of cardboard binding them together had torn, allowing them to jangle against each other. And they were heavy.

I closed the bag and pushed it across the desk as he returned from his nervous pacing. Leaning back in my chair, I eyed him across the desk. He put forward a convincing case, but I just couldn't buy what he was selling.

"If you're so reformed," I said, "why would you choose Joe Dilber for your new name? Both Joe and Dilber are names of thieves in the Charles Dickens story, *A Christmas Carol*."

The man dressed as Santa smiled. "Have you read *A Christmas Carol?* Or seen the movie?"

"No," I admitted.

"Then I guess you wouldn't know that Old Joe and Mrs. Dilber are *reformed* thieves by the end of the story. Like Scrooge, they repent of their evil ways and try to do good for the rest of their days." He paused. "Like me, Molly. I'm trying to make up for past mistakes."

He rose and held out his hand. "For Christmas sake, won't you give me the benefit of the doubt?"

I didn't stand or shake his hand. After a moment, he retracted it and sighed. "All right. Fair enough. I wish you a merry Christmas, Molly."

He left my office.

All the while, as I gathered cracker wrappers from my desk and whisked the crumbs into the wastebasket, guilt gnawed at me. Was

I misjudging the man? Would his true repentance be sullied by my doubts? Was I a Scrooge at heart?

Or was he scamming me?

I finished the day's work, accepted the receipts from every department, walked my rounds, and made my short trek to the night deposit box with Victor Tatum.

Then I went home and read *A Christmas Carol*.

I arrived at Hardison's Department Store on Christmas Eve with a renewed conviction that Floyd Rickles was a black heart with designs on Orkin's stock of jewelry. Charles Dickens had convinced me of that.

I stopped by Jewelry to ensure that Mr. Orkins was still on board for our stakeout. Beneath the glass counters, diamonds winked, gold sparkled, and a multi-colored array of gems beckoned anyone with an eye for glamor or glitz. I knew there was a lot more in the back room, locked behind sturdy wire mesh.

I drew Orkins aside and whispered, "I'm more certain than ever that Santa's coming tonight. He'll arrive with his big red bag empty and fill it from your department."

Mr. Orkins had developed an enthusiasm for our mission. "I think we should hunker down in Sporting Goods," he said. "We can sit in camp chairs and use night vision binoculars to scope things out."

"Good thinking. I'll meet you there twenty minutes after closing."

All day the store was filled with last minute shoppers, and I got a flutter in my chest every time I thought about what I planned to do that night. By late afternoon I was in a jittery state. I closed my office door and took five minutes at my desk to meditate, to calm myself, to think about my purpose and visualize my success.

Feeling better, I placed the large pouch for deposits on my desk and opened the door, preparing to meet the parade of managers with their day's receipts. They came soon, quick on each other's heels. The store was closing early on Christmas Eve and everyone was anxious to get out and celebrate.

"I'm going to a party tonight," said my friend Kayla from Women's Clothing. "You should come with me, Molly!"

I put the bundle of cash she'd given me into the pouch on my desk. "Thanks, but I already have plans."

She gave me an impish grin. "Whatcha doing? Anything exciting?"

"It ought to be," I said. "I'll tell you about it later. Have fun at your party."

When the last manager handed over the day's takings, I secured the pouch and locked it in the safe. I felt sick to my stomach and slightly dizzy. This was it.

Showtime.

I found Mr. Orkins in the camping gear aisle, already seated in a canvas chair with another beside him for me. He handed me a pair of binoculars as I eased myself carefully into the unwieldy chair. Orkins had pulled an enormous wire basket of rubber balls and a life-size cardboard cutout of a hunter into the aisle to shield us from view. A real camouflage expert.

The store was darkened, all the overhead lights extinguished. Without the Christmas music piping in over the sound system, a magnified silence filled the space and it felt weird, lifeless. I'd spent plenty of time in the store after hours, but tonight an ominous feeling hung over me. I shivered.

Mr. Orkins turned to me, his eyes wide in the dim light. "What about the tracker thing?" he asked. "Did you bring it?"

"It's already in place," I said, remembering how I'd slipped it behind a paper label where Rickles would be unlikely to notice it. "Let's not talk," I suggested.

Orkins nodded.

We sat in the dim and eerie silence, occasionally lifting the binoculars to our eyes. Hours passed and my stomach began to be uncomfortably empty and my bladder uncomfortably full. Glancing at my phone, I saw it was past midnight.

Christmas Eve had come and gone.

Still, the wee hours of the morning loomed and that's when he'd surely strike. Another half hour passed and I had to admit I hadn't considered my bathroom needs when putting this whole plan together.

"I have to use the restroom," I said. "Are you okay on your own?"

"Of course, dear. I'm having the time of my life."

Surprised, I realized he meant it. Quiet on the outside, our Mr. Orkins sizzled with adventure on the inside where imagination reigns.

"Remember, just call 911 if you see anything."

"Got it."

I hesitated. "As long as I'm away, do you mind if I make the nightly deposit? It'll only take about ten minutes."

"Do what you need to do. I'll be fine."

I used the bathroom and felt a hundred percent more prepared to deal with Floyd Rickles. Which was good, because as I rounded the corner and moved toward my office, I caught sight of Santa's red suit disappearing through the exit at the end of the corridor.

And the bag slung over his shoulder looked full.

With a sinking sensation in the pit of my stomach, I hurried to my office, imagining the doorknob was still warm from those thieving fingers wrapped around it.

He'd been there. Inside my office.

My hands shook as I dialed in the combination to the safe. The pouch I'd prepared was the largest of the year, stuffed with all the cash and receipts from the final day of the holiday season, earnings from every department. I'd had to squeeze to fit it into the safe.

Snapping the levered handle of the solidly built metal box, I swung the door open, holding my breath.

The safe was empty.

Well, almost empty. A slim electronic tablet rested on the floor of the compartment. I looked into it and saw...myself.

The tablet was a monitor for a camera, and when I looked up at the impish elf on the shelf, I saw the tiny device mounted there, where it could record the combination as I turned the dial.

Floyd Rickles. He must have planted the camera during his pacing the day before, when he'd come to make his confession and petition for my good will. His fingerprints must be on it, and on the safe. Incriminating evidence.

And then I remembered his white Santa gloves. There would be no prints.

I noticed something else in the safe. A Christmas card, addressed to me. I opened it.

My dearest Molly,

I must say I've enjoyed renewing our acquaintance. Please accept this assurance as my gift to you:

You were right. You warned others, you tried to stop me. No blame can fall to you.

You get to be the one who is correct, moral, upstanding, and good.

And I get to be the one who got away.

Again.

We each got what we wanted. Merry Christmas!

Santa

I dropped the card and it fell to the floor atop my Turkish rug. Collapsing into the chair beside my desk I covered my face with my hands and tried to control my breathing. This felt too much like those last arguments with Felix. Too much like my divorce.

He was the one who cheated, who broke the rules. He was the one who lied and hid things and pretended he was someone he wasn't. My only compensation was getting to feel like the virtuous one.

It wasn't enough. I wanted more.

Smiling, I stretched my arms to the ceiling. I laughed. I thought about how I'd meditated on the situation, changing my mind at the last minute about where to plant the tracking device.

Instead of slipping it among the jewelry, I'd tucked it behind the deposit slip on a stack of banded bills inside the pouch. Then I'd called

Mark and let him know what I'd done. He told me he'd be waiting, watching for the tracker to move.

He'd wait all night if he had to. He'd do that for me.

Thanks to Charles Dickens and Detective Mark Adams, I was having a merry Christmas, after all.

I put on my coat and used the same door through which Santa had exited. Outside, I stood on the sidewalk and looked up and down the block. About sixty yards distant, a dark blue Crown Victoria sat crosswise in the road with a patrol car. The light bar cast dancing shimmers into the night, like red and blue blinky bulbs on a Christmas tree.

I saw no sign of Floyd Rickles.

Across the slick, frost-crusted surface of the street, I ran to where Mark stood talking to two officers in uniform. My heart thundered at the thought they might have missed him, but when Mark saw me he grinned and pointed to the patrol car.

"Santa's going in the clink," he said. "Approach with caution—jolly is not a word I'd use to describe him right now."

Circling to the back of the car, I looked through the window and saw them. Hard, ice-cold, like blue marbles.

Not Santa's eyes.

Only the eyes of an unreformed and captured thief.

I turned away and Mark joined me, taking my cold hand in his, rubbing some warmth into it. He smiled and the warmth spread, filling me with hope and joy.

Putting in a call to Mr. Orkins in sporting goods, I let him know we had our man. He sounded disappointed to have missed the action but wished me a happy holiday. I returned the sentiment and ended the call.

Then I invited Mark home for Christmas dinner.

Green Storm Rising

Eluf crouched inside the tiny hut, coaxing fire into the frozen twigs and bits of paper he'd tossed into the pot belly of the ancient iron stove. It slumped in the corner like an old man gone to fat, creaky with age and temperamental. At last, a few licks of flame rose and caught on the kindling with a gentle crackle, giving Eluf hope for a nice blaze by the time Betina arrived.

He turned and surveyed the pile of quilts and blankets stacked on a mattress in the opposite corner. On the other hand, the cold might drive her more quickly beneath the sheets and that suited him fine. The thought of Betina's skin beneath his fingertips, her lips, roughened by the arctic winds, moving along his collarbone and up to nip at his earlobe, made his breath come faster and he watched the vapor puff out of him like a dragon's breath.

He would be like a dragon in bed tonight.

But they had to be careful. Meeting like this, in secret and only once or twice a month, made Eluf all the hungrier for her. But it had to be like this. At least, until they could figure out what to do about Betina's husband.

Eluf plumped the pillows on the low mattress, wrinkling his nose at the smell of unwashed bedclothes that wafted up from the tangle of blankets. Ah well, nothing he could do about it now. He scooped the binoculars from the seat of an old wooden chair and stepped outside.

The midnight sky rose above him, green and magnificent, shifting lights as magical as fairy dust. Greenland, in December, always brought the Northern Lights and their brilliance allowed him to see through the binoculars. Not sharp detail, as in daylight, but he could make out the village below and see smoke rising from chimneys, the outlines of shops and houses, the church steeple and village maypole like two masts of a great ship against a heaving emerald sea.

And in the nearer distance, a dark figure moving up the hillside to meet him, her alluring curves hidden beneath layers of coats and sweaters. He looked forward to removing every one of them.

The dancing lights above him brightened and sharpened, their radiance becoming harsh in a way he'd never seen before. He shielded his eyes, but the glow intensified into a searing flame of color that tore through the sky like Thor's firebolt.

Eluf squeezed his eyes shut and sheltered his head beneath his arm. The storm of brilliant color passed with a boom he felt in his gut, though he heard nothing. The sky now was white, washed clean. He focused the binoculars downhill and was relieved to see Betina hurrying toward him.

Shifting his gaze to the village below, he stared, refocused, and stared again.

It had vanished.

Where before had stood houses and shops, a school, a church, a post office, there was now only a scattering of ash, stirred by a restless wind.

Eluf gaped for the merest moment before the binoculars bonded to his face with a suffusing heat and he and Betina turned to dust.

Agent Talmadge Bannerman stared at the screen on the wall above the conference table. Silence hung in the room like a heavy cloak for one and a half seconds before cacophony broke forth, everyone talking at once.

Men and women dressed in dignified military uniforms and distinguished business suits gesticulated violently enough to put out the eyes of their neighbors, who were gesticulating wildly in turn. More than one coffee cup tipped and spilled, sending hot brown liquid across the polished table. There was a sound of shattering glass and a crunch as someone rolled their chair over the resulting mess.

Tal, a newly-minted member of the Department of Homeland Security team, waved his hand for attention and cleared his throat. Beside him, his partner, Carl Wrigley, took things a step further.

"Hey!" he shouted, the pink of his scalp deepening under the stress of the situation. "Before we all go ballistic, could we get another look at that footage, Secretary Livingston?"

The room fell into a tense quiet, tinged by the smell of coffee and fear. Assistant Secretary Pete Livingston pushed a button on the remote control and replayed the satellite surveillance recording.

Tal watched the grainy image of a far-off village, shimmering under an eerie green light. The light intensified, pulling into a cone shape. There was a flash on the screen and the village disappeared. Nothing but a residue of light ash remained, gray against the snow and blowing in the wind.

Tal felt a shiver run up his back. This time, no one broke the stunned silence until the Secretary froze the image on the screen and said, "What you've just witnessed is only one instance of the phenomena. We know of at least two more."

"What is it?" a woman three notches up Tal's chain of command asked. Her coral-colored lipstick had smudged on one side, giving her mouth a lopsided appearance. "An alien attack?"

The Secretary had a face like an Easter Island rock carving. "We don't think so," he said. "Our mole in the scientific community has been tracking a troublesome development over the last several months. His team have focused their attention on a lab facility in northern Greenland."

The Secretary pushed a button and everyone's eyes swiveled back to the screen. Tal watched as the frozen wasteland of a vanished village was replaced by a frozen wasteland dotted by a fenced compound.

"We believe an astrophysicist by the name of Antonia Scylla has been developing and testing a solar weapon, powered by geomagnetic coronal emissions."

"What does that mean in English, Mr. Secretary?" asked a balding man across the table from Tal.

"The science behind it is rather complicated, as you can imagine. Put simply, she's found a way to harness the power of the Aurora Borealis."

"The Northern Lights?" someone asked.

"And presumably the Southern Lights as well. Aurora Australis."

"How is this possible, Mr. Secretary?" asked the coral-lipped woman, the boss of the boss of Tal's boss. He wished he could remember her name.

The Secretary's eyes narrowed. He turned to the man beside him. "Commander Johnson, you want to take this?"

A man in uniform rose and took control of the remote. A huge fiery ball appeared on the screen. It seemed to be covered in bright orange lava which splashed and glowed with a fierce intensity.

"The Auroras originate some ninety-three million miles away, on the surface of the sun," he began. "When massive explosions of electromagnetic matter occur—we call those CME's, Coronal Mass Ejections—they create a stream of electronically charged solar particles known as Solar Wind."

"And you're telling us we're feeling that wind from ninety-three million miles away?" Director Hawkins asked. He was Tal's immediate supervisor.

"Not feeling it," the officer explained, "but sometimes we can see its effects."

"I'll bet that village we saw disappear was feeling it," said the boss of the boss of Tal's boss.

The Secretary cleared his throat. "I'll bet that village didn't feel a thing. It all happened too fast. One second there, the next...vaporized."

The woman's face was pale. She bit her lip, transferring lipstick to her two front teeth. The officer continued his science lecture.

"Solar Winds move at extraordinary speeds, up to forty-five million miles an hour. Their energy causes a distortion in the earth's magnetic field and some of those charged particles work their way into our atmosphere around the magnetic poles, creating what we call the Auroras. Apparently, this Scylla has developed a way to focus the power of those particles into a weapon. Sources tell us she calls it a Geomagnetic Concentrator."

"Those same sources," the Secretary added, "have been calling it The Oven Cleaner, because it incinerates everything in its path without flame, leaving only ash behind."

Tal's chill of unease grew. News of this fearsome weapon was troubling in the extreme, but something he'd have expected to be way above his pay grade. Why had he and Carl been included in this conference? He didn't think he wanted to know.

But he was about to find out.

The DHS Secretary resumed control of the remote. "Thank you, Commander Johnson."

He pointed to the screen where a woman's face appeared, mid-forties with cocoa-brown skin and dark hair parted down the middle with one white stripe snaking down each side. Tal couldn't determine if the stripe was natural or artificially produced and he didn't spend more than a second on speculation. The mesmerizing eyes caught his attention and held it like a small child holds a puppy—by the neck in a suffocating grip.

"This is Antonia Scylla," Livingston said. He flashed another photo on the screen, a blonde woman, tall and sleek, near the age of fifty, but toned and elegant with glacial blue eyes. "And this," the Secretary said, "is the eminent physicist, Eudora Petrovna. We believe these two women have been neck and neck in a race to perfect a new weapon technology. It now appears that Scylla has won."

"Let me guess," said the boss of the boss of Tal's boss, gesturing to the blonde. "They call this one Charybdis."

"You pegged it, Director Miskin."

Miskin! That was it.

A new image replaced Eudora Petrovna, a jingling video showing a Christmas wonderland of a town with a gigantic statue of Santa Claus to welcome newcomers and candy cane street lamps lining the main avenues. Livingston froze the frame on a cheery sign at the town limits. It read: Welcome to North Pole, Alaska. Pop. 2103.

"Our inside man tells us Scylla has finished her preliminary testing. She now plans to make a more extensive, more public demonstration of the weapon's efficacy. She's alerted potential buyers of her intention to incinerate the town of North Pole, Alaska at the stroke of midnight on Christmas Eve."

"Letting the world know what she thinks about peace on earth and good will toward men," said the balding man across the table.

Livingston nodded. "When the demonstration concludes, she'll open the bidding and hand her Geomagnetic Concentrator over to the highest bidder. We need to stop all of that from happening."

He turned to Tal and his partner, Carl. Tal's skin prickled as if someone had just run nails across a chalkboard.

"You two," Livingston said, "are going into Scylla's base of operation to secure the weapon."

Tal stared. Carl seemed tongue-tied as well until he finally sputtered, "Why the two of us? You should be sending in a battalion!"

"Yes, we should," Livingston agreed. "But we can't risk it. Scylla's stronghold is in a wide snowfield about forty miles west of North Pole. There's no cover, no way to conceal our approach and if she sees us coming, she's liable to pull the trigger on her new toy and obliterate the target early. A couple of wildlife photographers rambling past on snowmobiles have a much better chance of getting close enough to get inside."

Tal groaned. "But why us?" he asked.

Director Hawkins fielded the question. "Both of you have experience in relevant scientific disciplines, as well as tactical training. Wrigley, you studied heliophysics as part of your doctorate program and participated in a number of field experiments."

His eyes shifted in Tal's direction. "Your work in the Epidemic Intelligence Service took you more than once into hostile territory, Bannerman. You performed well under the rigors of war and disease in Afghanistan, Ethiopia, and the Sudan. As well as being an epidemiologist, you studied veterinary medicine for a time. That knowledge may well prove useful on this mission."

"What do you mean, boss?"

Hawkins looked at Livingston. The Secretary said, "We've had reports of strange animal behavior in the vicinity of the compound. The weapon may be sending out frequencies or in some other way interfering with the animals. Wolves, in particular."

Great. Add crazed wolves to the list of hazards.

"We'll supply you with tranquilizers and a dart gun. You'll have a better idea of the proper dosages."

Tal gulped. His pulse throbbed in his ears. "Surely you can find someone more qualified than the two of us," he said, trying to keep his voice even, his tone reasonable.

There was a brief silence, then Director Hawkins asked, "How's your cousin Amy, Bannerman?"

"Amy? How do you know about Amy? And funny you should ask. I just got a postcard from her yesterday, letting me know she's settling into her new assignment at Eielson Air Force Base in...Alaska."

"Right," Hawkins said. "Eielson." He turned to Livingston. "Where's that located?"

Secretary Livingston looked apologetic, but that didn't keep him from answering. "Less than ten miles from the town of North Pole."

Tal knew they had him. Knew they'd always had him. He raised his chin and saw Carl do the same. They were going in, side by side.

The Secretary rubbed his hands together. "Frankly, gentlemen, we don't have time to find another team. Tomorrow is Christmas Eve."

Every head in the room tilted to look at the clock above the Secretary's head. It read 12:27 am.

The Secretary checked the time on his watch. "Strike that," he said. "It's Christmas Eve already. We have less than twenty-four hours, people."

To Tal and Carl he said, "Go home, pack a bag, say goodbye to your families. Your flight leaves the airfield at Joint Base Lewis McChord in three hours."

The weather, when they left Tacoma, had been pitch black and drizzling with rain. Four and a half hours later, when they touched down on the flightline at Eielson, the world was pitch black and pelting tiny popsicles from the sky. Tal shielded his face against the miniscule missiles as he stepped off the plane feeling groggy and disoriented. As if moving through a dream.

He wished that's all it was.

But the bite of the Alaskan wind left him in no doubt this was real. It was happening, and he didn't feel at all ready. By the look on his partner's face, Carl was processing similar sentiments.

They crossed the tarmac, slick with patches of ice, and entered the terminal, pausing to pick up a contingent of personnel assigned to assist them in preparing for the mission. As they moved through a maze of corridors, footsteps and voices echoing, Tal felt like a VIP with an entourage and gained a new empathy for folks whose lives have been derailed by public demand.

Their first stop was the canteen, where Tal and Carl were plied with a hearty breakfast, the last real meal they'd have for the foreseeable future. Tal tried to do it justice, but the lump forming in his throat made it hard to swallow. While they ate, a team of outfitters sized them up, asking questions about preferences and proficiencies.

When they finished eating, they were escorted to a large room stacked high with clothing, accessories, and equipment. By the time they left, both he and Carl had been dressed from the skin outward with layers designed to withstand cold while allowing mobility. In their guise as photographers, they didn't wear anything suggestive of the military.

On the surface.

Beneath their parkas, each wore a holstered weapon and a tactical chest rig containing extra mags, two knives, a headlamp, a Zippo fire starter, a set of wire cutters, and a multitool. The cameras they carried on straps around their necks were designed less for photo quality and more for visual reconnaissance. They incorporated smart binoculars with night vision capabilities.

They also functioned as radio communicators, creating a link between their two-man mission and base control. A burly Master Sergeant demonstrated how to operate the radio, talking them through a transmission.

"And that's all there is to it," he finished. "Unless they won't work, which is possible."

"What do you mean?" Carl asked.

The man looked suddenly uncomfortable, as if wishing he'd kept his mouth shut. "A major geomagnetic storm occurred on the sun's surface three days ago," he admitted, "creating a strong solar flare."

"So? How does that affect us now?"

"Well, that's how long it takes, sir, for the flare to reach earth. Big explosions and electrical storms on the sun can block electronic communication, foul up GPS, wipe out power grids and even push satellites out of orbit."

"Surely that kind of thing is a rarity?" Tal said hopefully.

The Master Sergeant shrugged. "I'm sure you're right."

Miskin approached, looking at her watch. "Sunup's in less than an hour. Time to move out."

Winter days in Alaska are short. As Tal and Carl piled into the back of an eight-seater van, the sky to the east glowed pink and blue like birthday frosting on a long white sheet cake.

"You've got a little less than five hours of daylight," Miskin said. "But that's just as well, Might be better to make your approach in the dark."

The van turned onto Highway 2, taking them through the town of North Pole. They passed the giant Santa Tal had seen on the video, and a visitor's center painted with red gingerbread trim and murals of holiday scenes spanning cream-colored walls. A candy-stripe maypole stood in front, next to another larger-than-life Santa with a sleigh and piles of gaily wrapped presents.

Decorated Christmas trees were everywhere, and even the golden arches of McDonalds rose on candy cane supports. The day was shaping into a fine one, clear sky stretching overhead like a blue china dome, and no snow fell but a thick blanket of white covered the ground, adding to the postcard prettiness of the town.

Despite the grimness of the situation, their driver had tuned the radio to a holiday channel and Tal heard the wistful tune of *I'll Be Home for Christmas*, played at low volume. His heart captured the moment, fraught with meaning, one of those psychic snapshots your mind takes that you never forget. Years later, you can ferret them out of your memory like an enchanted image that brings back the sights and sounds, the smell and touch.

The *feel* of the moment.

He thought of Bridget—the recent roundness of her belly, the excited sparkle in her eye, the home they'd made together.

The family they were making.

Yes, I'll be home for Christmas.

If only in my dreams.

They passed through Fairbanks, but Tal hardly got a glimpse of it. DHS Director Miskin had accompanied them on their journey and she sat on the van's bench seat, between Tal and Carl, a large tablet on her lap showing a map of the region. She began their final briefing.

"We'll drop you here," she pointed, "where you'll rent snowmobiles—Alaskans call them snow machines, by the way—and head into this area." Her finger moved to a wide blank spot on the map. "Scylla's compound is about twenty-six miles in."

She handed each of them a GPS tracker showing Scylla's location in relation to their own.

"If things go without a hitch," Miskin said, "you can get within spitting distance in less than an hour. Even moving slow so you can stop and take pictures. Remember, you're wildlife photographers."

"While I appreciate your optimism," Tal said, "do you have any insight into the kind of 'hitches' we might expect?"

"Were you a boy scout, Agent Bannerman?"

"I get it—be prepared for anything."

"Right," she agreed, "but while we're on the subject, here's a little present for you."

Reaching under the seat, she handed Tal a hard plastic case about twelve inches square and five inches deep. It bore an adhesive label which read: Camera Accessories.

"Merry Christmas!" she said, her smile brittle.

Tal snapped the latches and opened it to find a tranquilizer dart gun nested in foam, along with a dozen disposable needled syringes with pink fringed tailpieces. The lid of the case contained several vials of zolazepam and ketamine. He hoped he remembered the dosing guidelines.

The van pulled into the parking lot of a winter sport rental facility.

"We'll wait here and see you off," Miskin said as the driver swung the door wide.

Snow crunched under Tal's feet as he and Carl crossed the parking lot to enter the building. Red and green banners fluttered from the eaves, and *Jingle Bells* emanated from a speaker mounted on a lightpost. They got in line behind six happy-looking customers and waited to fill out paperwork so they could mount two rental snow machines and set off to save Christmas.

At least, for the town of North Pole, Alaska.

Keys in hand, they returned to the van for the last of their gear and final instructions. Miskin looked at her watch. Carl looked at his watch. Tal didn't want to think about the minutes marching on. He retrieved the dart case and an insulated bag containing water bottles and power bars. Both he and Carl strapped a pair of snowshoes to their backs.

"You have approximately thirteen hours," Miskin told them. "That gives you ample time to get there, find a way in, and secure the weapon."

"Without a hitch," Tal said.

"Right."

Tal strapped the gear onto the back of his snowmobile, slid onto the seat, and fired up the engine. It started with a growl that settled into a purr and he moved off into the snow, looking back to see Carl following. Miskin and the driver stood watching them. Nobody waved.

As the machine hummed across the field, Tal was glad of his helmet, warding off cold and wind and cutting the glare. The sun was directly overhead and brilliant in the clear sky, its radiance magnified by the endless bed of white. The helmets were also fitted with headsets so he and Carl could talk to each other as long as they stayed in proximity.

"You ready for this?" Carl asked.

"Give me a hundred years and my answer would still be no. Yet here we are. Ready or not."

As they traveled the terrain, they crossed paths with other riders out for recreation, and even passed a group snowshoeing and a couple of lone cross country skiers. Soon, however, company became scarce and tracks left in the snow less frequent.

The land was mostly flat, occasionally fringed by stands of frosted pines. As they progressed toward Scylla's position, the ground became more uneven, rocky in some places and filled with undulating hills in others. At first, it was fun flying over the hillocks, taking air, and landing with a thump but it grew old fast and Tal wished it would flatten out again.

"Tal! At your ten o'clock!"

He looked ahead to the left and saw them.

Wolves.

The hair on the back of his neck rose. Wolves are nocturnal creatures. They hunt at night, and Tal found this daytime appearance disturbing. Something else about their behavior raised a warning flag. Contrary to common belief, wolves tend to hunt solo or in mated pairs. This pack of eight was moving in a solid line, flanking their position.

He cursed. Some boy scout. He should have filled some syringes and kept the dart gun at the ready.

"Tranq gun's not going to help us here," he told Carl. "I wouldn't have time to stop and dig it out before they'd be on us."

He looked down at the speedometer and saw it went up to 120 mph.

"Wolves don't act like this unless there's something wrong with them, Carl. They don't attack humans in motorized vehicles."

"Should we shoot them?"

"I think our better bet is to outrun them. They can sprint up to forty miles per hour for a short time. We can speed over a hundred. Let's go!"

Tal turned the nose of his snowmobile slightly right and gunned the engine, crouching low over the handle bars. The machine churned through the snow, sending up a spray of white matter that hit Tal's face shield like pellets of sand.

Carl kept pace beside him.

Tal twisted his head for a quick glance behind and saw the wolves still advancing but growing smaller in the distance. Just a little bit farther at this speed and they could slow down and reorient themselves.

As the thought crossed his mind, both he and Carl crested a hillock and went airborne. The earth fell away beneath them and Tal's stomach heaved with the sensation of free fall.

His ears rang with the sound of metal smashing against rock.

Tal landed on a drift of snow with a hard crack that jolted him from the seat and sent the machine skidding away on its side. It came to a rest twenty yards away and sputtered into silence.

Tal lay on his back, eyes squeezed shut against the sun's glare. He heard a groan and raised himself on an elbow, peering around to locate Carl.

"You all right?" he called.

He saw Carl's snowmobile, mangled and smoking, where it had met not snowdrift, but rock. His partner had been thrown clear of the handlebars, striking another rock rising bare from the snow. Carl lay beside it, his leg twisted. His face, protected inside the helmet, was a grimace of pain.

"No," Tal answered himself. "I can see you are not."

Tal flipped the switch on his camera that turned it into a radio, and transmitted the signal.

"Base control."

Tal gave his call sign. "We've had an accident. My partner's leg is broken. You need to send someone in to get him."

"Copy. I see your location. We can get to you in ninety minutes. Hang tight, and we'll work on getting you a replacement. Over."

"Copy that. Get here fast," Tal said.

He signed off and rose, moving his limbs, cracking his neck, shaking off dirt and snow. Kneeling beside Carl, he checked his partner's pupils and reflexes.

"Are you hurt anywhere else?"

"I don't think so. Not bodily, anyway. I think my pride's taken a hit." He frowned. "You'll have to finish this one without me, Tal."

"I'm sorry, buddy. There's no one else I'd—"

"Tal! They've caught up."

Carl pointed up to the ridge they'd recently barreled over. A line of scruffy canine heads broke the skyline. Tal reached for his holster but before he could pull his gun, a rifle shot rang out, echoing across the snow.

The wolves fled.

A low hum registered on Tal's awareness. It grew to a crescendo, then dropped as a snow machine, unseen above them, idled. A face covered in a black balaclava stared down at them. It disappeared and the engine cut off. Tal heard the man's footsteps as he approached from a lateral angle. He kept his parka open, hand near his holster.

"Careful," Carl warned, his voice soft.

When the man appeared again, this time coming around to Tal's level, he'd removed the head covering, revealing features Tal associated with the word "eskimo." A native Alaskan.

Elderly, with white hair and a mapwork of lines and wrinkles on his face, the man greeted Tal with a hand signal. "You've had some trouble."

"Yes," Tal said. "My friend is hurt."

The Inuit said nothing for a moment as he peered up into the sky. Then he said, "A storm is coming."

Tal looked at the clear blue expanse above them. He didn't like to contradict the man, but really?

The man smiled, showing a row of crooked teeth. "You do not believe me, but that won't stop the storm from coming." He gestured to Carl. "If we splint his leg, I can take him into town on my machine."

"Help is on the way," Tal told him.

"That's good."

Again there was silence as the man surveyed the sky. In the west, Tal saw a single thin tail of cloud reaching into the blue.

Carl wriggled where he lay, as if trying for a more comfortable position. "When will this storm hit?" he asked.

The man shrugged. "Two hours, four hours. Maybe more. Best to get under shelter soon."

Tal thought about the town of North Pole, of his cousin, Amy, so close and maybe going into town for Christmas dinner or festivities. Population 2103.

He couldn't wait.

"There's something I need to do," he told the man. "Will you stay here with my friend until help comes?"

"Tal, you can't go on alone."

"And I can't spare the time waiting, Carl. Think about it."

Carl sighed. He spoke to the stranger. "I'd appreciate it if you stayed with me so my friend can go. Shouldn't be more than an hour."

"I'll stay."

Tal thanked the man and checked the GPS tracker. Righting his snowmobile, he pointed it in the proper direction and turned the key in the ignition. The engine coughed and quit.

He tried again, coaxing life into the machine. The engine ran, settling into its customary purr, and Tal pulled on his helmet. He gave his partner a thumbs up and sped away.

Once over the bluffs and out of sight, he stopped long enough to load some syringes, making the doses right for a 120 pound wolf. He packed them into his chest rig, along with extra vials and empty syringes.

He loaded a cartridge into the tranq gun and put it in a pocket of the parka. Zipping it shut, he felt more prepared.

He hoped he wouldn't encounter any crazed bears.

He continued on, figuring he must have covered nearly twenty of the twenty-six anticipated miles to the compound. The land grew flat again, wide open and clear. He was drawing closer to the destination dot on the tracker screen, but he needed to stop for a call of nature.

As he stood in the snow near his idling snowmobile, a tiny dusting of flakes, soft and feathery, fell from a sky fast filling with scudding clouds. Still, it was hard to believe they heralded something violent enough to be called a storm. He ate a power bar and drank half a liter of water. He was screwing the cap onto the bottle when he felt something strike him in the leg.

Looking down, he saw a white rabbit, fluffy as a snowball with shortened ears. An Arctic hare. As he watched, it launched itself at him again, mouth opened in a snarl. Tal's thick snowsuit and insulated boots proved impervious to the animal's attack and he shook it off, almost laughing at the absurdity of it.

Until he saw a dozen more creatures moving toward him, springing through the drifts like Santa's coursers.

Enough of them together could knock him down and though he couldn't bring himself to believe a drove of maniacal hares would be the death of him, he didn't want to stick around to find out.

Climbing back onto the snowmobile, he glided away, accelerating to 60 mph for some minutes. Hares can run as fast as wolves and he didn't want them catching up.

As he slowed, he checked the GPS tracker. The dot had vanished.

Tal knew the expanse of white could be disorienting. He could be heading a few degrees off target that would ultimately result in a total miss. Stopping the snowmobile once more, Tal got off and stood on top of a rock, holding the tracker up, turning it in different directions.

He shook the unit, tried resetting it, but the screen remained blank.

He remembered what the Master Sergeant had said about geomagnetic disturbances messing with GPS signals.

He'd have to go on memory and instinct.

As he stood atop the rock, orienting himself, he heard a cracking sound behind him and turned to see a fissure forming under the snowmachine. He'd inadvertently parked on a layer of surface ice.

The crack widened as Tal watched helplessly. The snowmobile dipped sideways, bobbed on water and slowly sank like a fat man lowering himself into the tub.

His transport was gone. His food was gone. The backup syringes and tranquilizing drugs were gone.

Tal was alone, twenty-odd miles from civilization, with darkness coming and a storm blowing in. Wild animals, driven to bizarre and dangerous acts by the side effects of a mad scientist's experiments roamed the vicinity. And the crazed woman planned to deliver her deadly weapon of mass destruction to the baddest of the bad.

But only after she'd demonstrated its usefulness on a town full of innocent and unsuspecting citizens.

On Christmas.

Somehow, in a twist he still wasn't sure he fully understood, the responsibility for stopping this from happening had fallen upon him. He had to get to her compound, wrest the weapon from her control, and render her unable to complete her plan.

Before midnight.

On foot.

Alone.

Standing on top of the rock, wind whistling through his helmet, Tal remembered the map on Miskin's tablet. She'd pointed to a barren-looking spot, far from anything else, but he remembered seeing hot springs denoted to the north and to the east.

Hot springs could make ice dependability uncertain, unleashing warmer temperatures beneath the surface. With everything buried under a thick white blanket, he hadn't realized he'd stopped the snowmobile on top of water.

His rock wasn't going anywhere, but was it on land—or sticking out above a lake or pond?

He still had the camera radio hanging from his neck and a pair of snowshoes strapped to his back. He activated the radio and gave the transmission signal, getting a stream of static in response. He tried again and heard only a confusion of static and garbled snippets, like scanning across the dial.

For six or seven minutes, he continued the effort, dismayed at how low the sun now hung against the horizon. His scant five hours of daylight were about to pass into night, and darkness would begin. The whistling wind took up strength, sending forth an occasional howl across the icy wilderness and the few flakes he'd seen before thickened and fell faster.

Removing his helmet, Tal sat on the rock and donned the balaclava and knit hat the outfitters had tucked into an interior pocket of his parka. He added a pair of goggles and pulled on the snowshoes, adjusting and locking the bindings to his boots. Facing away from the fallen snowmobile, he transferred his weight onto the snowshoes and started walking, waddling like a duck.

Without poles to help his balance and aid his steps, his progress felt achingly slow and his energy waned, sapped by cold, worry, and lack of nourishment. His cover as a wildlife photographer, always dubious, was now useless but a new, more convincing one, took its place.

He was lost.

His orienteering skills had always been good and he thought he was headed in the right direction but he was going on instinct and nothing more. As he plodded on, with the lonely wind whooshing along beside him, he saw a figure in the distance. The person drew nearer and Tal saw it was a cross country skier.

They hailed each other with uplifted hands and once within hearing distance, the man shouted, "Storm coming! Where you headed?"

Tal gestured. "My buddy has a place about three miles that way, but it's slow going in these snowshoes and getting dark." He appraised the man's blue eyes behind a pair of goggles and figured it was worth a try. "You open to a trade?"

"What? My skis for your snowshoes?" He shook his head. "You'd have to sweeten the deal."

Tal tried to remember how much he had in his wallet, dreading the thought of digging down through the layers to access it. "How about fifty bucks and a Swiss Army knife?"

"Basic model or primo?"

"Primo."

"Done."

They made the trade and as he started off on the skis, Tal realized the man had gotten the better of the bargain. The skis were old, worn, the bindings loose. But he now had poles and moved more quickly across the snowfield.

The man was barely out of sight behind him when the sun fell, as if someone had snipped the string holding it up, and darkness spread over the landscape like a sinister shadow. Tal shivered and stopped. He fished the headlamp from his chest rig and adjusted it over the balaclava.

He skied.

After an exhausting length of time, he estimated he was three or four miles from Scylla's compound and hoped she'd have a few lights burning to help him find it. Gritting his teeth, he burrowed beneath protective layers to expose his wristwatch. It was an old school model, unaffected by geomagnetic interference.

It showed the time was 5:57 pm.

Six hours and counting.

He pressed forward, the sky ahead of him shimmering faintly green, reminding him of bioluminescence he'd witnessed once during a long distant sea journey. The wind, now a constant force pushing against him, hampering his progress, sounded like the roar of a pounding surf, swelling and receding, tossing him in its sway.

Tal lost two hours swishing through the snow, encountering no one. Not even a crazed and ravenous wolf. He changed direction and set off again, faring no better. He began to imagine he felt every second ticking by on the watch against his wrist. Like a drum beat of doom.

He herringboned up a hill and stood at the top, scanning with his souped-up camera for light, smoke, anything that might indicate a structure and people.

But there was nothing.

Where had he gone wrong? Direction? Distance? A single degree off course, multiplied by distance traveled, compounded the original error. Sometimes irredeemably. If he didn't find that stronghold, get inside, and stop Scylla's wicked posturing for power, thousands of people would die tonight.

Maybe millions more tomorrow.

Tal closed his eyes, prayed for guidance, prayed for peace on earth, good will toward men. Christmas was a celebration of the hope for deliverance. He needed that hope now.

He opened his eyes to see lights shifting in heaven. Glistening, shimmering emerald crossed by the nebulous gray of moving clouds, like a brilliant and mysterious green opal. He remembered that the color green, according to Christmas symbolism, represents eternal hope and renewal of life.

Embracing that hope, he strained his eyes over the expanse of darkness beneath the glowing sky and saw the compound nestled in snow. Saw it so clearly it was hard to imagine how he'd missed it before.

Sending up his heartfelt thanks, Tal switched off his headlamp and glided down the hill. The glow from the sky gave him enough light to move by and he didn't want to telegraph his arrival to anyone watching.

His skis became more of a hindrance than a help as he neared the compound. He abandoned them, realizing that without any kind of cover—no trees, only razor-wire and chain link fence surrounding the building—he'd have to crawl the last hundred yards, keeping low.

The only object that might provide him any kind of cover was a small garbage dumpster standing just inside the fence near a side door, presumably leading to the kitchen. He slithered up to the fence and laid flat behind the dumpster, catching his breath and peering beneath the dumpster's wheels.

It stank.

That was a good thing, as it turned out. Tal watched as two booted legs rounded the corner, accompanied by four black-and-brown dog paws. From his vantage point, he could only see the man from the knee down, but he saw enough of the Doberman to be glad of the stench helping to cover his scent. The wind that had pushed against him during the trek now worked in his favor—whisking scent molecules away before the dog could get a handle on them.

What now?

When dog and man had passed around the far corner of the building, continuing their rounds, Tal wriggled along the fence line far enough to give him a good look at the metal door. It was sturdy, flush with the wall, no entry keypad or card slider. Not even a keyhole. Just flat metal, unadorned.

He slinked into position behind the dumpster just as the patrol came back into view. The man paused and gave three raps on the door. It opened and a changing of the guards took place, including the dog. This time it was a German Shepherd.

Tal pulled back the layers and looked at his watch. Straight up on 11:00.

Alone, and with limited resources, the only way he could think to get inside that door was to wait until the next changing of the guard and take down the men while the door was open so their fallen bodies would prop the door open long enough for him to gain entry.

Provided no one else stood inside, waiting to drill him in the head as he crossed the threshold.

Fortunately, the cold would shorten their shifts. He bargained on their changing every half hour. It had to be. Otherwise, he'd be too late.

He spent the next thirty minutes waiting for the patrol to round the far corner and using the wire cutters to snip through the chain link fence while they traversed the opposite side of the yard.

As 11:30 approached, Tal's stomach contracted. He was shivering from laying in the snow and worried that his hands might be too numb to shoot straight. His target was less than 20 yards distant, ordinarily an easy shot for him, but the cold and wind were negative factors he had to take into account.

He readied the tranq gun for the German Shepherd, about the same size and weight as the wolf he'd planned for. With the time it would take to reload and shoot, tranquilizing the men was not an option. For them, lead.

He crouched beside the dumpster as man and dog turned the corner. He anticipated their stop at the door, the metallic rap, the bar of golden light reaching across the snow as the door opened.

It didn't happen.

The man and his German Shepherd continued past and out of sight. And again, on the next circuit. And the next.

Plan A was a bust, and there was no Plan B. Tal felt numb in the brain, unable to scramble together any kind of scheme to get him inside the concrete building before midnight. The structure featured an observatory dome on top with a raised portion down the center which Tal knew would slide open to facilitate a telescope.

Or a death ray.

Even as he watched, a mechanical hum reached him in the wind as the panel moved, creating a large opening in the side of the dome. The whole thing swiveled to point east. Toward the town of North Pole.

The only thing Tal could do was stick with Plan A and hope for a miracle.

It was Christmas, after all.

Two minutes to midnight.

Tal had his gun drawn and ready to fire. The tranquilizer dart gun held a syringe for the German Shepherd and Tal hoped he could load up another for the Doberman before it sprang on him and ripped his throat out.

The snow now was heavy enough to add visibility issues to the challenge he faced. It eddied and blew, flying against the shifting green sky while the wind moaned and shrieked an accompaniment.

One minute.

Tal firmed his jaw, willing himself to go to that place beyond fear, where resolve and determination called the shots and cold calculation won the day. He'd been there a time or two in the past, but it evaded him now.

So many lives at stake, so many obstacles to clear.

Ten seconds.

The sentry stood at the door. Three metallic knocks sounded as Tal stepped out from behind the dumpster.

He aimed.

The door opened.

He fired.

The first guard dropped.

Before the other man could return fire, Tal sent three shots into his chest. He staggered, slumping forward, and fell. Both dogs were in the yard now, barking like mad, jumping against the fence.

If they found the spot where he'd clipped through, he'd be dog-meat.

The first guard rolled and lifted onto a shoulder. He fired. The shot ricocheted off the dumpster. Tal heard it beside his ear, like an angry mosquito.

The dogs continued to launch themselves, moving closer to the weak spot. Tal shot the Doberman in the chest, the pink fringe of the dart like a party favor against the dark coat.

The dog yelped, but had time for one more leap against the fence before he drooped to the ground and went to sleep.

The downed guard reclaimed Tal's attention, firing off two more shots. One pinged off a fence post, ringing it like a bell.

The other hit Tal in the chest.

He went down.

He couldn't breathe. He'd fallen with his face right next to the fence. The German Shepherd barked furiously on the other side of it, jaws snapping inches from his nose, foamy saliva spraying against his cheek.

Tal groped blindly on the ground for the other loaded syringe, found it. Lying on his back, fighting for air, he loaded the dart gun and shot the German Shepherd at close range.

He whined as he fell.

The guard had risen to his knees. Tal saw him take aim for the death shot. But Tal's prone position made a difficult target, whereas the guard now presented a pretty decent one.

Tal fired twice.

The guard's gray parka bloomed red as he fell, face forward, and stopped moving.

Tal lay staring up into the strange green sky, flecked with emerald snowflakes. He fought to pull breath into his lungs and finally felt them expand, admitting oxygen into his bloodstream.

But it didn't matter.

It was midnight.

He'd failed.

Majestic and wondrous, the aurora borealis shone forth in the northern sky. Tal watched, his brow knit in pain, waiting for the lights to brighten and coalesce, forming a cone with the power to incinerate in an instant.

When a minute passed, and then two, he pushed himself up from the bed of snow and checked his watch again.

12:05.

As he wondered if this was the Christmas miracle he'd prayed for, he remembered the dropoff point, when Miskin had checked her watch and Carl had checked his, coordinating. Tal hadn't looked at his own watch then. He hadn't wanted to acknowledge the fear that ate at him, tied to the marching of the clock.

Besides, no one really used watches anymore. Handheld electronic devices kept time for the world. He still wore his own wristwatch only because it had been his grandfather's.

And it was set to Pacific time.

Not Alaska time.

It was 11:05.

He jolted to his feet then bent over, groaning. His chest hurt, and now that he'd been given a reprieve, he paid more attention to it. He fingered the hole in his parka where the bullet had passed through and found the misshapen missile trapped in the canvas of his chest rig.

It had been deflected by the multitool, and maybe *that* was his Christmas miracle.

He zipped the bullet, a souvenir of his near-death experience, into a compartment for safekeeping and hurried to the door, still blocked open by the sentry's body. He approached cautiously, weapon drawn, but encountered no one. With all the noise of the firefight and the dogs barking, his arrival cannot have gone unnoticed.

But the halls were empty. He headed toward the other end of the building, where the dome was. Now that he'd made it inside the compound, he wondered how he'd breach the inner sanctum and secure the weapon.

He needn't have worried.

The door stood ajar.

Gooseflesh prickled along the backs of Tal's arms. Staying close to the wall, he edged to the door and craned his neck to peer inside. Antonia Scylla lay sprawled on the floor, face up, her thick dark hair with its two stripes radiating out from her head like sunbeams.

She was dead.

A tall slim blonde dressed in a royal blue jumpsuit stood beside a large bolted-down mounting device flanked by mirrors tipped at various angles. She was busy packing something into a case, but she looked up and saw Tal.

Without pausing in her work, she jutted toward him with her chin. "Al, if you don't mind," she said, her voice smooth, cultured as a debutante's pearls.

The man who'd been leaning on a counter, watching her pack, pointed a gun and fired at the doorway. But Tal had seen him first and was a better aim. When the man fell, the blonde merely sighed.

"Before you go shooting me," she warned, "you'd better hear what I have to say."

"You're Charybdis?"

She shrugged. "If you like. I learned about Scylla's accomplishment with the concentrator from my Russian friends. They want it. And if they don't get it before midnight, they're prepared to firebomb everything within a fifty mile radius of this place to ensure it doesn't fall into the wrong hands."

"Preemptive bidding, huh?"

"You could call it that. Don't bother trying to stop me."

Before he knew how it happened, she had a gun in her hand, firing off a series of shots that chewed through the doorframe and sent him hugging the wall.

Another blast of her gun and the sound of shattering glass. Then silence.

Tal risked a peek into the room. Eudora Petrovna had made her own exit.

With the weapon.

Outside, the storm had arrived in full force. Snow flew in a frenzy, as if infuriated by the howling wind, everything tinted green by the eerie lights.

Tal reloaded his gun, bunched his muscles, and leapt through the broken window, landing hard on his back. He shoulder-rolled and came up into a crouching position, gun raised and seeking a target.

Nothing.

He turned, squinting his eyes into the night, looking for a moving figure. That's when he felt the hard barrel against the nape of his neck.

"I never even knew your name."

In the instant before she pulled the trigger, a wolf howled, making both of them jump. Her gun hand jerked upward, queering the shot which grazed the back of his skull.

The howl was loud, the wolf was close. But where?

It appeared at the broken window, snarling. *Inside* the building.

Its muzzle was smeared with gore and Tal guessed it had come in the same way he had—through a hole in the fence and the open door.

Only, the wolf had stopped for a snack.

It leapt.

Charybdis screamed. She dropped the case and ran. Instead of pursuing her, the wolf went for Tal, knocking him to the ground, dislodging the gun from his hand.

Tal's layers of protective clothing impeded the wolf's fangs, but the effect would be temporary. Tal desperately felt for a loaded syringe. His fingers slid with frantic haste over the Zippo and the extra mags.

Finally, his hand closed around a tranquilizer cartridge. He didn't bother loading the pistol—simply pulled the cap off with his teeth and plunged it into the wolf's hairy hide.

The creature yelped in pain, snapping at Tal's face, but he pulled away and pushed the animal down. The wolf was weakening fast.

Tal snatched the weapon case in one hand, his gun in the other, and skidded around the corner, to the side of the building he hadn't seen before.

Charybdis was there, standing beside two parked snowmobiles. The storm was abating and Tal heard a faint rumbling overhead. He looked up.

Charybdis raised her gun and pulled the trigger.

Three times.

Four.

She'd pumped four bullets into the spare snowmobile, destroying it.

The one Tal might have used to get away with the weapon.

The smell of gasoline permeated the air as fuel streamed onto the ground through the bullet holes. The sleek scientist climbed onto the other machine and turned the key, holding Tal at bay with her gun.

"The Russians are circling," she said. "I may not have the weapon, but I've got twenty-eight minutes to get out of the blast zone, and a way to get me there."

As she sped into the night, her voice floated back on the wind.

"I still don't know your name."

As Charybdis disappeared into the night, Tal sagged against the concrete wall of the compound building. Above him, the sky continued its magnificent light display and for a moment he simply watched and allowed himself to be awed by the power and beauty of it.

How wrong that such splendor should have been used for evil, to destroy, to cheapen human life to the price a bidder would pay.

How tired he was. It seemed more effort than he could muster to lift his head anymore. He let it droop, chin reaching his chest. All his communication equipment was lost, ruined, or malfunctioning. He had no means of reaching anyone, no way to pass on any information.

At this point, the Russians represented the best case scenario.

Thinking about the ramifications of a world where such a weapon existed, Tal decided it was just as well the Russians would be blowing the incinerator sky high in—he looked at his watch—seventeen minutes.

He only wished he didn't have to go with it.

Another precious minute ticked by before Tal came to the conclusion that he wanted to do it himself.

He grabbed the weapon case and raced back, stepping over the sedated wolf to climb through the window into the observatory.

He was no rocket scientist, but a quick study of what he'd taken to be mirrors showed they were indeed some kind of reflectors. Removing the device from the case, he fastened it onto the mount as he'd seen it before Charybdis packed it away.

The weapon featured dials for setting latitude and longitude, as well as a timer. Its many smaller dials and buttons would forever remain a mystery. Tal entered the coordinates he'd seen on the GPS tracker before it fizzled out. The reflectors repositioned themselves and a beam like a laser pointer bounced off of them onto the weapon itself.

A raucous alarm sounded and red siren lights strobed across the walls. Tal set the timer, giving himself a six minute window, and pressed the button marked LAUNCH.

He ran.

Slogging through snow slowed him down. But the memory of what he'd seen on the satellite footage, the way the village in Greenland had burnt to a crisp and blown away in the wind, gave him the will to speed.

He had no idea how tight a circle the weapon drew around its target. But he was soon to find out.

The overhead green intensified to a brilliance more than he could bear. Dropping to the ground, he buried his face beneath the wing of his arm and squeezed his eyes shut. There was a *WUMP!* that Tal felt in his stomach rather than actually hearing. When he felt the light dim, he cautiously lifted his head.

The compound was gone.

Obliterated.

And the weapon with it.

He lay in the snow, weak with relief, thrilled to be alive.

The emerald shimmers continued their dance in the sky above, emanations from the sun, giver of warmth and life. In this season of joy, meant for peace on earth and good will toward men, he thought the world just might have taken one step closer to that hope.

The hum of an aircraft reached his ears, faint at first and growing louder.

It was midnight.

The hum crescendoed, beating against his eardrums as the chopper hovered over the site. Tal hugged himself and waited. Then it faded off into the distance. The Russians, it appeared, had seen the cinders and judged their efforts to be superfluous.

Now what?

Tal dragged himself to his feet, bone weary and happy. But also aware that he might not live out the night. He was freezing, hungry, alone without provisions, and in the middle of nowhere, with no way to contact help.

And there were wolves. Two of them, stalking him on the left. Not crazed or rabid. Just ordinary wolves.

But dangerous all the same.

He had only a few syringes left, a bullet or two in the gun, and then he'd be defenseless. He stumbled forward and was just thinking about trying to find where he'd ditched the skis when he heard a new sound. A low growl, rising in pitch and volume.

Turning toward it, Tal watched as a row of snow machines crested the hill, looking cinematic against the shifting green sky. The riders wore Santa hats streaming behind them as they advanced.

And they flew the American flag.

The night was full of Christmas miracles.

*Note: If you enjoyed this Tal Bannerman story, there's a sequel you should know about. *The Bermuda Triangle Blueprint Exchange* finds Tal on an enigmatic island deep in the Bermuda Triangle, chosen as a pawn in a high-stakes game orchestrated by a criminal mastermind. Step again into Tal Bannerman's shoes and prepare for a ride like no other!

INCREDIBLE CHRISTMAS CAPERS

Most years, when it gets 'bout Christmastime, folks want to hear me tell the story 'bout how I got here. Gives 'em a tickle, I s'pose, and I can't fault 'em none for wantin' a lift over the holidays.

So, I rummage up my mem'ries of what happened that night. Though, truth be told, I think on it often—wonderin' how things might of come out different, wonderin' if I played it the best I coulda done.

And mostly decidin' I just don't have a hound dog's chance in hell of ever knowin'.

Now, I done had me some crazy nights in my time—that's for damn sure—but on that night, when I crept up on that house in the inky black of winter, I musta been clean out of my mind.

I remember the smell. Damp leaves, dead on the ground and stamped into the mud. And the spicy scent of tree bark. That smell—that feel—always gives me a hankerin' for hot cider, and I'd a been a whole sight better off goin' home to mix up a cup.

But I thought I had me somethin' better to do.

Fool that I was.

The wind was moanin', blowin' the tree branches, makin' 'em squirm like that snake-headed Greek woman I learned of in my school days.

It was cold, too. Christmas cold.

I had the shivers so's I could hardly hold my jackknife while I scraped the putty out of one of them little panes of glass. The house was a grand one—not so big and fancy as some I seen—but just right for what I wanted.

I had me a funny feelin' about that house. A fine kind of funny, like I get with a stomach full o' warm oatmeal or a thick, gravy stew.

A signpost planted in the mulch bed warned skulkers like me 'bout an alarm system. But I had watched from the trees while a fellow pounded that sign into the dirt, and he weren't nothing but a salesman makin' a pitch. I figgered it for an empty threat.

And I guessed I figgered right, 'cause no bells started clangin' when I loosed that pane and sprang the window latch. It was a wide, low window, easy to crawl through, so I let myself in with not a single noise, save for a wee-bitty bump when I pulled the window shut to keep out the cold.

I stood on carpet so thick my feet sank down into it like I was walkin' on the beach. And there was a partic'lar odor in the room, good pipe tobacco and a whiff a men's cologne. A dull smear of light glowed in through the window, stars peepin' from behind those snaky branches, but not enough to see by, so I lit up my penlight and shone it round.

Stretching mostways across the room was a big desk, made of glossy wood glintin' red, and behind it, rows and rows of books on shelves. A home office, it looked like. Or maybe a library.

I crept to the door, chucklin' inside, thinking about that website I been watching of late—Incredible Christmas Capers. Folks sending in videos of pranks played on department store customers. Or showing off their houses and yards festooned with enough lights to keep the man in the moon awake all night. Or displaying their precious pets in elf costume or dressed up like The Grinch.

As Christmas grew nearer, all sorts of silly frolics showed up on that site, everyone tryin' for a laugh or a crack at best video of the week. But I bet they never seen something as daring as what I just done.

The door stood open to the rest of the house, and I peeked out, panning the light over a kitchen that winked back at me, lined wall to wall with marble countertops and shiny glass. And right next door, a dining room stuffed full of dark, heavy furniture smellin' like a lemon grove.

Beyond that, I saw the twinkling lights of the Christmas tree, rising like a mountain to the ceiling, with a whole village of fancy-wrapped, 'spensive gifts spread out beneath it.

I couldn't keep the big grin off my face as I tiptoed past the dining room to stand in front of that tree. At the tippy-top was an angel, smiling down at me as if ready to grant my every Christmas wish.

I knew it was a real tree, too. Not the kind you pull out of a box and put together yourself. I knew, 'cause there were needles on the floor and the air smelled like pine. A good, clean smell that made me think 'bout my campin' days.

Turnin' slowly, I took it all in, lickin' my lips, a little tug of excitement in my gut. But before I could twitch a muscle, I heard a wicked rumbling that made my blood chill up inside my veins, and my heart leapt up into my throat like a toad scrabbling to get out.

The garage door!

Stumblin' to the window, I pulled back the curtain just in time to see a slick black Mercedes glide by as it vanished into the three-car garage beside the house.

I had to get out. I needed to move.

But my legs felt glued to the floor, like they was bein' sucked down in a bog of hungry quicksand.

And then a breath in my ear sent a shiver down my back. "He'll catch you if you don't move now. Come with me."

My legs, still stuck to the floor, turned to jelly. A woman in a long white gown appeared right beside me, clear as day. A ghost, I thought, and I might of sunk down on the floor and howled, but she touched me.

And she was no ghost.

Twinin' her arm around mine, she pulled at me and somehow I began to move, though my legs felt like two rough-hewed logs, heavy and raw. She guided me up a curvy staircase, climbing so fast I had to work hard to keep up.

At the top of the stairs, she pulled me through a door and I could see right away that we were in her bedroom. It didn't feel proper, me being there with her, and she, dressed in only a wispy nightgown. But I had not the time or the space to argue the point.

Pushin' me into the closet, she shut the door, cuttin' off my protest and the dim glow from her bedside lamp. It was like being smothered in black velvet as her soft, hanging dresses closed around me, carrying her scent and her insistent manner.

I had hardly a moment to wonder or think what to do, when I heard a man's voice right outside the closet door. I held my breath and pressed my ear against the wood, listenin'.

"Looks like you had a good time at the party," the girl said. "Did you get enough to drink?"

Her voice sounded strange. Harsh, somehow. But the man answered mild enough. "Plenty. You know I like a good eggnog."

"And a good scotch."

He made a noise I couldn't tell the meaning of before he said, "You're not wrong. I'm going to bed. Goodnight, Cara."

"Goodnight...Dad."

I waited there in the dark, crowded closet, shakin' like a poplar in the wind, 'til he was good and gone, and then another minute to make certain sure before I tried pushing on the door.

It wouldn't budge.

"Hush," said the girl, her voice passing through the wooden partition like a spirit in the night, so faint I might of imagined it.

So, I hushed. And I waited, thinking surely nothing as bizarre as this had ever appeared on Incredible Christmas Capers. At least, nothing I ever seen.

At last, the door opened, and she pulled me into the bedroom. Her glance, lit by the bedside lamp, looked like a tease, but I was having none of it. I gripped her by the shoulders and whispered somethin' fierce.

"What the hell is goin' on?" I wanted to know. "What fool game are you playin'?"

She laughed and snuggled close. "Is that a knife in your pocket," she said, her hand pressed against my thigh, "or are you just happy to see me?"

A chill trickled through me then, and I wondered if the girl was looney in the head. I knew I had to get out of that bedroom, and I did. Only, she followed me, hangin' on my arm like we was goin' to prom.

"Don't be mad," she said while I clung to the banister so's I wouldn't fall down the stairs in the dark. "I did you a favor."

I didn't say nothin', just kept goin' down them beachy soft stairs.

"I saw you sneak to the window with your little knife," she said. "I had the phone in my hand, ready to dial 911."

I reached the bottom step and stopped, suddenly overcome with a powerful curiosity to know why she done what she done.

"And then," she said, putting her lips to my ear, tickling me with her breath. "I had a thrilling idea. I turned off the alarm and watched you chip away at that windowpane. I wanted to see what you would do."

A little zap of surprise hit me, and I said, "There's an alarm?"

She giggled and gave my arm a little slap. "Of course there's an alarm. My father wouldn't want to lose any of his precious things to a thief in the night."

In the sparkly lights from the Christmas tree, I thought I saw a hard gleam in her eyes.

"Then why let me in?"

"Because," she said, her grip tightening on my arm. "He deserves to be robbed."

She let out a little sob and chewed down on it, pressing her lips together. "You may not believe me," she said, "but I'm telling you, my father is a terrible man. A cruel, heartless bastard."

She pulled back the neck of her nightgown and showed me a dark bruise spreading like the sea on a paper map. Lifting her hair, she tilted her head so the purple lump rising behind her ear glowed like a plum in the festive lights of the tree.

For a minute or two after that, neither of us said a word. Tears shone on her cheeks, and she wiped them away with a corner of her nightgown.

"You won't be able to grab it all up," she said at last, wavin' a hand as if to take in the whole room. "But I can show you the most valuable things to take. The things that will hit him the hardest."

She paused. "Like he hit me." Taking my hand, she added, "You'd be giving me a gift."

I thought a tick or two 'bout what she said, then I nodded. "A Christmas gift."

She smiled, and I saw the reflection of the twinklin' lights in the whites of her eyes.

Flappin' an arm toward the gifts under the tree, she said, "Forget the wrapped presents. Too big, too hard to carry. Here's my father's real treasure, anyway. Pocket-sized."

She crossed to a cabinet and fetched a key from a china pitcher shaped like a rooster. My own granny used to have one similar. Un-lockin' a drawer, she pulled it wide and showed me a wonder—dark blue velvet filled with little nooks and crannies, each one aglimmer with gold or silver.

I swallowed hard. Even better than what I come for.

Scooping up a handful of the coins, she shoved them into my pocket, and I helped by taking the rest.

Then she seized my hand and fastened her eye on me. "This isn't even the best of it," she said. "He keeps the cream of his collection in a coffer inside his bedroom closet."

I shook off her hand. "No, please and thank you," I told her. "This'll do just fine. And to all, a good night."

I was fixed to leave out the way I come, but she pressed herself against me, hip to hip, her hand wandering once more along my thigh.

"One coin from the coffer upstairs is worth everything you have here, and more. And should my father wake," she said, fingering the jackknife folded tight in my pocket, "you have the means to take care of the problem."

And now, I knew she was crazy. Unbalanced. Cuckoo. A queer shiver worked down my spine like a crawling hand, making me cold all over.

I wanted outta that house in the worst way, but before I could shake loose, we heard a creak and footsteps on the floor above and my heart cranked into overdrive.

"Cara, is that you downstairs?"

Her fingers bit into my arm as she pushed me behind the sofa. "Yes," she called. "Guilty. I hope I didn't wake you."

Crouching down with my cheek pressed up against cold leather, I heard her father come down the rest of the steps. I held my breath, wishing I'd a got out while the gettin' out was good.

"No, you didn't wake me. I couldn't sleep either. Why don't you make us some cocoa?"

"Sure thing, Dad."

After a moment, I heard the rattle of a kettle in the kitchen and knew I was alone in the room with her old man. Panic welled up in me and I fought a daft itchin' to make a run for the window and damn the cost of my foolish actions.

Faint scufflin' and poppin' noises told me he was doin' something over by the cabinet and I prayed he wouldn't open the blue velvet drawer and raise a hue and cry. When the crackle of an old LP filled the room with Bing Crosby singing *White Christmas*, I near fell over with relief.

I heard a rustle as the man settled into what I could only guess was his favorite armchair. Cowering against the smoothness of leather, I listened hard until Bing took up with *God Rest Ye Merry, Gentlemen*.

And then I heard something else that made my scalp tingle like that time my brother, Joe, dared me to stick my finger in a light bulb socket, and I done it.

An awful gasp. A dreadful groan. And then silence, save for Bing and the hiss of vinyl under the needle.

I didn't want to look. With every inch of my soul, I wished I'd a stayed home. But I had to move. I had to know.

So, I peeked out from behind my leather shelter, and I saw a man sprawled in a recliner, his yellow flannel pajamas stained red from the knife stickin' out of his chest.

My hand flew to my pocket, but the clang in my ribcage told me the truth before my fingers touched denim.

I was a doomed man.

Scramblin' up from the floor, I ran for the kitchen door, plannin' to disappear like a vapor into the woods behind the house. Before I got two steps across that plushy carpet, I heard a screechin' and a cryin' that sent a zing straight to my gut.

The girl. And she was 'parently on the phone to 911, screaming bloody murder. In the distance, I heard the wail of a siren and that lit a fire under my feet that shot me out the back door like a streak of lightnin'.

I run across the shadowy yard, trippin' on a garden hose, stubbin' my shins on flowerbeds and fancy pottery. I fell once, going down hard on a brick-paved patio littered with lawn furniture. The copper taste of blood filled my mouth, and I knew I done knocked a tooth loose. But I scrabbled up and kept on runnin'.

In yonder woods, the dark got so thick I had to stop scurryin' along for fear I'd crack my skull on a tree trunk. I slowed down and crept careful, but it done me no good. I could hear 'em comin,' shoutin' and scufflin,' gettin' closer with every tick.

And there in the wood, pressed up against the trunk of an old maple, I saw what a fool I'd been—beginnin' to end. I got an inklin' that girl maybe wasn't tellin' the truth 'bout how she got those bumps and bruises. For all I knew, she picked 'em up in a car crash.

For the man had seemed a decent fellow to me, and I knew *her* for a liar. I begun thinkin' maybe she wanted dear old dad out of the way for some other kind of reason. Like early access to an inheritance maybe.

There I stood, my pockets full of a dead man's gold, my jackknife in his chest, and I knew I'd pay for what I done. Truth is, I was ready to. I knew I was goin' to jail, and I was willin' to pay the price for my ambition and my stupidity.

But not for murder.

That's why, when the police come and grab me, I went gentle into the night. I let them pat me down and empty my pockets. I watched them put all the little pieces they found into their official evidence bags and mark down where they come from.

I sat still and quiet, the shackles bitin' into my wrists all the way to the jailhouse. I held my peace and waited for my court-appointed attorney.

'Cause I had something to show those lawmen. I broke into that house on nothin' but a lark. A dare. I meant to tape somethin' special for Incredible Christmas Capers that'd never been done before. I thought to earn me the best video of the season award.

That's all I went for.

That's why I borrowed Joe's GoPro camera and strapped it to my chest with the lens peepin' out from a buttonhole in my shirt, fixed there with a piece of duct tape.

That's why I went in with a fully charged battery and a virgin mem'ry card, ready to record the whole damn bodacious adventure for Caper fans everywhere.

That's why I think—after everything I been through—I deserve the award for best video of the season. When all is said and done, penalty paid and parole granted, I think it would be only fair.

Don't be surprised if someday I win that Incredible Christmas Caper award, after all.

And To All A Good Night

S heriff's deputy, Randall Steadman, watched as soft flakes, white and feathery as eiderdown, fell against the windshield, melting to slush as the wipers caught and spread them across the glass. The blades squeaked and stuttered, leaving behind long streaks and blotches. He made a mental note to replace them as soon as he and Vivi returned from their Christmas holiday.

A jazzy piano version of *We Three Kings* played on the Navigator's sound system. Steadman kept the volume low, wanting the festive music to be a mood enhancer rather than a main attraction. He liked it when Vivi talked, sharing her thoughts as she stared out the window, a child-like expression of wonder lighting her lovely face.

The snow let up and they passed through the Bavarian-styled town of Leavenworth, Washington in the gentle sunlight of early afternoon. Vivi leaned forward, eyes wide, taking in the fairy tale setting, and Steadman followed her lead. Picturesque cottages stood sandwiched between life-sized gingerbread houses and half-timbered inns with garland-strewn balconies. Shop windows glowed with displays of pastries, confections, jewelry, and clothing.

Despite the cold, Vivi lowered her window and drew in a deep breath. Steadman did the same, appreciating the crisp freshness, almost tasting the hint of pine and spice in the air. An octagonal bandstand stood at the center of the square, and a group of musicians dressed in lederhosen tooted out a brassy holiday greeting to the milling crowd.

"When I was a girl, we lived in Yorktown for three years," Vivi said. She rolled up her window and leaned back against the leather seat, a wistful look on her face. "All three of those summers we bought season passes to Busch Gardens. The Old Country, they called it."

Steadman smiled, raising his eyebrows as an invitation for her to go on.

"I loved going there. I pretended I really was in Europe. This reminds me of those days. I can almost imagine we're in Germany."

Steadman found her hand, squeezed it. "Someday we'll go," he said.

Vivi rolled her eyes.

"No, I mean it. Let's plan on next summer. I'll make the time, you make the arrangements."

"It'll just end up being another busman's holiday. Like this one."

"What do you mean—like this one? Bennett invited us to come and relax, enjoy Christmas with his family in this storybook environment. No investigation involved."

Vivi's lips pursed and she sighed, but she squeezed his hand back. "We'll see."

As the main town fell away, the road grew icy and Steadman kept both hands on the wheel, guiding the SUV around bends until they reached the turnoff to the Grayson property. The gate stood open and they crunched over the snow-frosted gravel of the drive, lined on both sides with oak, maple, and fir. As they rounded a curve and the house came into view, a missile of snow hit the windshield, making Steadman clutch reflexively at the steering wheel and drawing a squeal from Vivi.

Steadman braked and activated the wipers again, clearing the window in time to see two young people in snowsuits bearing down on them, flanked by a capering yellow Labrador.

"Sorry, sir!" the boy said, his cheeks and nose red from cold. "That was meant for her."

He gestured to the girl, who grinned and lobbed a snowball, laughing with glee as it splatted against the side of his beanie-covered head. She fled and he followed, chased by the dog. Steadman pulled the car around to the side of the house and parked, getting out to stand and stretch, shaking out the kinks of a long drive.

The children approached, faces still cheery but more formal now. The dog sniffed at Steadman, greeting him with a cold, wet nose against his palm.

"You must be the sheriff," the girl said. "I'm Olivia. Bennett's my uncle."

"I'm not a sheriff," Steadman told her. "Only a deputy."

"*Chief* Deputy," Vivi corrected, pulling her case from the trunk.

"Can I help?" the boy offered. "I'm Todd, Olivia's brother. And that's Gomer," he said, indicating the yellow lab.

"Steadman!" A voice boomed from the doorway and Steadman turned to see Bennett lumbering toward them. He clasped Steadman in a rib-shattering hug before bowing over Vivi's hand. "So pleased to meet you Mrs. Steadman."

"It's Vivi. Thank you so much for inviting us, Bennett."

The children ran ahead, each carrying a piece of luggage, and Bennett ushered them in through the side door.

It was very warm inside and Steadman shed his coat, hanging it on a peg in the entry as seemed the custom, judging by the haphazard arrangement of outerwear. The air smelled of gingerbread and wet dog. He smiled at Vivi and took her hand as they followed Bennett into the kitchen.

A woman bent over the center island, icing bag in hand as she applied raisins and gumdrops to a row of gingerbread men. Todd, at her elbow, argued that he should be allowed a glass of brandy-laced eggnog.

"You're thirteen, Todd. You'll have cocoa, like your sister."

The boy grumbled and bit the head off one of the cookies. The woman's lips thinned into a grim line and Todd slunk away, a sullen look on his face.

"This is my Aunt Desiree," Bennett said. "Des, meet Steadman and Vivi."

Desiree gave them a distracted hello. "Welcome to the nut hatch. Give me a minute to finish this, and I'll show you up to your room."

"My sister Karen and her husband are out doing some last-minute shopping," Bennett said. "But come meet my dad."

They passed through an arched doorway into a high-ceilinged room with two large windows overlooking a snowy field bordered by woodlands, a twelve-foot Christmas tree centered between them, sparkling with gold and silver ornaments. A fire crackled in the grate and a vinyl record spun on the turntable, sending forth the strains of an orchestra playing carol classics. Two men sat in front of the fireplace, and as they approached, one of them—a white-haired man wearing a cardigan—rose and stepped forward to meet them, his movements slightly hesitant. Steadman noted his sallow complexion, the wince he tried to hide, and realized Mr. Grayson was a man past his prime.

"Dad, this is my friend, Steadman. I've told you how he helped me with the ranch in Mason County. And his wife, Vivi."

"Right. Good to meet you, Steadman. Vivi. Call me Hunter." He fixed an intense gaze on Steadman. "I appreciate how you cleared up that cattle rustling business for Bennett. He speaks highly of your abilities."

Steadman cleared his throat, a bit embarrassed. "You make it sound like I'm John Wayne instead of just a county sheriff's deputy doing his job."

Hunter chuckled. "Have a drink with us?" he asked, gesturing toward the other man. "George brought around a bottle of single malt."

"George is our neighbor," Bennett explained. "Rents a little cottage we have on the property."

Steadman nodded a greeting and George raised his tumbler. "Happy Christmas!"

The man looked to be in his late seventies, but still sported a full head of grizzled iron-gray hair, though the skin under his eyes bagged and his hand, holding the glass, shook badly enough to make wavelets in the amber scotch.

"Where's Penn?" Bennett asked.

"Oh, you know how Penn likes to get outdoors," Hunter said. "He went for a walk."

Desiree came in, dusting her hands on a wide, black apron. "Let me take you up so you can get settled, have a rest and a bath before dinner."

Steadman motioned for Vivi to follow Desiree up the staircase while he brought up the rear. As they reached the landing, Olivia came out of a room at the end of the hall. She caught sight of them and jerked to a halt, a wash of pink coming into her cheeks.

"Olivia." Desiree's tone was forbidding, disapproving. She approached the girl, holding out her hand. Slowly, Olivia placed a key on the older woman's waiting palm and opened her mouth to speak, but Desiree cut her off with a sharp motion. "Let's not have any hysterics this year, all right?"

Olivia nodded and turned without a word, disappearing into another room off the corridor.

"You're in here," Desiree said, inviting them in with a sweep of her hand.

The room was spacious, flanked with three tall, narrow windows looking out on what must be a flower garden in spring and summer. The hardwood floors gleamed in the late afternoon sun and a faint scent of lemon oil lingered in the air. A high four-poster bed was spread with a handmade quilt crowned by a mound of plump pillows.

"This is lovely," Vivi said. "Thank you so much."

The sound of Desiree's footsteps had barely faded before Vivi was in the adjoining bathroom, running the tap into a round marble-trimmed tub. Steadman left her to it and wandered back onto the landing. He saw Olivia's door was open and strolled by, glancing in to see the girl standing at an easel, brush and palette in hand.

"You can come in," she said. "I could use a second opinion."

Steadman smiled, coming round in front of the easel, and stopped, dumbfounded. He didn't know what he'd expected, but it wasn't this. The fabric of the canvas seemed to be punctured and peeling away, making way for a perching bird so realistic he thought if he made a noise it might fly away.

"It's trompe l'oeil," Olivia said. "It tricks the eye."

"It certainly does," Steadman agreed. "It's remarkable."

Olivia placed her palette and brush on a table. "It's only a copy," she said. "I'm imitating the masters so I can learn their technique." She blushed. "At least, that's my goal."

She opened a book and showed Steadman a photo of the original. "I'm trying to learn how to create optical illusions, deceive the eye into seeing three dimensions when there are only two there. It's difficult. My paintings lack depth."

"You're very talented," Steadman said. "I've no doubt you'll master the technique." He hesitated, letting his curiosity get the better of him. "That room your aunt caught you coming out of...?"

Olivia snapped shut the book. "That's Aunt Zena's studio. She's the reason I paint. I want to be like her, but *Great* Aunt Desiree doesn't like me going in there."

"Bennett never mentioned he has a sister who paints."

"No, he wouldn't. No one talks about her anymore, not since she committed suicide six years ago. Just before Christmas."

Again, Steadman found himself floundering for words. Olivia seemed to realize she'd just dropped a damper on the holiday and made an attempt to lighten the mood.

"She was a wonderful artist, my Aunt Zena. I think she could have been great." She wiped her brush with a paint-stained rag. "To me, she *was* great and I think about her every time I paint. She had a fantastic studio, full of beautiful books and materials and all her incredible paintings. I always thought it would be mine some day. It seemed obvious that it should be."

She swirled the brush in a jar of cloudy water. "Desiree thinks my time would be better spent on something practical, like biology or solving equations. Last year, when we came for Christmas, I snuck into the studio and everything was gone. Erased, as if Zena never existed." She paused, drawing a deep breath through flaring nostrils. "I pitched a fit."

Steadman felt an echo of what she must have endured. The deprivation and disappointment. "I suppose that's what Desiree meant by hysterics."

Olivia nodded, chewing on her lip as she eyed his wrinkled trousers. "I'd change before dinner if I were you," she warned him.

Taking the jar with her, she closed herself into the bathroom and turned the lock.

Steadman took Vivi's arm as they descended the staircase for dinner. Vinyl still rotated on the turntable, but the music now was Glenn Miller and a couple wearing red sweaters jitterbugged beside the Christmas tree. Steadman guessed they were Bennett's sister, Karen, and her husband. Olivia's parents.

A delicious aroma filled the room. Not the smell of roast turkey, as he'd expected, but garlic and spice. Like a Chinese restaurant. Hunter and another man had pulled up chairs in front of a display case filled with bits of polished rock. Steadman paused behind them, mystified by their talk of gravity separation and troctolites. Hunter caught a glimpse of him and motioned him over.

"Steadman, may I introduce Pennington Smith, family friend and fellow rock hound. Penn, meet Sheriff Steadman."

Steadman shook hands, not bothering to correct Hunter's error. He'd found that in most social situations, people didn't draw a distinction between sheriff and deputy. He pointed to the display case.

"You've got a beautiful collection there."

Hunter beamed. "I do indeed." He fingered a slice of amethyst geode. "I'm hoping to pick up a few lumps of coal in my stocking this year."

Penn laughed, clapping his friend on the shoulder. "Been a bad boy, have you?"

The smile left Hunter's face and he began putting the bits of rock back in their places. "I believe dinner's ready. Shall we go in?"

The long dining table, decked with a red damask cloth and tasseled runner, held an array of platters, tureens, and bowls, all brimming full of Chinese fare. Steadman spotted egg drop soup, stir-fried vegetables, barbecued pork, spring rolls, Kung Pao chicken, and at least three varieties of rice. As everyone took their seats, Steadman turned to Desiree, who seemed to be in charge of the kitchen.

"Did you order in, or is this all homemade?"

She gave him a tight-lipped smile. "Homemade, sir, but I didn't do it all myself. Karen's husband, Leo, barbecued the pork and the children put together the spring rolls."

Penn grinned, pouring himself a glass of wine. "I brewed the sake."

Karen snatched the bottle from him. "You did not! And besides, sake is Japanese. This is plain old Napa Valley."

Everyone laughed and the meal began, dishes passing clockwise around the table, plates filling, silverware clanking. Each place-setting included a pair of chopsticks, but Todd was the only one who used them. With limited success.

"This family is steeped in tradition," Bennett said, slicing into a piece of pork. "We make a ceremony out of selecting and chopping down the Christmas tree. We decorate it with the same ornaments every year, accompanied by Bing Crosby and hot wassail. You've missed that bit, but I hope you'll be part of our Christmas letter tradition." He chewed, sweeping his hand around to indicate the meal. "And, of course, this dinner."

As he paused to drink, Karen said, "Most families in Leavenworth celebrate Christmas Eve with roast goose or Kartoffelsalat and sausages. But for us, it's always a homemade Chinese meal." Sadness tinged her smile. "Because that's how our father proposed to our mother—on Christmas Eve, over Peking Duck and fried rice."

"Dad says Mom burned the duck," Bennett added, "but we don't carry tradition that far."

"She did burn the duck," Hunter said, "but it was delicious anyway. She never missed a year, prepping for days ahead, spending hours in the kitchen. Not even when she went into labor with Karen."

"Or thought she did," Karen explained. "False alarm. I was born on New Year's Eve instead."

"Bringing us a whole year of tax benefits, clever girl," Hunter said, raising his glass. "To your mother."

We all lifted our glasses, toasting the family matriarch. Steadman remembered Bennett telling him that Emma Grayson had died of cancer when he was in his teens.

"How I miss her," Hunter murmured.

A moment of silence passed before Olivia said brightly, "I'm ready for my fortune cookie."

She reached into the bowl and selected a cookie, peeling away the wrapper and breaking it open to reveal a slip of paper. Smoothing it out, she read: "Old crimes cast long shadows—death waits around the corner." Her face crumpled. "What a horrid fortune! Somebody else open one. Let's get something jolly going."

The bowl passed round the table, but as everyone broke open their cookies, it became clear that all fortunes read the same: death waits around the corner.

"What do you make of that?" Bennett asked.

Penn cleared his throat. "Someone's idea of a joke."

"If it's supposed to be a joke, it's not a bit funny," Desiree said, pushing back from the table, stacking dirty plates for a trip to the kitchen.

Olivia threw her crinkled wrapper into the empty bowl. "The most reasonable explanation points to a bored employee on the fortune cookie assembly line."

Todd gave her a withering look.

"Let's forget it," Leo said, "and move on to the fun and games. It's Christmas Eve!"

Everyone rose and helped clear the table. Steadman noticed the slight frown furrowed on Vivi's forehead and thought she must be sensing the same faint underlying tension that gnawed inside him. He kissed the top of her head and took her armful of dirty linen napkins. "I'll see these make it into the hamper."

He'd noticed the laundry alcove tucked into the side entry where he and Vivi had come into the house. Away from the hubbub, the dark silence of the mud room seemed full of portent. Steadman dumped his load of linens and stood beside the coats and galoshes, listening, feeling, sensing a hum he couldn't identify. Or do anything about.

Returning to the den, he found the group gathered around the fireplace, their images reflected in the large picture windows either side of the tall Christmas tree. They played charades and six rounds of speed Scrabble, and then it was time to hang the stockings and say goodnight.

"Don't forget to write your Christmas letters," Karen reminded them. "I've put stationery and envelopes in all your rooms. You too," she said to Steadman and Vivi."

"It's kind of a personal time capsule we make for ourselves," Bennett explained.

"Wonderful idea," Penn added. "I get a kick out of opening them up a year later."

Olivia settled onto the sofa beside Steadman. "We write a letter to ourselves, saying what we hope to accomplish or what we wish for the coming year and then, the next year, they magically appear in our stockings and we open them and see if our predictions came true."

"Or we get a good laugh out of it," Todd said.

"Or inspiration for the year to come," Karen added.

"It sounds like an excellent tradition," Vivi said, turning to Karen. "Thank you for including us."

In their room, lit by starlight and the soft glow of a desk lamp, Steadman changed into pajamas and sat thinking about what to write in his letter. The sound of Vivi's pen, scratching so effortlessly away annoyed him. She folded her paper and slipped it into the envelope, licking it shut and scrawling her name across the cream-colored front.

"That's it. I need some sleep." She yawned and padded across to place her envelope on the desk, giving him a goodnight kiss before climbing into bed.

Steadman stared at the sliver of woods and sky visible through the tall, narrow window in front of him. He loved his life, his job, his friends, his family. There wasn't much more he could wish for except happiness for him and those he loved.

In the end, it was simple. He wrote his letter and went to bed, snuggling up next to the warmth of his wife, listening to her even breathing, thickened with just the hint of a snore. Better than any white noise machine. It put him right out.

In the morning, he woke to learn that Desiree Grayson was dead.

Once more, the family gathered in the den. The fire still crackled, providing the only sound, the only warmth on that cold, silent Christmas morning. Turntable still. Gifts under the tree, unopened. Chelan county sheriff's deputies moving up and down the stairs with respectful nods and apologies.

Steadman felt a weight in his chest. He'd brought Vivi here for a carefree celebration of the hope of mankind, never for a moment thinking it would turn into something like this. Still, Leavenworth was miles out of his jurisdiction; it wouldn't become a busman's holiday.

Or would it?

Vivi was right far too often.

Karen came into the room, carrying a tray. "Let's get something hot into you," she said, passing out mugs of coffee and cocoa. Steadman used the cup to warm his hands, letting the fragrant vapor rise to his nose like a healing mist.

"Does anyone want breakfast?" Karen asked.

No one did.

At length, the officer in charge came to speak to them. He was a large man, tall and big-boned with slightly drooping jowls giving him a hangdog expression. He positioned a chair near the fireplace where he could meet everyone's eye.

"I'm very sorry for your loss," he said. "I'm sure this is not how you wanted to spend your Christmas. I'm Chief Deputy Morgan, and I'd like each of you to introduce yourself and state your relationship to Desiree Grayson."

When that was finished, he closed his notebook and looked up, his face solemn. "I'm sorry to deliver such sad news, but it appears Ms. Grayson took her own life."

"No," Hunter said. "She wouldn't."

Olivia, too, shook her head, her face ashen. Karen began weeping quietly and Vivi placed an arm around her shoulders.

"Are you sure?" Penn asked.

"We'll be looking more closely at the evidence," Morgan said, "but all indications point that way. I'm sorry." He pulled an envelope from his jacket pocket. "She left this."

"It's her Christmas letter," said Olivia.

"Or," Chief Morgan said after a moment's silence, "it could be something else." He handed the envelope to Hunter. "Would you open it, sir, and read it? We'll need to take it with us, but you should know what it says, since those were Ms. Grayson's last words."

Hunter took the envelope, his hands noticeably shaking. Pulling a penknife from his pocket, he used it to slit the envelope, sliding out the cream-colored sheet of paper. Steadman watched his eyes move down the page, the stony features of his face unmoving. The only sound in the room came from Gomer, the yellow lab, who whined softly from his basket by the fire.

Finally, Hunter cleared his throat and read:

My dear future Desiree,

This letter—as always—will be a short one. I must acknowledge, as I have every year, that nothing in the past can change. As much as I might wish to, I cannot reverse the mistakes I've made. All I can do is try to atone.

Perhaps this year I can bring myself to do what needs to be done.

With that hope in mind, I close my Christmas letter with love in my heart for my family. All I've ever done is to keep and preserve them.

Sincerely,

Desiree

Bennett rose and paced to the window. "That's hardly a suicide note," he said. "She addressed it to her future self. Why would she do that if she wasn't planning to have a future?"

"And yet, it's clearly an expression of deep regret," Chief Morgan said. "Most notes left behind by suicides are. Can anyone tell me about the past mistakes she refers to?"

No one spoke.

"Well," he said, gently extracting the letter and envelope from Hunter's clutched hands, "there are a number of ways to interpret what she said. We'll look into it further."

He returned the letter to his jacket pocket. "Chief Steadman, may we speak in private?"

Hunter grunted an assent when Bennett asked if they could use his office. Steadman followed Chief Morgan as Bennett led them into a large square room filled with mahogany furniture. His legs felt stiff, as if made of wood, yet his head seemed light enough to lift off his shoulders and float away. He'd dealt with situations like this before, but this one had blindsided him.

As Bennett left, closing the door behind him with a decisive click, Chief Morgan sank into an armchair beside a small table, motioning Steadman onto the sofa.

"I'm glad to have you on the scene, Chief Steadman, though I doubt you feel the same right now."

Steadman said nothing, and Morgan continued. "It's my belief that Ms. Grayson took her own life. The evidence points to a self-administered combination of potassium cyanide solution and sleeping pills. We've seen this method used before. The cyanide ensures the job gets done, and the sleeping pills send the victim to sleep before the symptoms set in.

"She had a bottle of cyanide crystals on her bedside table, along with a vial of sleeping pills and a water glass, not quite empty. And there's the letter. A bit odd for a suicide note, yet that sentence about bringing herself to do what needs to be done...perhaps this is it."

"It's possible," Steadman agreed.

"One lawman to another," Morgan said, "is there anything here we should be aware of?"

Steadman sighed. "My wife and I just arrived yesterday afternoon. The only one of the family I've had any dealings with before is Bennett, and I'd say he's an upstanding citizen and a good man. I can't really speak for anyone else here, though I think young Olivia is a sharp one."

Morgan shifted in his chair. "You'll let me know, won't you, if..."

"There is something," said Steadman. "This isn't the first suicide this house has seen. Six years ago, Zena Grayson—that's Hunter's younger daughter—took her life. Just before Christmas."

Chief Morgan's eyebrows bunched together, almost touching. "Really?"

"That's what the girl, Olivia, told me. Apparently, the family has a deep respect for tradition." He paused. "Any chance this could be murder?"

Morgan rose. "There's always a chance," he said, "but I don't think that's what we're dealing with here." They shook hands. "We'll get out of your hair now. I hope you can salvage some Christmas cheer, Chief Steadman."

Bennett waited in the hall. "My turn," he said, steering Steadman back into the office and waving him into a chair. "You helped me before, Steadman. I'm asking for your help once again. I don't think my aunt committed suicide."

And there it was. Vivi's instincts on target, as usual. Busman's holiday.

Steadman rubbed a hand across his face. "You understand what you're implying?"

Bennett nodded, his face grim. "Murder."

Steadman gritted his teeth, thought about how this could go. He didn't like it. Vivi wouldn't like it. But he recognized he was in a unique position to help the family.

Or do them harm.

"This could get messy," he warned Bennett. "If I'm to do any good, you're going to have to toss the skeletons out of the family closet. I need you to tell me everything that might be relevant, and a lot of things that probably aren't. No way to tell, at this juncture."

"I know, Steadman. I appreciate this."

Steadman leaned forward. "Let's start with Zena's suicide."

"How did you—"

"Olivia told me."

Bennett turned to gaze out the window, a band of sunlight accentuating the tightened muscles of his jaw. "I don't want to talk about this in the house. Let's take a walk."

"All right."

Gomer followed them as they left through the mud room door, running ahead to make some yellow snow. The day was fine, with a clear azure sky and sunlight radiating off heaps of fluffy white, making

Steadman squint. Neither spoke as they crunched over the gravel drive and set off down a woodland trail, frozen earth hard beneath their feet, the dog scampering beside them.

"If Olivia told you, then you must know Zena was an artist. A good one, too. She was so young, but already attracting attention from a few galleries in Seattle. That's where she met Alex."

Bennett stepped over a fallen bough, pausing to tap the snow from his boots. "Zena was never a paint-by-numbers type of girl, but she stuck to formula when it came to Alex. They met, fell in love, got engaged, and she brought him home to meet the family."

He stopped mid-stride, biting his lip, face twisted in grief. "She was so happy, Steadman. Full of life, energy, and so much promise. Alex seemed a decent sort to me, but I'm afraid Desiree didn't consider him of our same 'social caliber.' She said he was a gold digger, after the family fortune.

"Dad didn't like him either, but I thought it was the standard 'no one's good enough for my daughter' business. He had Alex investigated, but he came out clean except for a dropped charge of statutory rape during his freshman year in college. His girlfriend was only seventeen, but it was consensual. The girl's father lodged the complaint, and Dad took it to heart."

Bennett started walking again, pushing violently at a barren branch crossing the path. "It hurt Zena so much to see their reactions, but I know she thought they'd warm to him. And for a while, it almost seemed they had. Zena brought Alex several times for weekend visits and the ruffled feathers appeared to be settling. And then, during one visit, Dad took Alex out shooting."

Steadman felt the doom in that sentence and feared to guess what happened next. He kept silent and waited for Bennett to go on.

"While they were gone, Desiree came to Zena, showed her a torn blouse and ripped stockings. Bruise marks on her arm. She claimed Alex had forced himself on her. Zena said she didn't believe it, but when Dad and Alex got home there was a confrontation."

This wasn't what Steadman had expected to hear, but just as bad.

"Zena was on a bed of nails between her family and her fiance. Alex saw her momentary doubt in him and I think it broke him. He left. Dad said that only confirmed his guilt."

Bennett scooped a brittle stick from beside the path and broke it in half, hurling the pieces into the underbrush.

"None of us ever saw Alex again. Three days later, his body was found in the woods outside Seattle. He'd been shot. Police said the wound appeared to be self-inflicted, but no gun was found on the scene."

A ray of sunshine broke through the twined, snow-clad branches overhead. The trail they'd been following descended out of the woods, skirting the snowy field Steadman had seen from the windows of the house. A stooped figure in a shaggy sweater tramped through the drifts on the opposite side of the field. It was George, the man who rented the cottage. He waved and Steadman waved back.

"Zena went into a decline," Bennett continued. "She stopped painting. She stopped eating. Had trouble sleeping. She blamed herself for Alex's death and eventually she swallowed a handful of sedatives and a solution of cyanide crystals."

"Sleeping pills and cyanide? You need to tell Chief Morgan about this."

"I will," Bennett said. "But I don't see that it proves anything. Des has always felt a measure of guilt over Zena's suicide, but I don't think she'd take the same way out."

Bennett stopped walking, put his hand on Steadman's shoulder.

"I'm afraid, Steadman," he said. "I'm afraid someone in my house killed her."

Steadman stood alone at the edge of the snowy field and watched the yellow lab gambol in the drifts, kicking up sprays of snowflakes. The sheet of white glistened under the lowering sun and somewhere in the distance, a church bell pealed, the faint sound traveling far in the thin, crisp atmosphere.

Fishing his phone from his pocket, Steadman pulled in a deep breath of pine-scented mountain air as he waited for his partner, Deputy Frost, to pick up.

"Merry Christmas, boss!" Frost said when he answered.

"And the jolly same to you, Frost. I trust all is well back at the fort."

"Well enough. I haven't been called in to deal with any holiday crises, so I'm at my mom's house. We just finished a fine dinner."

"Is Lily there, too?"

"She is."

"Fantastic. I could use some help, and you two are the very ones I need."

"Whoa Chief, I thought you were on vacation."

"I thought so too, but...stuff happens."

He explained the situation and Bennett's request for help, waiting while Frost noted down the names and basic information.

"We'll see what we can dig up," Frost assured him. "You know what a research hound Lily is."

"I hate to ruin your holiday."

"No worries, boss. Gives me an excuse to spend more time with the lovely Deputy Jamieson."

Steadman signed off and trudged back to the house. He had to tell Vivi what was going on, though he felt sure she already knew. Then, he had to persuade each member of the household to speak with him, despite having no official standing in the case. He hoped being a friend to Bennett would be enough to open those doors.

And the place he should start was at the top—with Hunter Grayson.

"Suggesting that someone murdered Des is preposterous," Hunter said, when Steadman had him alone in the office. He raked a hand through his thinning, white hair. "But so is the idea that she took her own life. I just don't know what to think."

"Is there any reason someone might want her dead?" Steadman asked.

Hunter stared out the window with unfocused eyes before slowly shaking his head. "No, it doesn't make sense."

"What about money? Who inherits her property?"

"Our parents left the family holdings to Des and I equally. I'm not even sure Des made a will, but one way or another, I suppose her share will come to me." He gave a derisive grimace. "Not that it will amount to much. Ranchers like us are a dying breed, Chief, and if you think I might have murdered her for the money, you're way off base."

Steadman left the man at his desk, head sunk into his hands, shoulders shaking. Mourning his sister.

He found Karen and Leo in the kitchen, pulling together a supper of leftovers.

"No," Leo told him, "I can't think of a reason anyone would kill Des."

Steadman hesitated, leaned against the counter to catch Karen's eye. "She clearly acted as the matriarch of the family. Might there be someone who resented her for that, felt it wasn't her rightful place? She wasn't your mother."

"Me, you're suggesting?" Karen said. "You're not only barking up the wrong tree—you're miles away from the forest. I was thrilled to leave her in charge of everything. Less worry for me. We're a family who loves tradition, Chief Steadman, but tradition requires a lot of work and planning."

"What about you, Leo?" Steadman asked. "How was your relationship with Desiree?"

Leo stood at the stove, head bowed over a skillet of reheated vegetables so that Steadman couldn't properly see his face. But there was no mistaking the flush that crawled up the back of his neck.

"I avoided the woman, if you want the truth. We were pleasant to each other but..."

"Leo wanted into the family business when we married," Karen explained as she turned spring rolls on the oven rack. "But Des voted him out. It's always left the tinge of a bitter taste." She lifted the tongs, waving them at Steadman. "But you're wrong if you think Leo had anything to do with her death. They mostly just ignored each other."

Steadman wondered if that was true, but didn't want to pursue the subject in front of Karen. She leaned her head through the arched doorway into the den. "Penn, would you mind setting the table? Dinner's nearly ready."

The man rose from his seat near the fire. "Not at all, dear lady."

Steadman helped with plates and silverware. "What's your connection with the family, Penn?" he asked, keeping his voice casual.

"Just an old friend and fellow rock enthusiast alongside Hunter. That's how we met." He moved around the table, laying napkins on each plate. "I've got no family of my own, and the Graysons are kind enough to take pity on me. Especially over the holidays."

"It's not pity," Olivia said as she came down the stairs. "We like having you around."

"Oh, mercy, girl. You make an old man blush."

How long have you known the family?" Steadman asked.

Penn paused to think, rubbing the stubble on his chin. "Must be four years now, maybe four and a half."

Steadman couldn't think of a reason Penn might have for murdering a woman who treated him like family. He hadn't even been around when Zena died, so if Desiree's death was somehow connected to that—as the fortune cookie hinted—it seemed unlikely Penn could have anything to do with it.

Vivi came down and wrapped Steadman in a hug that warmed him to the heart. Her hair tickled his nose, smelling sweet and fresh like peaches and cream. Bennett, Todd, and Hunter arrived behind her and they all sat down to dinner.

"Sorry about the leftovers," Karen said. "I'm not sure what Des had planned..."

She bit her lip and Vivi spoke up. "I'm a fan of leftovers. Especially when they were so good the first time. An encore never goes amiss."

After dinner, Steadman drew Bennett aside. They moved into the mudroom where they could speak undisturbed.

"I've made a few gentle probes," Steadman said, "but nothing's popped up on the radar so far. I've asked my partner to do a bit of digging, but we need more to go on. What can you tell me about Alex? Last name, where he's from, anything."

Bennett thought. "Alex Bantry," he said. "Grew up in England, somewhere in Yorkshire. He came to the U.S. for university, graduated from Stanford, I think. When he met Zena, he was working on a masters in architecture from U-Dub."

"Okay," Steadman said, texting Frost an update. "Anything else? What about the old man in the cottage—George?"

"George! You can't seriously be considering that angle," Bennett said. "We hardly see the man except from afar on his daily walks. He's rarely been in the house, and what earthly reason could he have for harming Des?"

"None at all. Of course you're right. I'm just thinking out loud." Steadman hesitated. "As far as that goes...forgive me Bennett, but thinking as a lawman for a moment, rather than a friend, I have to ask—is there any reason *you* might have for killing Desiree?"

Bennett took a step back, brows rising on his forehead. "I suppose I opened myself up to that when I asked for your help. You were unapologetically thorough over that cattle business and I can see it's part of your formula for success. I won't hold it against you for asking."

He stood for a moment, face puckered in thought. "I guess there is," he said at last. "Deep down, I always felt like Des was responsible for Zena's death. I tried to get past it, but part of me has always blamed her. I reckon that's as good a reason as any for killing her, but I didn't do it, Steadman."

"I believe you."

Steadman looked past Bennett's shoulder to the hodge-podge of winter coats and boots in the entryway, the ordinary trappings of a family living together, sharing their lives.

"But I think," he said, "it might point us to the reason someone did."

The day after Christmas passed in slow, dismal disarray. No one seemed to know how to move forward without Desiree holding everything together. The azure clarity of the previous day was gone, blotted out by wisps of sullen gray stretching over the sky like wool batting, and the air felt flat, subdued.

Steadman and Vivi spent the afternoon keeping Olivia company, watching her paint. The girl wore a red and white striped man's shirt as a smock, dotted with dried bits of paint in all colors. A slight resinous odor hung in the air and Olivia hummed to herself as she brushed and daubed at the canvas. Steadman sensed that painting gave her a way to escape the gloom hanging over the house, and he was glad.

He swayed gently to and fro in a rocking chair while Vivi sprawled on her stomach across Olivia's bed, nose in a book she'd brought from home. Neither of them was allowed to look at the work in progress on the easel, but Steadman knew Vivi would be delighted at the end of the session when she saw Olivia's painting. The girl's talent, at such a young age, was a marvel.

Steadman had felt the undercurrent of Olivia's resentment toward her aunt, and he knew by sad experience that some fifteen-year-olds were capable of killing. But he could not bring himself to consider Olivia—or her brother, Todd—as a suspect in Desiree Grayson's death. In truth, he didn't want to consider anyone in the house a suspect, yet he didn't believe the woman had killed herself.

A shadow fell over the room as the feeble sun dimmed behind a cloud.

"I'm losing the light," Olivia said. "I might as well finish for the day. The sun drops fast in the mountains and the fireworks will be starting soon."

Vivi rolled over and stretched, letting out a long, audible yawn. "Fireworks?"

"It's Zweiter Weihnachtsfeiertag," Olivia announced, stumbling a little over the strange syllables. "Second Christmas Day. Germans celebrate on the 25th *and* the 26th, so in Leavenworth, they do too. There'll be a big fireworks display tonight. I'm sure we won't be going into town to party this year, but we'll be able to see some of the fireworks from the front porch."

"Never mind the fireworks," Vivi said. "I want to see what you've painted."

Olivia laughed, wiping her hands on a paint rag. "All right, you can look. But keep in mind, it's not finished."

This time, Olivia had painted what seemed to Steadman like a photograph, so sharp and realistic were the details. It was a brick archway framing a cobblestone street and courtyard.

"It should feel like you could step through the archway," she explained, "but I haven't quite got the perspective right."

"It's amazing," Vivi said. "I've got goosebumps."

Steadman couldn't pull his eyes from the painting. "Remarkable things are in your future, Olivia. It's none of my business, but I'd say leave the biology and equations to other folks and pursue your talent with all your might. The world needs what you can bring it."

From behind him came a choked sob, and Steadman turned to see the girl's face twist with grief. Vivi rushed to Olivia's side as she crumpled into tears, drawing her onto the bed, stroking her hair as she cried.

"Let it out, sweetheart," Vivi crooned. "You've been through a lot. Just let it all drain out."

Steadman knew he'd become superfluous. He let himself out and found a quiet spot to call Frost. His partner didn't pick up and he ended the call without leaving a message. Downstairs, he found a desultory knot of people in front of the fireplace, watching the dwindling flames lick at a whitened pile of char.

"I found a roast in the freezer," Karen informed him. "We'll eat a late dinner after the fireworks." She turned to Todd. "Run down to the cottage and see if George wants to join us on the porch."

Todd left. No one else looked up or said a word.

Vivi and Olivia came down just as the first booming sprays lit the overcast sky. As if grateful for something to distract their minds, everyone rose and bundled up for the front porch. Except Hunter.

"I'm not feeling up to it," he said. "I think I'll turn in early."

Todd returned, alone. "George must be out with friends," he said. "No one answered the door."

Penn pulled on a bright red and green cardigan of the ugly Christmas sweater variety and a ridiculous hat like a spangled dunce cap.

"Just my way of bringing a little cheer to the occasion," he said, forcing a grin.

Leo raised his glass of whiskey. "And here's my way."

They filed onto the porch, pulling wicker chairs and loungers up to the railing, watching plumes of color sparkle and smoke against the clouds. Steadman's phone vibrated in his pocket and he excused himself to take the call.

After greeting Frost and explaining all the booms and pops and fizzles in the background, he clicked his ballpoint and got down to business. "I'm sure you'll email me a report," he said, "but give me a rundown now, while I've got you on the phone."

"Sure, boss. Lily's still checking the line on Alex Bantry, but I managed to get a look at the file on Zena Grayson's suicide."

"And? Any suspicion it might have been murder?"

"None, Chief. If anything pointed to murder, it wasn't in the file."

Steadman jotted notes as Frost filled in details about the Grayson family finances and background—no surprises there. As he was getting ready to sign off, Frost grabbed his attention.

"Hold on, Chief. Lily just uncovered something you might find interesting. That Pennington fellow is originally from Leeds—that's in Yorkshire."

"Like Alex, you mean? Yes, that is interesting. He doesn't speak with a British accent."

"That's not all, boss. Hold on to your hat for this one—Pennington Smith was born under a different name. Peter Bantry."

"Hell's bells. Gotta go, Frost. Thanks!"

Steadman rejoined the family on the porch. Standing back, he watched the man in the absurd hat and sweater enjoying the firework display. The constant pops and sputters, the smoke-filled sky, and the heavy smell of gunpowder in the air told Steadman this was the finale. When it was over and the rest of the group drifted into the house, Steadman invited Peter Bantry to stay and chat on the porch.

Taking seats, they smiled across at each other, a sizing-up moment which Steadman decided to break.

"Tell me again," he said, "about your connection with the Graysons. I'm not sure I heard you right the first time."

Before the man could respond, Olivia burst onto the porch. "Please come! Something's wrong with grandfather."

Steadman rushed into the house, Penn right behind him. Hunter's bedroom was empty, bedclothes rumpled, a few pillows tossed onto the floor. The door to the adjoining bathroom stood slightly ajar.

"I tried to open it when he didn't answer," Olivia said, "but something's blocking the way."

Steadman pushed against the door, straining to peer through the three-inch gap, seeing enough to make him take out his phone and dial Chief Morgan's number.

After a brief explanation and urgent summons to the sheriff's deputy, Steadman gathered everyone once more into the den. Peter Bantry was nowhere to be seen.

"Anyone know where Penn went?" he asked.

"I don't remember seeing him up in dad's room," Bennett said. "It'd be hard to miss him in that ridiculous sweater."

"Stay here," Steadman said. "Wait for Chief Morgan. I'll be right back."

Steadman found the room Desiree had allotted to Pennington Smith. The vibrant hat and cardigan lay on the bed. Checking the closet and bathroom, he found toiletries and clothing still in place. He pulled aside the curtain and saw Penn's car parked beside his own.

Everything left as it should be, but Steadman knew the man was gone.

Taking the hat and sweater, he returned to the den. "Was Penn present during the firework display?" he asked the group.

"What's going on?" Karen asked. "Has something happened to Penn?"

Steadman ignored her question. "Let's go out on the porch," he suggested. "I want you all to show me where you were during the fireworks."

Leo shot Steadman a look of annoyance, but he joined the others as they put on coats and gloves and took their places on the wicker furniture.

"Where was Penn?" Steadman prompted.

"He sat here," Karen indicated. "I could see him just over my right shoulder."

"Did he stay there the entire time?"

"I remember him oohing and aahing when the whole thing began," she said. "And he applauded like a wild man when it was all over. So, I guess he was here the entire time."

"But you didn't turn and look directly at him?"

"No."

Olivia stood and donned the hat and sweater. She held Steadman's gaze for a moment before dropping her chin in a tiny nod, letting him know they were on the same wavelength.

"Bear with me," he told the group. "I'd like to try a little reenactment. Olivia will play Penn's part."

Leo sighed, his breath vaporizing in the cold night air, but each of them stared obediently into the sky. Karen's chair angled to the left for a better view, and Olivia took the chair to her right, set back slightly.

"The fireworks begin," Steadman said, and they all murmured appreciatively. "Don't turn your head, Karen. Can you see Penn from the corner of your eye?"

"Yes."

"Okay, keep watching the fireworks. Tell me if you see him leave."

Steadman watched Olivia slowly move the hat from her head, letting it rest on the knobby back of the wicker chair. "Fireworks are booming," he said. "Imagine them in the sky. Red, green, gold."

Olivia slipped out of the sweater, leaving it draped across the chair, representing a flattened version of a man. She moved quietly to stand beside him.

"Okay, keep watching the lights in the sky, Karen. Is Penn still beside you?"

"Yes. I see the hat in my peripheral vision."

"Of course," Steadman said. "And your attention is on the mesmerizing display anyway, not on the man in the silly hat."

"Yes," Karen admitted.

"Okay. Now, turn and look at Penn."

Karen swiveled her head and gasped.

"Trompe l'oeil," Olivia announced triumphantly. "It tricks the eye."

Tricks the eye.

There was a lot about this case that tricked the eye, Steadman realized but before he could pursue the thought, the doorbell rang and Olivia ran to admit Chief Morgan and his men. The family, numb and chilled, returned once again to the den to watch the scene of deja vu play out, deputies moving up and down the staircase with equipment, evidence, and—finally—the body.

Steadman turned the pieces of the case in his head, looking at them from different angles, trying to discover how they'd all been tricked. Then he went up to have a word with the man in charge.

"Shot through the temple," Morgan told him. "Another case of apparent suicide. The body was slumped against the door, blocking it shut. There's no way someone could have gotten out of there."

"The window?" Steadman asked.

"Latched from the inside. The gun was there, finger still twined in the trigger guard, signs of GSR on the hand. The sound of the shot must have fit in with the fireworks. Crazy as it sounds, it looks like we've got another suicide."

"No," Steadman said. "You don't. And neither was the last one."

Morgan ran a hand across his forehead, regarding Steadman with eyes like a sad bloodhound. "I'm sorry, Chief. I have to go where the evidence leads me."

"I know that," Steadman said. "But this is murder."

He took a breath and squared his shoulders.

"And I can take you to the murderer."

The moon had risen, wide and nearly full behind the ragged cotton-wool clouds. It cast light enough for navigating the front drive, but once the lane disappeared into the trees, Steadman and Morgan switched on flashlights and followed their searching beams along the graveled road.

A chill wind shook the bare branches overhead, rattling them like Ezekiel's dry bones. Steadman's shoes slipped on an icy patch and Morgan reached a hand to steady him.

"You're telling me this man they call Penn murdered two members of the family?" Morgan said, sounding skeptical.

"That's what I'm saying."

"Why would he do that?"

"Because he believes Hunter Grayson and his sister, Desiree, are responsible for the death of his son and future daughter-in-law."

"You mean Zena, the girl who poisoned herself six years ago."

"Yes. Her fiance was Alex Bantry, son of Peter Bantry. Known to the family as Pennington Smith."

Morgan gave a low, incredulous whistle. "Peter, Penn, whatever you want to call him—you know where he is?"

"I know where he *was,*" Steadman admitted. "His still being in the hidey-hole depends on whether he's decided to brazen it out or make a dash for it. Either way, I know the man who can help us find him."

The cottage rose before them on a slight incline as they left the main drive. German-style, with half-timbered trim and a peaked roof made of overlapping circular tiles, Steadman thought it looked like a gingerbread house, enchanted by moonlight. And, as in the fairy tale, it had been a trail of breadcrumbs that led him there.

Steadman raised his fist and pounded three times on the sturdy wooden door. He waited a full minute, then lifted his hand to knock again, just as the door opened. George stood before them in striped pajamas, rubbing sleep from his eyes. He yawned and squinted at his wristwatch.

"It's two-thirty," Steadman said. "Sorry to wake you. May we come in?"

Without a word, the old man stepped back, allowing them entrance. In the tiny living room, he switched on a pair of low-wattage lamps and sank into a chair, waving Steadman and Morgan onto a plump velvet loveseat. Stifling another yawn, he said, "Has something happened up at the house?"

"Yes," Morgan told him. "I'm afraid Hunter Grayson is dead."

"What! Another suicide?"

"So it appears."

George's hands were shaking. He clasped them in his lap. "This is terrible. That poor family. I'm happy to help any way I can, but why—"

"We're looking for Pennington Smith. He disappeared when Hunter's body was found."

George's mouth dropped open. "And you think...what? Something happened to him? Or he's somehow involved in Hunter's death?"

"We know he's involved in Hunter's death," Steadman said. "He killed him."

George stared. His face left the mellow pool of lamplight as he leaned forward, resting his elbows on bent knees. "I don't believe it. Why?"

"We can go into the reasons later. Right now, I want to speak to Peter Bantry."

A pained expression crossed the old man's face. "You've lost me, now. Who's Peter Bantry?"

"He's the man who can explain everything that's happened, and you're hiding him, George."

George wagged his head, like a man struggling to wake up. "One of us must be dreaming. Where would I hide a fugitive in this tiny cottage?"

"Right here, George," Steadman said, leaning forward to pinch the man's cheek. He pulled, and a strip of graying, wrinkled skin came away, leaving a slightly healthier swath of cheek beneath.

The man sputtered, swatting Steadman's hand away.

"Yes, all right. You've got me," he said, dropping the fake American accent in favor of his native British tone. "But it doesn't matter. I've done what I came here to do."

The man composedly peeled away the thin layer of latex, like a salon treatment facial. Steadman noticed his hands had lost their shake and the ice-blue eyes peering at him were steady and resigned.

"You might feel better talking about it," Steadman suggested.

Peter Bantry nodded. "No reason not to," he agreed. He rubbed his hands over his face and loosened the gray wig from his head, tossing it onto the coffee table.

"My family was everything to me," Bantry said. "I was devastated when Alex died, and then that lovely girl, Zena. I met her first, you know. In Prague. I was an engineering consultant, called in for a project in the Czech Republic. Zena was there, studying art. I used to watch her painting in the park during my lunch hours and I knew she was the one for Alex. I introduced them."

"I thought they met in Seattle," Steadman said.

"They did. I pulled some strings and interested a few galleries in Zena's work. I'm an engineer who specializes in problem-solving, so I solved the problem of getting the two of them together by engineering a chance meeting. I knew once they met, the rest would follow."

Steadman realized the man must have carried a burden of guilt since the ball he set rolling had smashed into smithereens.

"When my wife was killed in a car accident less than a year later, I decided to strike back. I paid someone to beat up the drunk who hit her. After that, how could I let the death of my son go unavenged? I hired a private investigator who unearthed enough information to make me think someone in this family was responsible for sending Alex to his death."

Peter Bantry stared into the darkness beyond the lamp's dim glow. "I learned about geology and befriended Hunter Grayson at a rock show, slowly working my way into the family until I became part of the furniture and could poke around at will."

He paused. "Three weeks ago, I found Zena's suicide note."

Rising from the chair, he took a sheet of paper from the pages of a book and tossed it on the coffee table next to his abandoned wig. Steadman opened it, letting Morgan read over his shoulder. It told how Zena had discovered the rape accusation was a scheme designed by her father and aunt, to get rid of Alex. The note concluded:

I cannot shoulder this guilt. I should never have doubted my darling Alex. I go now to be with him.

"Desiree had it hidden away," Bantry said. "Probably to use as leverage against her brother if need be." He grimaced. "I started planning how to kill the both of them."

"How *did* you pull it off?" Morgan asked. "Both deaths appeared as genuine suicides. You would have got away with it if Chief Steadman hadn't been here."

"My misfortune, then." Bantry sighed. "I approached it like an engineer with a problem to solve. With Desiree, I simply coated the adhesive on the envelope for her Christmas letter with a solution of potassium cyanide. She poisoned herself when she licked it shut. Poetic justice, I thought. For Zena."

He sat again, smoothing his crumpled pajamas.

"The cyanide was diluted enough not to take effect right away. Desiree swallowed her normal sleeping pill and once she'd fallen asleep, I placed a water glass with the remainder of the solution and the vial of crystals on her bedside table, making sure to leave her fingerprints wherever it made sense. Those ambiguous phrases in her letter were just a stroke of luck."

"And Hunter?" Steadman prompted. "How did you manage that?"

"Logistical engineering," Bantry said. "I led Hunter at gunpoint into the bathroom and I shot him. Then I opened the window and fired another shot out the window using his hand to establish gunshot residue. I counted on the noise of the fireworks to disguise the sound of the shots."

"But how did you get out?" Morgan asked. "The window was locked from the inside."

"Of course it was. I refastened it and left through the door. I ran a large bath towel underneath the door and positioned Hunter's body on the towel, leaning against the door but with enough room for me to get out. Then I shut the door and pulled the towel through, drawing his body tight against the door. Worked a charm."

"Okay," Morgan said, "but how did—"

"I've said all I'm going to say about it," Bantry broke in. "Now I have a question for Chief Steadman: what gave me away?"

Steadman thought for a moment. "It was the first thing you ever said to me, though I didn't catch it at the time."

"What did I say?"

"You greeted me with 'Happy Christmas.' Americans say *Merry* Christmas. Then later, I realized I'd never seen Penn and George together. The real kicker, though, was Olivia's trompe l'oeil, the creation of an illusion. You used that sort of misdirection to fool Karen into thinking you never left her side during the fireworks. And on a larger scale, you created George, the perfect way to make Penn, the murderer, disappear into thin air."

"Not so perfect, as it turns out."

"No," Morgan agreed. "Peter Bantry, I'm arresting you for the murders of Desiree and Hunter Grayson."

Steadman stayed to watch the contingent of lawmen drive off with their confessed killer. He felt suddenly very tired. The moon had dropped behind the trees and it was the coldest, darkest part of the night. Just before the dawn.

He walked back up the drive, shoes crunching on the gravel, breath misting in the beam of his flashlight. Gomer greeted him from his basket in the mudroom with three thumps of his tail against the floor.

Steadman looked around once more at the jumble of coats, hats, boots, scarves, and mittens which seemed to him a symbol of the family. The Graysons had been badly damaged during this holiday season, but really the wound had been struck long ago. Now, maybe, the healing could begin.

"A merry Christmas to all," Steadman murmured softly. "And to all, a good night."

He hung his coat on a peg and climbed the stairs.

Vivi was asleep. She'd lived through too many of his late-night excursions to wait up for him, and he was somehow touched by her willingness to let go and sleep. It showed her confidence in his ability to make it safely back to her.

He climbed into bed, pressing his cold form into the sleepy warmth of her body. She stirred, drawing him close, and they curled together, breathing as one. Before Steadman drifted into unconsciousness, he sent up a brief prayer of gratitude—for the season, for life. For Vivi, no illusion, no trick of the eye.

She was the real deal.

He slept.

If you liked this story, you may be interested in reading the thriller novel that introduced Chief Randall Steadman to the world. *Steadman's Blind* has the Chief caught up in a pursuit that will change his life forever. Or end it. Gripping and fast-paced, this explosive tale explores the limits of trust, the price of redemption, and the lengths one will go to protect the innocent.

There's also a whole series of Steadman and Frost mystery short stories. Be sure to check them out!

A Very Krampus Christmas

Tal Bannerman stared out the rain-streaked plate glass fronting the office building on Tukwila Boulevard. Not a snowflake in sight. Gray sidewalks, gray skies, and a scudding array of towering, charcoal-tinted clouds. Nothing outside the norm for the Seattle area.

Ordinarily, Tal popped his vitamin D pills and powered through like everyone else, but with Bing crooning softly in the background and a merry sprinkling of Christmas lights amongst the shrubbery in the circular drive, Tal wished for weather of a more festive variety.

He craned his neck, glancing up at the giant clock high above the lobby's granite floor, a silent reminder that they all worked against the inevitable march of time. Here, in Homeland Security, a never-ending lineup of lawbreakers were fed into the system like deadfall through a wood chipper. On a good day, that felt like a satisfactory tradeoff for his efforts, making the world a tidier place.

On those other days, it simply felt like shoveling a thicker layer over a mass of noxious weeds.

The smart click-and-slide of smooth soles against wet polished stone turned Tal's attention to the approaching figure, a trench-coated man holding out a peace offering in the form of Danish pastry.

"You're late," Tal said.

Agent Carl Wrigley shrugged and thrust the fragrant pastry under Tal's nose. "I'm sorry."

His mouth watering from the buttery aroma, Tal grabbed the Danish from his partner and tore a large bite from one corner. "I know you are. I can tell because you brought me baked goods instead of the regular spinach smoothie."

"You're welcome for the pastry. As for the smoothies, you'll thank me when you're a spry eighty-year-old."

"All due to your revolting concoctions?"

"Indubitably. Let's get upstairs, the old man's waiting."

"Know anything about the new case?"

Tal noticed the slight hesitation before Carl answered. "Only the roughest sketch. Let's get moving."

Stepping off the elevator, Tal ducked under a low-hanging sprig of mistletoe and skirted the ribbon-trimmed noble fir standing guard in Reception. The sharp, piney smell triggered memories of fresh mountain air and campfire sing-alongs, remnants from his boy scout days. Before he had time to wonder if he was now nothing more than an overgrown boy scout, the director's secretary, Felicia, waved them into the inner office.

Plush carpet pillowed his feet as Tal stopped to stare at the cascades of homemade cut-paper snowflakes decking the wide windows, setting the scene for Rudolph and his eight tiny reindeer pals as they pulled Santa's sleigh across the glass expanse.

"My granddaughters," Director Hawkins explained, "practicing their scissor skills." He gestured them into seats and leaned against his massive Cherrywood desk, arms crossed, impatience etched across every feature. Tal expected a rebuke for tardiness, but Hawkins refrained.

"Time is of the essence, Agents," he told them. "I'm handing you a case that deals with some of the lowest scum you can imagine. Real nasty characters."

"Lawyers?" Carl inquired.

The director raised an eyebrow. "Among others. Nice little holiday case. You'll feel like you're in Oliver Twist, but with a higher class of thief. We've been watching this pile of snakes for a while now, trying to figure out which head to cut off for greatest effect." He paused. "We think we found it."

"What's the deal, boss?" Tal asked.

"We've uncovered an organization of scammers with foundations set up to front fake drug research companies, funnel bribes to government officials, and run a network of moles within the system. They pop up with one operation, skim billions, and then disappear inside a series of smoke and mirror corporations, only to pop up later and start all over again."

Tal's toes curled inside his shoes. "Sounds like a cold-blooded crew," he said.

"Hang on," Hawkins continued, "it goes from cold to downright arctic. Their most profitable play involves running cons on marks with loved ones suffering a terminal illness. Those people are vulnerable, desperate, willing to give whatever it takes for the hope of a cure."

Tal felt his blood heat, rising up into his face, his tongue growing thick at the back of his throat. He swallowed, clenching his jaw until he felt able to speak and then stood, bracing himself against the chair.

"I don't think I'm the man for this job," he told Hawkins. "Someone else—"

The director held up a hand, cutting off the suggestion. "Agent Wrigley assured me you could handle it."

Tal turned an accusing eye on Carl, who only shrugged and said, "I can't think of anyone better suited."

Bunching his toes, Tal worked to release the anger, get a grip. He was a professional and this was his job. Scowling, he dropped back into the chair and aimed a defiant glance at the director. "Go ahead. What's the plan?"

"An organization that large and that slick must maintain records in order to keep everything straight and have hard dirt to hold over the head of anyone looking to stray. The plan is to steal a copy of those records without anyone the wiser so we can coordinate a crackdown on multiple fronts, catching a handful of the more lethal snakes before they can slither away."

"How do we do that?" Tal wanted to know.

"We've got a few moles of our own," Hawkins said. "After more than three years of infiltrating the organization, they've identified the head man as Meinard Schlimme. He owns several residences here and overseas, but he's spending the holidays at his palatial home in Leavenworth."

"By his name, I'm assuming he's German or of German descent," Carl said. "Leavenworth makes sense, then. If you can't go home for the holidays, bring home to where you are."

Tal snorted. "Isn't that a little like Tiger Woods golfing at the mini putt-putt?"

Tal and his wife, Bridget, had visited Leavenworth Washington last holiday season and enjoyed the Bavarian-styled village in the Cascade mountains. Quaint and cute, with an alpine feel, but only a reflection of the real thing. Still, in such a place, a man like Schlimme could feel like a king.

And behave like one.

"Schlimme is an American citizen, second generation, but with solid roots still in Bavaria. He's throwing a big German-style holiday gala this Saturday evening. Our source believes the records we seek are on the premises." Hawkins retrieved a stack of folders from his desk and passed one to each of them. "You'll find press passes inside, along with a detailed dossier and instructions."

Tal opened the folder and fingered the plastic-encased press card.

"Bannerman, with your handsome mug, you can pass as a TV newscaster," Hawkins said. "And Wrigley, you're his cameraman. Schlimme considers the party a good photo op. He 'supports' a number of charitable operations and likes everyone to know about it."

"And by 'support,' you mean he uses them to launder money," Tal suggested.

"You sound like you know the man."

"Unfortunately, I'm starting to."

"I expect you both to know everything possible about him and his operation before Saturday's shindig." He shooed them out of his office. "Go read up. And remember, it's imperative you get in—and out—undetected. Schlimme can't know he's been compromised."

In Reception, under cover of the Christmas tree, Carl pulled Tal aside. "Look, I'm sorry—"

"Forget about it. We've got a job—let's get to it."

"Okay, but Tal—"

"Drop it, Carl." Tal pushed past, tamping down the storm that seethed inside his chest. He hurried to the elevator, determined to steer the conversation down a different road.

"How's that new stove working out for you?" he asked. Last weekend he'd helped Carl install a coal-burning stove in the basement rec room of his home. "That thing was a bugger to haul down the stairs."

Carl grinned. "Wasn't it, though?" His smile twisted into a grimace of disgust. "Speaking of swindles, I got one in my own backyard. That truckload of coal I ordered is nothing but clinkers and rocks. Sarah's furious and I've got a pile of useless crap where the kid's sandbox is supposed to go."

"Call the guy. Send it back," Tal said.

"What guy? He's disappeared, phone number goes nowhere."

"Ouch! The scam-buster gets scammed."

"I know, right?" Carl lowered his voice. "Keep it under your hat, okay buddy?"

"We keep at this any longer and I'm going to owe my wife an explanation," Tal murmured.

"Stop flapping your lips. I'm almost done."

Tal shut his mouth and breathed in through his nose, detecting a slight whiff of the tuna Suzanne always had for lunch. She was leaned in so close he could see the tiny pencil strokes in her eyebrows.

"Attention to detail," she said, "can make or break a cover. A proper newsman wouldn't go before a camera with such a shaggy mustache."

Tal heard the faint scything of the nail scissors as she snipped a few more hairs. "There!" Suzanne declared. "Now you're ready."

She snapped open a compact and held it up, inviting his feedback. He inspected his mustache but couldn't tell where her ministrations had made a difference. "Looks great, Suzanne. Thank you."

Bells jingled in the background as "Sleigh Ride" came in through the intercom at a volume calculated to raise morale without disturbing output. Tal watched Suzanne pack her tools into a cosmetics bag and return to her cubicle next door, giving him a thumbs up.

He leaned back in his chair and stretched his arms wide, tightening his core muscles and letting out a ferocious, jaw-stretching yawn. Friday afternoon. Go-time for the job was fast arriving and over the intervening days his attitude had made a one-eighty. He was looking forward to slicing the head off the snake and watching the ice-cold reptilian blood drain away, leaving only an empty husk.

He saw the top of Carl's head bobbing above the line of cubicles as he approached, scalp shining like a bright pink beacon through thinning blond hair. Tal knew that shade. It meant Carl was excited about something. Or upset.

Carl dropped into the chair beside Tal's desk, out of breath, furrowed lines on his forehead drawn into a vee. "The op is cancelled."

"What!" Tal's stomach plummeted like he'd eaten a stone for lunch instead of ham on rye. "What do you mean, the op's cancelled?"

"Schlimme pulled our press passes. No one's getting in except expressly invited guests."

"They're closing ranks," Tal said. "Why?"

Carl shrugged. "We've got guys inside his organization…"

"And he's got guys inside ours," Tal finished. "So what do we do?"

"There's no time to scramble a new plan before tomorrow's party," Carl said. "We'll have to wait for another opportunity."

"No way. This is it, Carl. We're getting in. I don't care if we have to dig a tunnel through the sewer system. We're—"

Carl leaned forward, his voice quiet yet urgent. "Dying on this sword won't make Elizabeth any happier, Tal. Or bring Ryan back."

"Leave my sister out of this," Tal warned.

Carl shook his head. "Can't be done. You know she's right in the middle of it. Schlimme might even be the one—"

"I'm convinced he *is* the one. The one behind giving Elizabeth false hope before smashing it into sharp little pieces. The one behind scamming her out of every penny she had. The one behind prescribing her son the snake oil that—"

Tal's throat closed up. He pressed his palms into his eye sockets and fought to control his breathing.

"Okay," Carl said, "you may be right about that. But going in hot isn't going to help the situation."

"How did you think I'd be going in, Carl? We may be dealing with the most cold-blooded of all God's creatures, but *my* blood's hit the boiling point."

A silence fell between them, accompanied by "Drummer Boy" from the sound system. Tal's mind raced, weighing options, searching for a toehold into the fortress. He felt feverish, desperate to find a way inside that holiday party.

"Maybe we could—" Carl began.

Tal glowered. He made a sharp motion with his hand like a clam snapping shut. *"Shhh!"*

He thought harder, until he could almost smell the burning of his brain. At last, he took a deep breath and let it out slow, like the release of steam from a pressure cooker.

"I have an idea."

It reeked inside the mask, like a cheese had crawled up and died in there. Tal gagged and resigned himself to it, knowing Carl would never agree to switch costumes. He watched his partner put the finishing touches on his makeup, adjusting the saintly white beard and tall headdress of good St. Nick, buttoning the long, flowing robe.

"As I recall," Carl said, "on our first case together, *you* were the one wearing a dress and toting scripture."

"I remember it well," Tal replied, "and I'd do it again in a heartbeat rather than wear this stinking goat head."

He turned to the mirror and stared at himself, transformed into the very devil. The mask featured terrifying horns sprouting up from sparse black hair. The skin, gray and wrinkled, was marred by deeply carved grooves as if the creature clawed itself in its sleep. Two deepset eye sockets featured green glass marbles with elongated black pupils.

The mouth was the worst, lined with rows of sharp, rotted teeth and a long forked tongue. Tal saw his own eyes peering out at him from well-hidden slits in the bags and creases below the creature's eyes. He roared at himself in the mirror and was gratified to see Carl flinch a little.

He was Krampus, the terror of Christmas in Bavaria, dodging the footsteps of the benevolent St. Nick, distributing lumps of coal to naughty children and carrying off the worst of them in his big burlap sack.

"Tonight the devil claims his own," he said.

"Don't let the costume go to your head, Tal. The only thing you'll be carrying away in that sack is a flash drive full of data."

"And may the data send him to hell."

After learning about the entertainment Schlimme had arranged for the evening, Tal and Carl had hijacked the van en route to the party, procured the costumes and props, and paid the actors enough to send them home and keep them quiet. Tal's only regret was that he'd let Suzanne trim his mustache for nothing.

"All right," he said to Carl, "let's get in and get this done."

"You have to dance first."

"Dance? What are you talking about?"

Carl waved a sheet of paper. "It says here, on the agenda for tonight's entertainment—Krampus Dance. They'll be expecting it. Might look suspicious if you don't follow the program."

"And how is Krampus supposed to dance?"

"Like I know? Look it up on YouTube."

"I don't have time for that. I'll make something up."

An expressionless guard at the front gate powered open the wrought-iron portal and let them through, not even cracking a smile at their elaborate dress. Carl drove up the mile-long carriageway and around to what they guessed was the service entrance. He parked the van.

"Check it out," Carl said. "The guy's got a bowling alley back here."

"Also racquetball and a nine-hole golf course," Tal added, nodding toward a signpost. "Fine little swimming pool, too."

He gazed at the keyhole-shaped pool, flanked by red bricks in a herringbone pattern, groupings of chairs and glass-topped tables scattered along its edges. "Something tells me he'll miss all these niceties when he gets where he's going."

The oom-pah sound of an accordion band spilled out of the enormous house, billowing into the misty night. The moon, silver-gilded by fog, floated in a blue ink sky, casting fairy beams of a quality even Schlimme couldn't afford to buy. Beautiful lighting, a pity the night was too cold for an outdoor party.

Checking to make sure they had everything they needed, Tal and Carl walked up the path and entered the lair of the beast.

Staff and guests stood aside to let them pass, a courtesy granted by their imposing costumes. Some applauded, others just stared. The noise of a party in full swing led them to the center of the action, a ballroom as big as a baseball diamond. Laughter and music, all of it loud and hearty, rose up around Tal. He felt stifled, unable to breathe through his cloying mask with so many bodies moving around him, sucking up oxygen.

People gathered around a stage at the far end of the room, clapping rhythmically and hooting with mirth. A band played and someone sang into a microphone in German. Tal didn't recognize any of the words, but he got the gist of the song and understood why everyone laughed.

Three trench-coated men stood center-stage, heads bowed, their legs suspiciously bare beneath the hems. Each time the singer reached the chorus, the men lifted their heads and opened their coats, revealing themselves naked save for a strategically placed tin pan struck by a foot-operated mallet. Each gong-like loin-covering was tuned to a different note and the men played out the chorus like a burlesque of handbell ringers.

When the song was finished, a tall man in black lederhosen stepped to the mic and hushed the applause. His face was flawlessly tanned and distinguished streaks of silver graced the thick hair waving back from his temples. He smiled, showing a perfect set of white, shiny teeth.

"Honored guests, the time of reckoning has come. Naughty or nice, it's time to pay the price." He paused. "Although, now I think of it, no one very nice made my guest list this year."

More laughter and applause. Schlimme beamed at them like a proud papa. "I see that Good Saint Nick and his evil twin Krampus have arrived." He turned to Carl. "All right, Nick, anything you'd like to say to my guests tonight? This is the best attention you'll get from them all year."

Clutching an oversized Bible, Carl made his way to the mic. He raised the Bible in one hand. "The good book says to love one another and show forth good works of charity." The crowd stood restive, unimpressed, waiting for something more entertaining. Carl pressed on. "Each year I ask the children if they know how to pray. I ask you now—can you pray? Do you know how?"

A low, grumbling hum started somewhere at the back of the throng and grew to a resounding chant. "Kram-pus! Kram-pus! Kram-pus!"

The band started up, echoing the demanding beat, adding in the sounds of heavy metal and whining guitar. Someone pushed Tal and he found himself propelled to the front of the crowd.

"Dance! Dance! Dance! Dance!"

Tal shimmied his hips, wondering what the Krampus dance was supposed to look like. The band picked up speed and he whirled and dipped, keeping time with the frenzied music. Seen through his tiny eyeholes, the people swarming around him appeared as demons, sickening him with their leering grins and grotesque gesticulations.

The heat inside his shaggy costume built until he could bear it no longer. He held up his burlap sack and made a few threatening passes as if to capture and carry off one reveler or another. Beating his chest, he threaded through the horde of people, escaping into a wide and breezy foyer with a ceiling high enough to easily accommodate the twenty-foot Christmas tree that stood at one end, surrounded by an array of wrapped presents.

Carl burst through the door in his wake. "That was some good dancing, goat man."

Tal ignored the comment. "Let's find an empty room. I've got to get out of this mask."

"No time for that now. Something tells me our welcome mat won't be out for long. We need to get what we came for and beat it."

"I can't breathe."

"If you're talking, you're breathing. Let's go."

The dossier they'd both studied included a blueprint of the house plans and an assurance that the records they sought were housed in a vault in Schlimme's personal study. Their first pass revealed a guard seated outside the door, but they'd prepared for that possibility.

Carl approached, holding out a beribboned box with chocolates, nuts, and little candies shaped like fruits. The candies were coated with sugar, and the sugar was supplemented with a sedative.

"Good soul, faithfully discharging your duties," Carl said, addressing the guard. "Accept my humble gift." He bowed and presented the box. The guard took it, poking suspiciously at the contents.

"And I brought the beer," Tal roared, holding out their contingency plan.

At this, the guard's face lit up. He popped the cap off the brown bottle and took a long swig of the specially prepared beverage.

Nine minutes later, he lay snoring on the hardwood floor. Tal and Carl dragged him into a nearby room and draped him over the sofa, arranging an assortment of beer bottles around him. When he woke up, he wouldn't remember what happened, but the evidence suggested he'd be out on his ear.

Their next obstacle lay in cracking the keypad outside the study door. Both he and Carl donned latex gloves. Using a special laser scanner, Tal determined which numbers were used in the combination and ran a pressure analysis to reveal their order.

He punched in the code and the door beeped open.

"That worries me," he told Carl.

"Why?"

"Too easy, too old-school to be guarding such sensitive information."

Carl shrugged. "Some guys still keep their money under the mattress. Sometimes the old ways are the best ways. Especially to someone from a traditional background like Schlimme."

"I hope you're right," Tal said. "Keep a lookout while I try these password suggestions on his computer."

Slipping inside, Tal removed the goat head mask and let his eyes adjust. Schlimme's inner sanctum was dark, cave-like, the walls lined with granite tiles of storm cloud gray. Squat, solid furnishings sprouted from the floor as if anchored by roots stretching beneath the slate-tiled floor. Tal felt the hair on his arms rise up, responding to some kind of low-grade energy source. The air thrummed with an almost sub-aural buzz.

"This place is ultra creepy," he said aloud, the words sounding dull as if dampened and swallowed by the room before they were even out of his mouth. He sat at the desk and woke the computer screen, waiting for it to present him with a password request.

If Schlimme used a randomly generated password, there was no way he could hack in with his limited skills. What they needed now was a big dose of good fortune. Christmas providence. Using a variety of information sources, their inside man had put together a list of the most likely passwords. Tal hoped one of them would work.

One did.

Heart beating faster, Tal connected the flash drive and searched the directory, deciding to take it all and sort it out later. There was room on the drive, but was there time? Hawkins was counting on them to get in and out again without detection, sounding no warnings, giving none of the key players a chance to bug out.

He started the download and paced, watching the progress bar creep along at an agonizing rate. Poking his head out the door, he got a thumbs up from Carl. Still all clear.

Breathing a little easier, Tal returned and watched the green light fill in the last of the progress bar. With shaking hands, he ran a quick program to erase all traces of his intrusion before disconnecting the flash drive. He zipped the drive into its protective case and turned to go, but froze, staring in confusion.

The room was changing. The faint hum he'd noticed on entering rose in pitch and volume and a blue glow emanated from around the doorframe. The reason for Schlimme's low-key security measures became clear. He was less worried about someone getting in, and more concerned about someone getting out.

Tal was sure—almost sure—well, eighty percent sure that *he* could get out unharmed. But the drive containing the data would fry. A one-hundred percent certainty.

He slammed a fist down against Schlimme's solid desktop, feeling the vibrations up to his elbow. He was *not* leaving without that data. The monster must be stopped. Not one more family harmed. Not one more nest egg stolen.

Concentrating to shut out the hum and engage his brain, Tal considered his options. Leaving the flash drive on the desk, he approached the glowing door. He gulped and opened it, shoving a fist through the threshold, flexing his hand. He felt all right.

Stepping through the doorway, he motioned to Carl.

"All done?" Carl asked.

"Data's downloaded, but I can't get it out."

"What do you mean? What—"

"No time, Carl. I need you to go back to that hall with the Christmas tree. Bring me two presents."

Carl stared. "Any two?"

"No, listen carefully. I need a large present, wrapped in foil paper. This is important, Carl. Look for shiny foil wrapping. The old-fashioned kind, if you can find it. Not that mylar stuff."

"Okay. And the other present?"

"Make it about the size and shape of a shoe box. Cardboard. Got it?"

"Got it!"

Tal sweated inside his shaggy goat man costume until Carl returned, bearing two gifts.

"All right," Tal said, grabbing the boxes. "Hang tight and be ready to run."

Back inside the sanctum, Tal removed the foil wrap from the large box. No thrifty maiden aunt ever unwrapped a present so carefully. He had to make sure there were no nicks or tears marring the smooth surface of the foil.

He tore the wrapping paper off the smaller box and emptied its contents into his burlap sack. Placing the flash drive into the cardboard vessel, he encased the box in foil, using tape from Schlimme's own desk drawer to secure the paper.

Carl stuck his head in. "It sounds like the party is breaking up. Are you almost finished?"

"Almost," Tal said, handing him a paper clip. "Straighten that out for me, will you?"

"What are you doing?"

"I'm making a Faraday Cage. Basically, it's an electronic isolation chamber, allowing electrical pulses to go *around* the container, instead of through it."

"Right. Why?"

"See how the doorframe is bathed in blue light?"

"Oh, I get it. Bzzzzt!"

"Exactly. Give me the clip."

"Sure. What's it for?"

"It's the ground."

Tal taped the straightened clip to the foil-wrapped box, like a miniature lightning rod. He attached a binder clip to the top of it.

"Time to go," he said. "Let's hope this works."

Gritting his teeth, Tal stepped through the doorway, holding the makeshift Faraday Cage in front of him. No sizzling sounds accompanied the short journey, but he'd leave it to the folks in IT to let him know whether his contraption was a success.

Letting out his pent-up breath, Tal stuffed the box into the filthy burlap sack designed for hauling away the worst of the worst. At last, it was fulfilling its destiny.

He looked around Schlimme's personal snake hole, making sure it looked the same as when he'd first stepped in. With a grimace, he replaced the Krampus mask and strode down the hallway and out of the house, followed by Good St. Nick.

Christmas Eve arrived in Seattle, bright and sunny. No crystalline snowflakes, but a far sight better than shades of gray.

Tal turned from the window, entranced by the smell of gingerbread wafting in from the kitchen. He passed the Christmas tree, decked with gold beads and candy canes, topped by the angel his mother had made when he was just a boy. The tree leaned slightly to the right and somehow, that enhanced his feeling of holiday cheer. He smiled.

His wife, Bridget, appeared in the doorway to the kitchen, holding out his phone. "Hawkins has been trying to reach you," she told him. "You'd better call him back."

Tal turned down the music, a piano medley of carols, and punched in the number. "Sorry I missed your call, boss. What's up?"

"Got a Christmas present for you, Bannerman. I thought you'd like to know we rounded up Schlimme and five of his henchmen last night. And arrest warrants out for twenty more. We're shutting down their operation for good."

"Sir, you couldn't have delivered a more welcome Christmas gift. I'm thrilled to hear it."

Hawkins cleared his throat. "You and Wrigley do great work. I'm putting you both in for a commendation."

"I don't know what to say."

"How about Merry Christmas!"

The doorbell rang as Tal ended the call. He watched Bridget embrace Carl's wife, Sarah, and coo over the new baby. Carl's two-year old toddled toward the Christmas tree and certain disaster. Tal had total confidence the women would successfully handle it, and stepped out to join Carl on the porch.

"Just got off the phone with Hawkins," he said.

"Yeah, I got a call this morning, too. I'm feeling pretty good, Tal. You?"

"I feel great. So good, in fact, that I arranged a little surprise for you."

Carl narrowed his eyes. "Uh-oh. Am I going to like the surprise?"

"You're going to *love* the surprise." Tal leaned against the porch railing and squinted into the sun. "Remember that worthless pile of crap coal taking up half your backyard?"

"I wish I could forget it."

"Well, you can. Right about now, my buddy who owns a dump truck is emptying that load of rocks into Schlimme's swimming pool."

Carl's mouth dropped open. "Hot damn! You got to be kidding me."

"I kid you not, partner. My only regret is that Schlimme won't be around to enjoy it."

Tal braced himself as Carl slapped him enthusiastically on the back. They chuckled over the mental image of all those chunks of filthy coal tumbling into the bad man's pool, like the giant-sized Christmas stocking of a supremely naughty boy. After a moment, Carl sighed.

"I'm sorry. I didn't get you anything, buddy."

Tal turned, noting the sunlight on Carl's pink scalp, the scraping sound of a bare branch against the dining room window, the crisp brush of the December breeze against his cheek and the warmth he felt inside.

He thought about his sister, Elizabeth, and the child she'd lost.

He swallowed against the thickness in his throat and gave Carl's shoulder a squeeze.

"Oh, yes you did, my friend. Yes, you did."

SILVER SECRETS, CRIMSON TIES

A chill drip found its way down the back of his neck as Sheriff's deputy, Randall Steadman, ducked his head in the rain and ran ahead to hold the door for his family. They shuffled in from the cold and wet of the parking lot, shaking off in the sudden warmth of the vestibule like a litter of puppies emerging from their bath. Outside, strings of colored lights spiraled around the narrow spears of trimmed, potted evergreens that lined the walk in front of the pavilion, their effect more dismal than cheery in the sullen drizzle.

Once inside, the atmosphere underwent a dramatic change. Magical snowdrifts banked the walls, dotted with decorated trees and garlands of gold and silver. The hall shone with a million lights and above the buzz and noise of a bustling crowd, Steadman caught the strains of *I'll Be Home for Christmas*.

He felt a small hand slip into his own and looked down at his granddaughter, Arabella. Her eyes were huge as she gazed around at what must seem like a true winter wonderland to an imaginative four-year-old. Smiling, he hefted her up where she could get a better look at the tables and booths of Christmas crafts, goodies, and games.

"Smell that spiced cider," his wife Vivi said. She tucked her coat into the foot of the stroller occupied by their new baby grandson, Christopher. "I'm going to get us some."

She began threading her way toward a nearby refreshment stand.

"I'll help," offered Nadine, his son's wife, scooting after Vivi's disappearing form. Steadman stood with Ari and his son, Eric, taking in the scene.

At the front of the large space, a crimson-curtained stage rose above the crowd. In the center of the platform, ensconced in a golden throne, sat a plump Santa with a small, beribboned girl in his lap and a line of children waiting to be next. Ari caught sight of the spectacle and stared, a look of hesitant fascination on her face.

"Do you want to sit on Santa's lap?" Steadman asked her.

She shook her head, burying her face in his chest.

"But Ari," said her dad, "you can give him the Christmas list you made."

"Me and mama already sent it," she told him.

"Mail is slow this time of year," Eric said. "It might not reach him before Christmas Eve. You better hop up on his lap and tell him what you want."

She looked at her father scornfully. "We emailed it," she said.

He laughed. "All right, then. I guess Santa got the message."

Vivi and Nadine came back with the drinks and they milled through the crowd, sipping the hot, cinnamon-laced apple cider. Vivi bought a handmade sweater to send to their daughter in Colorado. Steadman watched as Eric helped Ari throw hoops over bottles to win a prize. She wrapped her small hand around the pint-sized fuzzy frog she'd won, her face shining with pride. Nadine found a booth selling patchwork Christmas stockings and bought five—enough for their burgeoning family, plus one to grow on.

While the women browsed a table of homemade candies, Steadman found himself looking over the crowd, unable to quell his lawman's eyes from their habit of observing and assessing. As they drew nearer the stage, he saw a young woman becomingly dressed as an elf helping the children to form an orderly line and escorting each to Santa's giant chair, helping them into his lap. A jolly voice boomed out an occasional message of good cheer or admonition over the PA system.

"I hope you've been good this year, boys and girls! I know Santa's been making a list and checking it twice. Maybe even three times. So, listen to your parents, help out around the house. Be good!"

A photographer crouched beside the stage, snapping shots of the children as they perched on Santa's plush lap. Another recorded videos. Freelancers, hoping to sell their products to parents wanting to preserve the moment with a professional's touch.

Steadman watched as the elf girl checked her watch for the third time in as many minutes. A frown furrowed her forehead, marring the impression of Santa's merry helper. After a fourth glance, she made her way to the onstage mike, putting a big, excited smile on her face.

"I think I hear Mrs. Claus coming," she said. Then, after a pause, "Let's clap for Mrs. Claus so she'll come out and greet us."

She started clapping and some of the children and bystanders joined in. No Mrs. Claus appeared.

The elf bit her lip. "I'll go see what's holding her up," she said and disappeared into the wings.

Steadman's sensors were now on alert status. He waited for the elf to reappear with Santa's errant wife. Instead, he thought he heard a muffled shriek, but the noise level in the hall was such that he couldn't be sure. He began making his way to the stage and as he reached it, he saw the elf girl standing just behind the curtain, her face pale and twisted with uncertainty. Tears glinted on her cheeks.

She stepped out and moved to Santa, interrupting a little boy's shopping list to whisper something to the jolly, red-capped man. Santa's face went slack. He absently pushed the boy from his lap and stood.

Going to the microphone, he said, "I'm so sorry, children. I must go at once. One of the reindeer has broken a leg!"

Groans, complaints, and concern broke out among the waiting throng as Steadman mounted the stage and pulled Santa and his elf aside. "I'm Chief Deputy Steadman," he told them. "What's happened?"

The girl covered her mouth with a shaking hand, unable to speak. Santa drew a deep breath, his mouth working, willing to tell though the words were slow to come.

"Let's take this backstage," he said at last.

The girl stepped back, allowing Steadman entrance to the nether regions of the stage, raising one trembling arm like a signpost pointing the way to tragedy. Steadman pushed past her, brushing against the velvety curtain as he passed into the dim area backstage.

He paused, letting his eyes adjust as they focused on a crumpled heap in the center of the floor. Santa beside him swept off his hat and held it to his heart, staring in horror at the flowing red fabric and tangled hair.

Mrs. Claus sprawled face down on the boards, a crimson scarf knotted tight around her throat.

A merry jingling of bells floated out over the clusters of laughing, jab-bering people as *Sleigh Bells* played. Steadman stood at the parting in the red velvet curtain, guarding the crime scene, watching the crowd. A spray of fresh pine boughs garnishing the stage like parsley on a plate tickled his nose with their resinous scent.

It hurt Steadman's heart to be the one putting a stop to the holiday gaiety, but after his partner, Deputy Frost, arrived with six uniformed officers apprised of the situation, Steadman stepped to the mike and cleared his throat.

"Ladies and gentlemen, kiddos of all ages, I'm sorry to announce that we'll be shutting down early tonight. There's been an incident, and we'll need everyone to record contact information with the offi-cers at the door as you leave, in the event we need to reach you."

He dealt with the usual unrest and questions that always arose after such a pronouncement. He'd already spoken with Vivi and said goodbye to his family, sending them home while he prepared for a late night. Steadman braced himself as Frost approached, looking as if he might cry.

Deputy Cory Frost loved Christmas. He loved it with the fervency of a football fanatic embracing the Superbowl. Anything that dented the joy of the season dented him.

"Mrs. Claus murdered?" he said, real pain in his voice. "Who would do such a thing? Who *could*?"

Frost's childlike joy in the season was such that Steadman almost wondered if he'd need to explain how the actress dressed as Santa's wife was not the genuine article. But as much as Frost revered the yuletide, he loved and respected the law and his part in upholding it to an equal extent.

The deputy straightened his spine. "What's the victim's name?" he asked Steadman.

"She's Jenny Conner, age 24. I've detained everyone from the theater company that supplied Santa and crew, as well as anyone attached to them who was present in the vicinity. We'll question them as soon as we've had a chance to go over the crime scene with the specialists."

The crime scene team arrived, setting up lights, snapping photos, combing the area for any kind of trace evidence. Coroner Smithson examined the corpse, confirming the time of death as within the thirty-minute window before Steadman had seen the body.

"Barring any surprises, I'm willing to say she died from strangulation. In addition to the muffler tied around her neck, note the petechiae, the purple lips and protruding tongue."

Steadman felt a wrench of regret. The woman—so young, presumably vibrant, talented, and full of potential—had been snuffed out like a Christmas candle. He dropped to a knee and lifted the end of the dark red knitted muffler—the murder weapon—with a ballpoint pen from his pocket.

"There's a silver thread running through the yarn," he pointed out to Frost. "That's pretty distinctive."

Turning back to Smithson, he said, "Unless there's anything else you want to bring to our attention, we'll speak with the possible suspects now."

The coroner waved him off, turning back to the victim. Steadman and Frost found the conference room filled with potential suspects and witnesses. Two uniformed sergeants sat among them, discouraging conversation. As they entered, a man in his early thirties rose and held out a hand to shake. His light brown hair was thinning on top, letting a patch of shiny pink scalp peek through, and a slight paunch hung over his belt line like a pan of rising bread dough.

"I'm Donald Townsend," he said, pumping Steadman's hand. "I'm the director of the company." He blew out a long breath, canting his lip so the fringe of hair at his brow fluttered in the exhalation. "We're all so shocked by what's happened."

A woman in a silver-spangled green Christmas sweater clutched a wad of tissues to her chest, red-rimmed eyes smeared with ravaged mascara. "I can't believe our Jenny's gone. It had to be some kind of maniac. A mad stalker or something. What sane person would do such a thing?"

"This is Jenny's aunt," Donald explained. "Gloria Foster."

"And I'm Ray Foster," spoke the man beside her. "Jenny's uncle. We were Jenny's guardians." He stared at Steadman, his jaw hard under clenched muscle. "Find out who took her from us," he said. "Find out why."

"That's what we intend to do, sir," Steadman assured him. "We appreciate everyone's patience and cooperation. We'll need to speak to each of you in turn."

There was a moment of silence as he let his eye wander among the company, picking up small details in appearance and demeanor. He paused on a young man at the near end of the table, seated next to the elf girl. His crown of thick, dark waves sported a Superman swirl, one errant curl hanging over his right eye. Everything else about him was Clark Kent. Pale, bespectacled, timid. He chewed gum but stilled his jaw as Steadman examined him.

He wore a dark blue wool blazer. Steadman's gaze stopped on the sleeve where rested a frayed fragment of crimson yarn.

Shot through with a silver thread.

'We'll start with you," Steadman said, motioning with an arm for the young man to join them in the hallway. A small office had been set aside for questioning and as they entered, Steadman pulled an evidence bag from his pocket and coaxed the fragment of yarn into it with his ballpoint. The young man stared, face lit with apprehension.

"Your name, please."

"Mungo Martinez," the boy murmured. Frost wrote it down.

Steadman summoned a picture to the screen of his phone. He showed it to Mungo.

"Jenny Conner was strangled with this scarf. Do you recognize it?

The boy's pale face went a shade lighter. He swallowed. "It's from the costume closet. I'm the stage manager, so I'm in charge of costumes and props. Nora—that's the elf—wore that scarf last night and it got caught in the hinge of a chair. I mended it this afternoon. That's why..."

He gestured to his sleeve.

Steadman studied the young man. As he watched, Mungo fished a silver gum wrapper from his pocket and used it to swath the chewed gum from his mouth, wadding it into a ball.

"Mungo," Steadman said, waiting for the boy to meet his eye. "Did you kill Jenny Conner?"

"No."

"Is the costume closet open to anyone, or do you keep it locked?"

"We've had problems with pilfering, so now we keep it locked."

"And who else has access?"

Mungo pulled at the piece of twine around his neck. "I keep my key here," he said. After a thoughtful moment, he added, "Donald must have a key, as well."

"Mm. Where were you at the time Jenny was killed?"

"I was in the audience." A wash of pink chased the pale from his face. "Watching Nora."

"The elf."

"Yes."

"Does she know you were watching her?"

The pink deepened to red.

"What I mean," Steadman explained, "is will she be able to corroborate your story?"

"Oh! Yes, sir."

"Fine, then. You may go."

Visibly relieved, Mungo rose and moved to the door, unwrapping a new stick of gum as he went.

They spoke with Donald next. The man had rustled up a cup of coffee from somewhere and its fragrance filled the small office, borne on rising vapor from the paper cup. Steadman noticed a slight tremor in the man's hands, but no more than might be put down to the stress of the situation.

Donald's light brown eyes maintained contact with Steadman's own, his face solemn.

"The scarf used to strangle Jenny Conner came from your company's costume closet," Steadman began. "Do you have a key to that closet?"

"Yes, of course. But I believe it's in my desk at our main location. I've never had to use it—Mungo's so good about seeing to everything prop-related."

"Where were you at the time of Jenny's murder?"

"I was in the sound booth, running the equipment."

"Will you show us?"

Donald escorted them to a small room lined with acoustic tile. A counter stretched down one side, supporting two laptops and an array of control boards for sound and lights. Four CCTV monitors spanned the wall above, showing different angles of the main hall.

"I manage the technical aspects from here, taking care of lights, music, and sometimes engaging the audience with banter or announcements."

"And what were you doing during the half hour before Jenny's body was found?" Frost asked him.

He shrugged. "Making periodic sponsored plugs, jollying along the little kiddies, spreading holiday cheer."

"Okay, Mr. Townsend. You may go."

Back in the office, they talked to the Fosters—first Ray, and then Gloria. Both claimed to have been shopping the stalls when Jenny had died. Steadman and Frost learned that Jenny's parents had both been killed in a plane crash when she was thirteen. Ray, her mother's brother, had taken her into his home and become her guardian. They also had a son present. Kelvin.

"We'll need to speak to him as well," Steadman told Gloria as she rose to leave the office.

"That'll be a treat," she remarked, her voice sardonic, as she closed the door with a decisive click.

Next to enter the room, however, was Phillip Quinn. Jenny's boyfriend. Tanned and toned, with the look of a blond Adonis, Steadman expected swagger and arrogance. But if there had been any before, it was lost in the tide of Jenny's passing. He looked bereft.

"I'm sorry for your loss, Phillip." Steadman leaned forward, trying to engage eye contact with the young man's downturned face. "I can only imagine how difficult this must be for you."

Phillip looked up, a pucker of pain crossing his tanned features. "Jenny was everything to me." He made a hopeless gesture. "I've lost it all. All I've ever wanted."

Steadman let a moment pass. "I'm sorry to ask you this, Phillip, but I must. Where were you during the half hour before Nora discovered Jenny's body?"

Phillip balled his fists, pressing them against his chest as if stilling a broken heart. "I was at one of the jewelry booths, buying Jenny a Christmas present. This," he said, digging a small velveteen box from his pocket. Inside was a delicate gold chain hung with a crystal unicorn. "She loved unicorns."

There was a rap at the door and one of the sergeants stepped inside. "I'm sorry to interrupt, Chief, but the photographer shooting videos stopped by to show us this. Thought it might be important."

Steadman gestured Frost over, and together they watched a video play out on the camera's screen. In the background, Mrs. Claus could be seen huddled furtively with a man as they whispered urgently together in a way that might be interpreted as intimate.

The man was not Phillip Quinn.

Steadman looked at the time stamp on the video. "That must have been right before she died."

Frost agreed. "Narrows the window even more than the thirty minutes the coroner gave us."

Steadman showed the video to Phillip, pointing out Jenny, her hand on the arm of a young man whose face Steadman recognized from the conference room. They'd be talking to him next.

"Any idea what that might be about?" Steadman asked Phillip.

Phillip's fists clenched tighter and his jaw jutted forward at an ugly angle. "I wondered," he muttered. "I wondered if she had something going on with Andre."

Had he wondered? Or had he *known* something more about it? Enough to drive him to murder?

"You can go for now," Steadman told him. "But stay in town. We'll need to speak with you again."

Steadman sent Frost to bring in Andre Reese. When the young man was seated with his ankles—encased in brightly printed Christmas socks—crossed in front of him, Steadman showed him the video.

"What's the story?" he asked, inviting an explanation.

Andre had the kind of face that plainly showed the skull beneath. His nose, looking sharp enough to cut paper, rose in the air as he contemplated the ceiling. With a resigned sigh, he said, "Jenny's been giving me money."

Steadman watched the young man fidget, waiting for more.

"I had some gambling debts. She helped me with them."

"How much money are we talking about?"

He drew a breath through his sharp little nose, making the nostrils pinch. "Thirty-five thousand."

Steadman heard the tip of Frost's ballpoint tear through paper as he recorded the amount. The revelation had startled him as well.

"She's been great to me. But..."

Again, Steadman held his peace until Andre cracked.

"I got into trouble again last week. I asked her for more money, but she refused."

"Where would Jenny get that kind of money?"

Andre stared. "She's loaded. And she'll really be rich when she turns twenty-five." He stopped. "I mean, she would have been."

"Explain."

"Jenny's dead parents had a ton of money. They left it to her in trust. She's been getting a very generous allowance, but she was to inherit the rest of it on her twenty-fifth birthday."

"Interesting," Frost said. "Who are the trustees?"

"Her Aunt Gloria and Uncle Ray."

Steadman's heart rate bumped slightly as he waited for Frost to note that down. Then he said, "Where were you during the half hour before Jenny's body was discovered?"

Andre looked at the wall, a pained expression settling over his features. "I don't mind telling you, but is there any way you could keep it from Ray and Gloria?"

"Why should we?"

"They think I'm a gold digger, just trying to worm my way somehow into the family money."

"And how does that relate to your alibi?"

He uncrossed his ankles and leaned forward. "I was with Kelvin. Their son."

Steadman hesitated. "When you say with...do you mean—"

Andre's eyelids lowered. "I mean *with*. We found an empty room down the corridor."

"And how long have you been *with* Kelvin Foster?"

The young man rubbed his temples as if warding off a headache. "Look, it's not cheap and dirty. I love him. We've been together almost a year, but we're keeping it secret."

"His parents don't know?"

"If they did, I might be looking down the barrel of a shotgun right about now."

Steadman sighed. "All right, Mr. Reese. That's all for now. Go home and stay out of trouble."

When the door had closed behind him, Frost said, "Holy smokes, Chief, we need to talk to the aunt and uncle again."

"And the boyfriend. This might cast new light on what he meant when he said he's lost everything he ever wanted."

A knock sounded at the door and a sergeant escorted Kelvin Foster into the room. Kelvin, barely past his teen years, had already developed lines around his mouth and forehead from a perpetually sullen expression. He had curly, strawberry blond hair and black square-frame glasses that magnified his blue eyes. He looked like the Mrs. Beasley doll Steadman remembered from watching *Family Affair* as a young child.

After sizing him up for a moment, Steadman said, "Did you kill your cousin?"

The blue eyes widened even more. "No! Geez—"

"You don't seem sorry she's dead."

"I'm—" He hesitated. "Well, I'm not." He raised his chin. "Except now she'll stay young and beautiful forever. People will speak of her in tones of reverence, while the rest of us age and wrinkle and fail in our dreams and desires." He flicked a speck of lint from his shirt cuff. "She always did get the better of me."

"How are your parents taking it?"

"Oh, they're real broken up. They always cared more for her than for their own son." A bitter smile touched his lips. "Of course, that might have been about the money. And since the money comes to them now, I think they'll somehow get over it."

Steadman let a moment pass. "Where were you when Jenny was killed?"

Kelvin gave him a smoldering look. "Down a dark hall with my boyfriend."

"Sounds almost like the two of you rehearsed it."

"Oh, we've rehearsed it, officer. We rehearse it almost every day. I think we're really getting it down."

Steadman ignored the innuendo. "You can go."

Kelvin saluted on his way out and Nora Cook came in. The elf girl.

Nora made a good elf with her petite figure and delicate features. She'd changed out of her costume and wore jeans and a pink sweater sprinkled with sequined snowflakes. Sinking onto a chair, she twisted her hands in her lap and waited for Steadman to speak.

"Walk me through what happened," he said. "From your point of view."

She explained how she and Jenny had worked the shift as elves, helping children, reassuring parents, posing occasionally for one of the photographers. About half an hour before the shift ended, Jenny went backstage to change into Mrs. Claus.

"She was supposed to come out and tell the children she needed Santa's help. We were all due a fifteen minute break. When she didn't show up, I tried to prompt her. And when that didn't work..."

"Right," Steadman said, "that's where I came in."

Nora chewed on her lip, brows drawn together like a pair of doves in flight. "Sir..." Her voice faltered. Clearing her throat, she tried again. "It was supposed to be me," she said. "I mean, it's my job to play Mrs. Claus, but Jenny wanted to try it. Donald wouldn't have liked that—he's a control freak, always on my case. But since he was in the sound booth, we thought he wouldn't even notice and no one else would care as long as the job got done."

She sniffed, running a finger under one eye. "I don't think I can live with the guilt if Jenny got killed because she was where I was supposed to be."

Steadman thought about the implications of what she'd just told him. "Jenny was strangled," he said. "That suggests this was a very personal crime, that Jenny wasn't a random victim. If it *was* a case of mistaken identity, can you think of any reason someone might want to harm you?"

She thought about it, hands clasped so tight the knuckles shone white. At last, she shook her head. "No. I'm just ordinary. Jenny's the one with all the drama and glamor."

She left, and Steadman turned to his partner. "What do you think?"

"About her? I agree that Jenny is far more likely to be the intended victim. There's no shortage of people with motives for wanting her dead."

"True. But why would the killer choose this venue, with so many people around? So many children?"

Frost closed his notebook and slipped it into his breast pocket. "Maybe it wasn't planned. A murder of opportunity. He was back-stage, picked up the scarf, and wrapped it around her throat."

"Smithson said the attack came from behind," Steadman said. "It could have happened as you say, but how did he get the scarf if it was locked in the closet?"

"It might have been Mungo the stage manager."

"Possibly." Steadman picked his jacket off the back of his chair and shrugged into it. He glanced at his watch. "Let Lily sleep but get her onto this first thing in the morning. Have her dig into the list of suspects. Is that it for tonight?"

"The only one we haven't interviewed is Santa."

"I sent Santa home hours ago," Steadman said. "Good Saint Nick wouldn't murder Mrs. Claus during a Christmas celebration. If need be, we can talk to him later. He has a pretty solid alibi, after all."

Frost grinned, shaking his head. "I don't know why all the guys down at the station keep telling me you're a Scrooge."

Saturday morning. Steadman had hoped to be sleeping in, waking up to a home-cooked breakfast, spending time at the kitchen table with Vivi and the spread-out pages of a newspaper. The death of a young woman had removed that option for him, but as he rolled over and silenced the perky alarm on his cell phone, the smell of bacon and maple syrup told him that all was not lost.

He dressed quickly and greeted Vivi with a kiss. As he drank coffee, he watched her assemble a sandwich he could take on the road—waffles, scrambled eggs, bacon, and a dollop of syrup.

"You're the greatest," he told her.

"Breakfast of champions."

"Am I?" he asked. "Your champion?"

"Every day of your life."

At the station, Frost was already waiting for him, using the time to hang Christmas stockings from the white board's accessory tray. Benny Goodman and his swing band filled the long desk-lined room with *Jingle Bells* and a peppermint candle burned beside Steadman's pencil jar, which Frost had filled with candy canes.

"Glad to see you're not letting a little thing like murder dampen your spirits, Frost."

His partner turned, fixing him with a solemn eye. "Things like murder make celebrating light and joy all the more important."

Steadman sat at his desk and drew a deep breath of peppermint-scented air. "Right you are, Frost. But don't be expecting some big fancy present from me."

"I am, boss. I'm expecting big things from you. Don't let me down!"

Steadman read over last night's reports while Frost trimmed a small tree set back in the corner of the room. The handbell tones of *Deck The Halls* resonated from Frost's pocket and he answered his phone, nodding and making notes. When he ended the call, he pulled a chair up to Steadman's desk.

"That was Lily. She's been busy."

"She didn't get any sleep last night, did she, Frost? You called her after we left?"

"Actually, boss. I called her much earlier, as soon as we had a list of suspects. She's been digging up the dirt ever since and she's uncovered a few items of interest."

"Such as?"

"She was able to find the details of Jenny's trust and confirm that Ray and Gloria Foster are the trustees. Also, we'll need a court order to access the extent of it, but our accountant source said it looks a bit dodgy, like some fraudulent handling might be at work."

"Excellent. Tell Lily she did good."

"I will, Chief, but there's more. She found the guy Andre owes money to—Pete Montell."

"Pete, The Heat, Montell. That's not good."

"No, it's not. And she found out how much he owes. Another twenty grand."

"No wonder Jenny stopped the gravy train. She realized it wasn't a one-time thing. Andre's got a habit."

"A habit that's led a lot of men into kill or be killed situations."

"But why strangle the golden goose?"

Frost shrugged. "Maybe they argued, things got out of hand, he grabbed the scarf..."

"Could be. All right, let's see what we've got."

Steadman drew up a chart on the white board, listing all the suspects—Ray, Gloria, Phillip, Mungo, Andre, Kelvin, and Donald—in the left-hand column and setting up check boxes for motive, means, and opportunity. He stood back and rubbed his chin while he thought.

"As far as means," Frost said, "I don't think we can rule anyone out. Mungo said they keep the closet locked, but it's not like it holds the treasures of the ages. He must have stepped away from the closet now and then when it wasn't locked. Or he could have forgotten to put the scarf away after he mended it."

"Speaking of which, we should check with Nora to see if she really did tear the scarf so it needed mending. Mungo might have made that up. What about opportunity?"

"Again, pretty wide open. Donald was in the sound booth, so that puts him out. And Kelvin and Andre alibi each other. But no one else can really be eliminated."

Steadman sighed. "As I see it, *none* of them can be eliminated. Kelvin and Andre might have been in it together. And the way technology is, Donald could have rigged something to make it sound like he was in the booth when he really wasn't. No," he thumped a fist down on his desk, "it comes down to motive."

"And everyone seems to have a motive. Except Mungo and Donald."

"Right. Tell Lily to keep digging."

"Oh, she is, boss." His phone chimed out again with *Deck The Halls*. "That's her right now."

He listened and Steadman watched the eyebrows rise on his partner's forehead.

"Lily found a Las Vegas marriage license," he reported. "Phillip and Jenny were secretly married last month."

Steadman let Frost drive. He wanted to think.

Yesterday's rain had receded, leaving the sky clean, the sun a lemon-yellow glow filtered through gauzy clouds. The crisp air, carrying a spicy scent from the moistened bark of pine, oak, and maple, made wearing a hat and jacket smart while precluding the need for mittens and heavy coats.

Typical Christmas-time weather for the Pacific Northwest.

Something felt backward about this case. Mungo seemed to have the greatest means and opportunity. But if he had a motive, they had yet to discover it. Donald also appeared to have no reason for killing

Jenny, and his opportunity for doing so was less straightforward than any other suspect. Everyone else involved had a plausible motive.

Except the elf and Santa himself.

Steadman found himself discounting those two. Was that wise?

Something bothered him about the whole business, something that set him on edge with a slight sense of foreboding and he wished to heaven he could put his finger on it.

Frost turned off on a dirt lane that led to the rented house Jenny had shared with Phillip. Her husband. A gravel driveway circled a fountain in front of the house, a water carrier in classical Greek fashion. It was dry.

Layers of dead leaves, brown and yellow, covered the ground beyond the gravel, and a large dog with curly black hair came to greet them. Friendly, tongue lolling, eyes peering out from the unruly fringe of curls.

Steadman held out a hand and felt the cold, wet nose meet his palm. "Where's your master?"

"Right here," Phillip said rounding the corner of the house. "I heard you pull up."

Frost stooped to give the dog a good ruffling. "Fine animal. What's his name?"

"Jasper."

Steadman gestured toward the porch. "May we go inside?"

Phillip's lips thinned. "I suppose we'd better."

Once seated in a room fashioned from an eclectic mix of elegance and folksy comfort, marble statuettes next to patchwork pillows, Steadman began the conversation.

"You left a few things out when we spoke yesterday."

"I answered all your questions."

"Perhaps. But the gaps you left might lead one to wonder if you're hiding something. For example, you neglected to mention that your girlfriend had become your wife."

Phillip flushed. "We weren't ready to share that with anyone yet, just enjoying being together and keeping it to ourselves."

"You also forgot to inform us that your wife was quite a wealthy woman. Now that she's dead, it seems entirely possible that you'll come into some money. Unless you're guilty of killing her."

"I'm not! I could never—" Phillip buried his face in his hands and spoke through his fingers. "I could never hurt her. I loved Jenny. I love her still. I don't think I'll ever stop."

"Her cousin Kelvin said that now she'll stay young and beautiful forever while the rest of us wither."

"Yes, that's it. We didn't have the chance to grow warts on our marriage. It will always remain in this perfect honeymoon state, preserved in amber. And I don't know if that's a good thing or a bad thing."

His shoulders shook and he kept the hands over his face a moment longer before throwing them off and straightening himself.

"If I'd married Jenny for money, why would I kill her now? All I'd have to do was wait a few months until she turned twenty-five and increase my return by thirty-fold. I'd be a fool."

"There could be any number of reasons," Steadman said.

"Maybe you argued," Frost contributed. "Maybe you thought she was cheating with Andre."

Phillip stared at them, a deep furrow forming on his Adonis-like brow. "I didn't kill my wife."

Deck The Halls broke the silence that followed, and Frost checked his phone.

"Excuse me," he said. "I need to take this."

Steadman watched his partner retreat to the front hall, speaking softly. He thought he knew who the caller was. Before he could say another word to Phillip Quinn, Frost hurried back into the room.

"We gotta go, boss."

As Steadman snapped his seat belt into place, Frost started the car and circled the driveway, accelerating onto the dirt lane.

"There's been another murder."

Steadman stepped out onto the balcony of the small apartment and pulled in a lungful of damp, cold air. The weather had changed on a dime, as it often did near the Puget Sound. Gray mist shrouded the sky, dimming the sun's light to a watery white. He stood at the rail and breathed, kicking himself mentally, wondering if he might have prevented this second murder by being faster, smarter, more on the ball.

Turning, he leaned back, letting the rail support his weight while he watched Frost and Smithson move around the body. A cheap artificial Christmas tree, decked with ornaments and homemade strings of popcorn stood just inside the glass, miniature colored bulbs giving off a dull shine. Steadman realized they must have been on at the time of the murder, the last thing she saw perhaps, as she lay helpless in a pool of her own blood.

It seemed the elf might have been the original intended victim after all.

He should have seen that. He should have given Nora's fears about that more concern. *I'm just ordinary. Jenny's the one with all the drama and glamor.* She'd said it and he'd thought it sounded right. He hadn't imagined this might happen.

But it had.

Nora Cook had been stabbed sometime during the early hours of the morning. Her neighbor had found Nora's cat yowling in the stairwell, his fur streaked with blood. When she'd called through Nora's open apartment door and gotten no answer, she called the police.

Steadman steeled himself and walked back into the living room. He crouched beside the Christmas tree and poked at the scattering of wrapped presents with his ballpoint pen, looking at the tags. To Nora from Mom. To Nora from Uncle Jim. To Nora from Santa. Ho, ho, ho.

He swallowed hard and rubbed a hand against his mouth. Bunching his muscles beneath him, he poised to stand but froze as his gaze fell on a torn scrap of wrapping paper poking out from beneath one of the gifts.

He prodded the gift aside and worked at the scrap, loosening it from the splintered floorboard where it was caught. Steadman imagined someone hastily snatching up a wrapped present in the dark, not noticing the tear. It might be significant. Or totally irrelevant.

Using his ballpoint, he smoothed out the crinkled scrap. It was the shape of a pennant, crimson-colored with raised silver-glittered stars, about two inches long. Different paper than any other under the tree.

He wondered what the tag on that gift had said.

"Hey Chief," Frost called. "I've got something here."

Steadman crossed to the body. The coroner had rolled Nora onto her side and Frost pointed to what he'd found beneath, in the place where she'd lain.

It was a small silver ball. A foil wrapper wadded around a piece of gum.

Mungo Martinez lived alone at the edge of town, in a small, utilitarian structure more hut than house. Painted dark brown, it blended well with the surrounding forest and Steadman thought it might have been a ranger shack at one time. The late afternoon was waning toward dusk and silence prevailed as the day birds tucked heads under wing and nocturnal creatures waited for night's curtain to fall.

Inside, the walls were hung with framed movie posters, mostly from classic films like *Casablanca* and *The Wizard of Oz*. There were no distinct rooms in the hut. The kitchenette in one corner gave way to a small sitting area and a twin bed and nightstand in the opposite corner constituted the bedroom. Only the bathroom was tucked away to one side with a door separating it from the rest.

Mungo had cooked something with garlic and onions for lunch, but he'd washed up. Not a dirty dish in sight. Steadman and Frost perched at the edge of a futon sofa, almost knee to knee with Mungo, who sat in a chair angled next to them.

"We found this at the crime site," Frost said, holding up the evidence baggie containing the foil-wrapped wad of gum.

Mungo winced. "I have a bad gum habit. I try to tidy up after myself but sometimes I overlook it. I'm sure there's more than one roly-poly packet like that backstage at the Pavilion."

"We're not talking about the crime scene at the Pavilion," Steadman told him. "The other crime scene. The one at Nora Cook's apartment."

Mungo's face went white in the space of a second. "What happened at Nora's?" he asked. "Is she okay?"

"No," said Steadman. "She's dead."

Mungo beelined for the kitchen sink, uttering a keening wail as he went. Leaning over it, he lost his lunch. Steadman had been right about the garlic and onions. But he would have sworn Mungo's reaction of shock and grief was genuine. The man stood over the sink, sobbing like a lost child.

When at last he'd regained some composure and wiped his face, he returned to the chair and dropped into it like he was made of jelly. "We were in love," he said. "Nora and I. She was the sweetest thing, the best thing in my life. I can't believe she's gone. Why?"

"That's what we're trying to figure out, Mungo," Steadman said. "Who knew about your relationship with Nora? Were you keeping it a secret?"

Didn't anyone in this group know how to have an open relationship?

"I wouldn't say a secret, but we were keeping it private. It's no one's business but our own."

"Maybe," Frost said, "but is there more to it than that? If you want us to find out who did this to Nora, you need to tell us everything you know."

Mungo went to the kitchen for a paper towel and blew his nose into it before answering. "Nora didn't want Donald to know. He was always trying to pry into her life, to control her."

Steadman remembered. "She told us he was always on her case, wouldn't leave her alone."

"That's true," Mungo said. "She just wanted a part of her life he couldn't crack into."

Steadman stood. "Thank you, Mungo. You've been very helpful. I'm truly sorry for your loss."

As they left the hut in the woods, the night creatures began to stir.

The gloom of night deepened as Steadman drove toward Donald Townsend's residence. He owned a house near Mason Lake, a fifteen minute drive out of town. The house was not large or grand, but it sat high on a hill and featured a picture window overlooking the lake.

Donald stood in the window, watching their approach.

He invited them in and offered to make coffee. As they settled onto a plump, floral print couch in the living room, Frost stared around him, a look of disgust on his face.

He mouthed the words, letting Steadman read his lips. "No Christmas decorations."

That, in itself, was a crime as far as Frost was concerned.

The smell of fresh coffee followed Donald as he carried a tray into the room and Steadman took up his cup, thanking the man. Frost ignored the coffee but helped himself to an Oreo.

Steadman swallowed a mouthful of the hot brew and put his cup down. "I'm sorry to inform you," he said, "that Nora Cook was killed early this morning."

There was a clatter as Donald lowered his cup to the coffee table. "What? How? What happened?"

"She was stabbed in her apartment."

"Oh my," Donald said. "I'm so sorry to hear that."

"Where were you between midnight and five a.m., Donald?"

"Me?" He lifted his coffee and took a sip. "In bed, sleeping."

"Is there anyone who can corroborate what you say?" Frost asked.

The man gave a thin smile. "I live alone, deputy. My wife left me last summer. So, the answer to your question is no, but I assure you I never left my bed."

Steadman drained his cup and leaned back into the corner of the sofa, arranging the pillow beneath his arm. His hand scraped against something papery, slightly rough beneath the skin of his finger. He drew it forth, revealing the gift, wrapped in shiny crimson paper covered in glittery silver stars. He pictured Donald standing at the window and seeing them come, belatedly remembering this incriminating parcel lying on the couch, hastily shoving it down between cushion and pillow before answering the doorbell.

Steadman read the tag aloud. "To Nora from Donald." He turned the package over and saw the tiny, pennant-shaped tear in the paper.

"That's awfully sweet of you, Donald," he said, holding the packet out of reach as the man made a swipe for it. "I'll see that it goes in with Nora's personal effects."

"You have no right to take that!"

"I do, and I am." He gazed around the room. "What else might I find here, Donald? If I really looked?"

"I want you to leave now," Donald said, his face red as a brick. He shooed them toward the door. "And you'll need a warrant if you want to look at anything more."

As they walked back to the car, Frost said, "That's not strictly true. We don't need a warrant to search the sound booth at the Pavilion. It doesn't belong to him."

"Exactly what I was thinking," Steadman agreed.

What a difference a day makes.

Steadman had asked that all the suspects be assembled back in the hall of the Pavilion where twenty-four hours earlier, Jenny Conner had been murdered. The booths and tables lay vacant, their wares abandoned until further notice, and Steadman hoped they'd be able to get the holiday reveling back on track soon.

Yellow crime scene tape stretched across the stage area and Steadman invited the assembly to be seated on a group of folding chairs in front of the stage, noting that one of the chairs retained a bit of silver-laced crimson in the jaw of one hinge.

The place seemed too quiet without the piped-in Christmas carols, the noise of the crowd, Donald's cheery jests and greetings. The gathered company sat glum and enervated, drained by the stress and anguish of the day.

Steadman stood before them, Frost at his side.

"For those of you who haven't heard, Nora Cook's body was found this morning by a neighbor. She'd been stabbed to death."

Only Donald and Mungo seemed to have known about the second murder. Shock and distress traveled over the group in waves, and Steadman waited for it to settle before moving on.

"I've called you here because you all deserve to know what happened. Let's focus, for a moment, on Jenny's murder. In truth, any one of you could have gotten ahold of the scarf, the murder weapon. And nearly all of you have some kind of motive."

He turned to Ray and Gloria Foster. "You've been controlling Jenny's trust fund for the last eleven years. That's a lot of money, and a lot of control. Tempting to overstep your authority, and I think that's just what you did, using money from the fund to improve your own lifestyle."

"We didn't do anything wrong," Gloria said. "We're family. We used the money to benefit the family Jenny was part of."

"That remains to be seen," Frost told her. "After an official audit is conducted." She sank back onto her chair and crossed her arms, like a scolded child.

"Phillip Quinn stands to benefit financially from Jenny's death," Steadman said. "As he is her husband."

A series of gasps rippled over those gathered. Ray Foster stood up so fast his chair tipped over. "What are you saying? Jenny married him?"

"Yes, Ray. That's what I said. But you'll have to take it up with him later. For now, sit down and listen."

Ray locked eyes with Phillip and both men looked ready for a fight, but he returned to his chair, glowering.

"However," Steadman continued, "if Phillip had married her for the money, he would have waited until she came into her full inheritance before killing her. No, Phillip had another motive."

"He thought she might be romantically involved with Andre," Frost said. "But that was unlikely, since Andre is in a relationship with Kelvin."

"What!" Gloria Foster shot back out of her chair. "That can't be true." She stared at her son.

"It's true, mother," he assured her. "You may as well know that I've invited him to join us on that Mexican cruise we're taking next month. For the benefit of the family."

Gloria Foster was speechless, her face blotchy with fury and disbelief. She dropped back to her chair and threw her hands up in surrender.

"And since we're talking about Andre," Steadman said, "he's been borrowing large sums of money from Jenny and yesterday she cut him off." He turned to Andre. "I'm sure that made you angry. Angry enough to kill her, since her refusal put your own life at stake with Pete, The Heat, Montell."

"Killing her wouldn't get me what I need. She would've come around, I know. Jenny was a good sort. I'd never hurt her."

"*You* might think Jenny was a good sort, but your lover certainly didn't," Frost said. "Kelvin hated her, felt displaced by her. Jealous."

"Bitterly jealous," Steadman added. "Enough to kill."

"You may be right about that," Kelvin admitted. "But I didn't."

"Then we come to Mungo, who had easy access to the murder weapon, but no discernible motive."

"That goes for Donald, as well," Frost said. "He had a key to the costume closet, but no reason to kill Jenny."

"But every one of you had opportunity," Steadman said.

"Except for me," Donald pointed out.

Steadman nodded agreement. "Except for you. *Unless* you engineered some way to keep speaking from the sound booth even when you weren't there, giving yourself an alibi. Maybe something like this," he said, pressing a button on his phone.

Donald's voice, clear and jolly, came through the PA speakers: *I hope you've been good this year, boys and girls! I know Santa's been making a list and checking it twice. Maybe even three times. So listen to your parents, help out around the house. Be good!*

"Wait! Where'd you get that?" Donald said, his voice a strangled squeak. "I—"

"You...what, Donald? Erased it? I know you tried," Steadman told him. "But you should have destroyed the flash drive. Buried it. Thrown it over a bridge. Lucky for us, you didn't."

"You left it in the sound booth for us to find," Frost said. "Our technicians were able to restore the erased file."

"Thing is, Donald—we weren't even looking at you as a serious suspect until Nora died. If you'd left it at Jenny, you might have got away with it."

"But you never meant to kill Jenny, did you?" Frost said.

Donald glared at them in silence.

"It was Nora you were obsessed with," Steadman continued. "And when you found out she was putting you off while welcoming Mungo's attentions, you decided to kill her and frame him for her murder."

"Those CCTV units are so grainy," Frost said. "You didn't realize Jenny and Nora had switched roles and Nora's elf was still out front with Santa."

"In the Mrs. Claus costume, with her back turned to you, you thought Jenny was Nora. You crept up behind her and slipped the scarf around her neck, pulling it tight. If she made a noise, it was lost in the hubbub."

"And you killed her!" Phillip shouted, barreling toward Donald, knocking him to the floor. He pulled back a fist and Steadman moved forward to stop him.

But not as fast as he might have.

By the time Steadman and Frost had pulled Phillip off the Christmas killer of two young women, Donald had a bloody nose and a swollen eye that would turn a nice shade of black. The bereaved husband sat on the floor with his head in his hands. His wounds would take far longer to heal than those he'd inflicted on the killer.

Steadman signaled a pair of deputies who stepped forward to cuff Donald and read him his rights. The party broke up and Steadman clapped Frost on the back.

"Good job we did, wrapping this up."

"Yeah." Frost looked down at his shoes. After a moment, he said, "Could we have prevented Nora Cook's death?"

A weight sank in Steadman's chest, but it was the sort of question he'd asked himself a million times over his years on the force.

"I don't know," he answered, "but if we took the guilt for every bad thing done by crooks and murderers, we wouldn't be able to do our job at all. I gave it my best, used the skills I've learned, worked late into the night and hit it again early in the morning. You did too."

Frost lifted his head and sighed. "We all make our choices, don't we."

"We do. And we can only be responsible for our own, Frost. I believe in love and mercy, and that's what we rely on. Maybe not as lawmen, but as humans. And at the end of the day, that's what we are."

Frost stuck his hands in his pockets. "My apartment's just around the corner. Are we going back to the station tonight?"

Steadman considered. "It's late. Heck—it's Sunday by now. Go home, Frost. We'll write up reports on Monday."

"Thanks, Chief."

"Consider it my Christmas present."

Frost gave him an incredulous look. "Really? That's it? Merry Christmas, now get out of here, kid? You're not getting off that easy, boss."

Steadman laughed. "What do you want from me?"

"I want to hear you sing a Christmas carol. I want to watch you dance a little jingle bell rock. I want to see you kiss your wife under the mistletoe!"

Steadman laughed. "Done and done," he said. "You set the time and place, I'll bring the wife."

"And I'll bring Lily."

"Of course you will."

Steadman, bone weary but essentially happy, climbed behind the wheel of his car and headed home.

To practice his bit under the mistletoe.

DUET FOR PIANO & CHISEL

In her travels as a concert pianist, Riley had visited Spain six or seven times. She'd worn a polka-dotted dress and danced the Sevillana during Feria. She'd caught handfuls of pelted candy at the Three Kings' Day parade and gone tapas hopping until dawn. Once, she'd even climbed to the top of a craggy rock in Tarifa and looked across to Africa before rappelling down the cliff-face and nearly breaking an ankle.

But she'd never been to a bullfight.

Now, watching the man with the scarlet cloth, she could almost feel the rumble of the ground vibrating under clashing hooves as they raged toward the swinging cape. Not more than ten feet in front of her, the man holding the cloth danced out his convincing presentation, wielding the cape with fierce concentration, brows drawn together on his forehead, a glimmer of arrogance in his eyes. Riley felt both fascination and embarrassment, but she couldn't look away.

The most compelling feature of the spectacle was that it took place on the polished marble floor of the Mackenzie mansion on the shores of Washington's Lake Sammamish, off I-90. The tinkle of champagne glasses and murmured conversation punctuated by bursts of laughter swirled around Riley. Strings of colored Christmas lights festooned the walls and a twelve-foot Noble fir, decked with tinsel and ornaments, stood sentinel over the gathered party.

Most of the guests in their cocktail finery hadn't noticed the man in the corner stamping his feet and flourishing the blood-red muleta as if a roaring applause spurred him on. Those who had, watched with interest or thinly veiled derision.

No one stepped forward to put an end to the display.

With a satiny rustle, a woman arrived at Riley's shoulder and spoke into her ear. "It's called Utilization Behavior. Be a dear and hold these for me, won't you?"

She handed Riley two flutes half-filled with pale champagne and stepped toward the man, gently taking the cape from his fingers and returning it to the hook from whence it came, next to an ornate matador's costume and an elaborate sword made of Toledo steel. A dazed look crossed the man's face, as if he'd just woken from a dream. It was followed by a wash of red as he noticed his audience.

The woman—Riley recognized her as Robyn Vaughan, the concert pianist known for her mastery of Mozart—squeezed his hand. He gave a self-conscious shrug and exited down the hall toward the powder room. Robyn spread a defiant smile over the onlookers, smoothed the skirt of her designer gown, and returned to Riley's side, retrieving the flutes and taking a sip from one of them.

"Let's count ourselves lucky he didn't pull down the sword," she said, her lips twisting in a wry grimace. "David lost a small piece of his brain to a surgeon's knife a few years back and it changed him in many ways. Utilization Behavior—or UB, as it's called by the men in white coats—is a neurological disorder that presents its sufferers with an irresistible compulsion to handle objects, using them in an appropriate manner, but not always in the appropriate venue or moment. It's given David quite a lot of grief since the surgery. Let's not mention it when he comes back."

"Of course," Riley said. A server appeared, bearing a silver tray with a single glass. Ginger ale, rather than champagne. Riley never drank alcohol. She took the glass and nodded her thanks to the young man before turning back to the woman.

"I'm so happy to meet you Ms. Vaughan. Your performance this evening was magical. I've never been able to master the left hand articulations in that Mozart Sonata."

Robyn laughed, raising her glass. They clinked. "So you say, Riley Forte, but I'd hate to face you in a battle of the Brahms. You've got me there—hands down."

"Nice one." Riley smiled, acknowledging the pun and the compliment to her night's performance. "Why don't we meet over Shostakovich—home field advantage to neither one of us."

Shostakovich was a contemporary composer, while Riley specialized in music from the Romantic period and Robyn favored the Classical masters. Riley dipped into the Baroque on occasion, and she adored many of the twentieth-century musicians, Debussy and Barber first among them.

"I'll give it some thought," Robyn said in reply to her challenge.

Riley sipped fizzy liquid from her fluted glass, savoring the mild flavor. Her own concert career, derailed after the death of her husband and son, had been regaining traction since the harrowing events surrounding Mt. Rainier's eruption last year. She'd like to credit her nimble fingers, but knew she owed a great deal of her current success to her mysterious new sponsor.

Playing here tonight was a case in point. An important local charity event for the arts, the concert drew a great swath of attendees including some who made the earth rumble under their indomitable footsteps. Others floated in on their coattails or just needed a place to blow off the holiday blues. Riley supposed some of the guests even came to support the fundraiser's stated cause.

Across the crystal rim of her glass, she caught sight of the novelist, Abraham Gentry, setting up at a table stacked with glossy hardbacks of his latest release. Tonight's benefit was meant to raise funds for the Proctor Bingham art gallery and the rising generation of local artists but Abraham, with a barren twenty-six-year stretch between his hit debut novel and this current book, looked determined to corner some action for himself.

As Riley watched, a bit of hubbub arose between the novelist and a woman garbed in gold lame, most likely his wife. Their words were lost in the general buzz, but Riley imagined their content, based on the pantomime. An important item was missing. Abraham blamed his wife. She spiked the ball back in his court and washed her hands of the matter.

Riley heard a soft snort from Robyn who stood next to her, tipping her champagne glass, eyes turned in the same direction. "Overcast, with a chance of rain," she said. "Definitely some thunder."

As the drama continued, a woman whose long auburn ponytail brushed the shoulders of her tasteful pantsuit stepped into the fray and pointed across the enormous living room toward the imposing front door. Whatever she said convinced Abraham to lay off his wife. He pulled something from his pocket and stalked off toward the field where valets had parked the guests' cars.

"Did I miss anything?" asked David, returning from the bathroom. Before Robyn could answer, Riley's escort, homicide detective Nate Quentin, arrived from the patio where he'd retreated to take a phone call. Introductions were made all around and the foursome fell into comfortable chatter.

"I know what the ladies do, and how marvelously they do it," said Nate, "but what's your line, David?"

Riley thought David looked slightly embarrassed. "I'm a sculptor," he said.

Nate's eyebrows went up. "Really? How interesting. What medium do you work with?"

"All sorts."

Robyn, an impish grin on her face, placed a hand on Nate's shoulder. "What do you think of that piece?" she asked, indicating a nearby sculpture of a woman in a yoga-like posture, face turned toward heaven.

As she studied the figure, Riley felt an almost physical radiation from it, a manifestation of serenity as pure as if the sculptor had pared down to a vital, essential truth. The piece was fashioned from rich, warm-toned wood, streaked and whorled with a gorgeous natural grain. The curvaceous surface, polished smooth, invited touch. Nate complied.

"It's fantastic," he said. "It almost glows, like it's lit from within."

Robyn slipped her arm through David's. "I love it, too," she said. "It's a David Peeler."

Riley gasped. "You made that?"

David, his face tinged pink, nodded. The woman with the auburn ponytail hurried past, her heels tapping out a crisp rhythm on the hardwood floor. She fluttered her fingers at David and he waved back.

"Who's that?" asked Nate.

"That's Layla Haversham, a curator at the Seattle Art Museum."

"Do you have any pieces in the museum?" Riley asked.

David looked startled. "No," he said. "I mean, not inside it. Have you been to the Olympic Sculpture Park?"

"We were there last weekend," said Nate.

"Did you notice the colossal typewriter eraser poised to roll down and rub out the Space Needle?"

"How could we miss it? Is that yours too?"

David grinned. "No." Then changing the subject, he beckoned to one of the ubiquitous tray-bearing servers. "I'm starving," he said, scooping up a handful of canapes. They smelled delectable, scenting the air with the aroma of bacon and green onions. Riley's stomach growled.

Nate stuffed two cheese-topped rounds with caramelized onions and roasted red peppers into his mouth, speaking around them. "These tiny toasts are great, but they do not a man-sized meal make. How about we all go out for a late supper?"

They agreed on a restaurant and made their way to the parking lot. As Nate opened the car door for Riley, a dark-colored Cadillac rolled past and she recognized the face behind the wheel as the auburn-haired curator. Riley eased herself into the car and adjusted her trailing skirt so Nate wouldn't slam the door on it.

She watched him settle into the driver's seat and fire up the engine, leading the little two-car caravan down the twisting road toward Seattle, the red taillights of the Cadillac in front of them piercing the dark like two burning eyes. Frost glazed the blacktop, and a light fog drifted between the towering pines. Riley hoped it wouldn't thicken as the night wore on.

"Your Tchaikovsky was excellent tonight," Nate said. "Best I've ever heard it."

"It's the first time you've ever heard it."

"And the best."

Riley laughed. The road was challenging, edged with guardrails to protect against steep drop-offs, lined with wrenching curves and sudden slopes, but Nate handled it well, though a little speedier than she liked. The Cadillac's taillights grew smaller and more distant.

"That car's traveling awfully fast," Riley said, and a little shiver passed through her. The receding red dots disappeared around a curve and when Nate reached the same spot, negotiating with care, Riley was dismayed to see how far ahead the taillights had advanced.

"Nate, something's wrong with that car. I'm afraid—"

She broke off with a scream as the Cadillac went airborne, hanging for a moment in the dark sky, the slanting beam of its headlights playing against the shifting fog. Then, tipping at an impossible angle, the car plunged into the abyss, the red-eyed taillights winking out forever.

Strains of merry holiday music poured from the speakers of David's eight-year-old Toyota. He fiddled with the volume control, squeezing the knob's ridges between his fingers as he reduced the rich tones to a mere background murmur. He was not in the mood for "Deck the Halls."

A week had passed since Layla's accident. He hadn't known her well, but she'd been a fan of his work and he'd always found her frank appraisals helpful. Her death, so stark and sudden, had dropped a shadow over his holiday spirit, thicker and darker than the rain clouds crouching over Seattle.

"Why are you looking so grim, David? We had four lovely days of sunshine in a row, and that's as much as can be expected from a northwest December. Stop scowling."

David shot a brief glance at Robyn in the seat next to him. She wore a poinsettia red dress and sparkling gold earrings shaped like tiny Christmas wreaths, her pale, wispy hair caught up off her neck in an arrangement of pins and cascading curls that was utterly charming.

"I'm not scowling," he said. "I'm concentrating on my driving. I don't want to end up in a heap of scrap metal like poor Layla." He shuddered, feeling the creases in his forehead deepen. He knew Robyn was justified in calling it a scowl, but he didn't care. "I'm still seeing the Caddy leap off that cliff in my nightmares."

Silence from the passenger seat. The monotonous swish and thump of the windshield wipers sounded like a dirge. City blocks passed by in varying shades of gray, gilded by streetlights and slashes of crimson, all too reminiscent of the dying taillights that had quashed their dinner plans a week ago.

"It was awful," Robyn said at last, her quiet words letting him know what hellish thoughts had occupied her mind during the interval. "She must have been terrified in those last moments."

David felt a surge of gratitude. It had been an appalling experience for all of them. Seeing the crumpled remains of the car, still rocking at the bottom of the incline, illuminated in eerie sienna tones by Nate's headlamps as he maneuvered his car to the very edge. The hurried 911 call, the rescue crew and police, the undignified way Layla's body, strapped in a harness at the end of a rope, had risen to meet their horrified expectations before being zipped into a body bag and bundled into the back doors of the waiting ambulance.

Yet, as bad as all of it had been, Robyn had made the trip up from Portland to spend another weekend with him, and neither one of them wanted to sever the tender ties of friendship that had started to form with Riley and Nate. As if reading his thoughts, Robyn initiated a slight shift in subject.

"I'm glad we're cashing in that raincheck for a dinner date. I don't have a lot of real friends in the concert circuit, and I could use one. Besides, I understand Nate's been assigned to investigate Layla's death and I'm curious to know what's going on with the case."

David clasped her hand. "I'm glad, too." He paused, swallowing an unaccustomed lump in his throat. "Thank you, Robyn."

"For what?"

For what? For reaching out to him when he had no friends in the art world, when he thought he'd lost everything worth having, when his erratic behavior turned others away. Words could not answer her question.

So he said nothing.

He steered the car into the restaurant parking lot, an old-fashioned Italian place that got good reviews, and killed the engine. Inside, Riley and Nate were already waiting for them at a corner booth lit mostly by a wax-encrusted Chianti bottle topped with a flickering candle. The air was laced with the scent of garlic, and a tantalizing sizzle emerged from the kitchen each time the door swung open. That sound was like Pavlov's bell for David. His mouth watered.

They exchanged greetings and small talk, ordered drinks, and settled in to peruse the menu, but David couldn't focus on the printed offerings. He fought the impulse to reach across Robyn and grab the lute that rested on a small shelf above the table, meant strictly for décor. Part of him knew that. It was the rest of him that struggled with the urge to seize it and pluck its strings.

The waitress delivered their drinks. Robyn gave her an imploring smile.

"May I ask a favor?" she said, taking the lute and passing it across the table. "Would you mind putting that somewhere else for now?" She dabbed at her eyes with a napkin. "My allergies are terrible. Something in the lacquer must be aggravating them."

"Of course!" The waitress hurried away with the offending instrument and David squeezed Robyn's thigh under the table. She fluttered her eyelashes at him, but David sensed the tension of suppressed curiosity beating over her in waves. As soon as the server took their orders and retreated, the dam broke.

"So Nate," she said, eagerness animating her voice, "have you figured out who killed Layla?" She paused. "I'm inferring it was murder."

"Oh, it was murder all right," said Riley. "And I think the novelist did it."

"With the candlestick, in the library?" Nate said, giving her a pointed glare.

Robyn leaned forward, a knife clutched in one fist and a fork in the other, licking her lips. "Come on. Serve it up, Detective."

Nate laughed. "Show me some mercy, woman. You know I can't discuss an ongoing investigation."

Robyn's lower lip trembled in a beguiling pout, her eyes taking on the look of a hungry puppy. David knew that look. They'd be hearing some details of the case.

Nate sighed, relenting a bit. "I'll tell you what I can," he said. "An unknown suspect cut the brake line on Ms. Haversham's Cadillac, and the OnStar system was disabled. She died at the scene of the crash."

"And the writer?" Robyn pressed.

"We do consider Abraham Gentry a person of interest, but we're pursuing other lines of investigation, as well."

A brief silence fell over the table, broken only by the soft tones of The Ukrainian Bell Carol and the clink of cutlery. Robyn clicked her tongue in disgust.

"That's it? I got that much from the morning paper. Have a heart, Nate. You've clearly told more than that to Riley."

Nate squeezed his eyes shut and let out a long-suffering groan. Leaning forward, he opened his eyes and pinned Robyn with an intense gaze.

"You remember last year's serial killer, The Puget Sound Slasher? Riley was indispensable in helping me solve that case. Believe it or not, her musical training has equipped her to recognize patterns and remember data on a par with many computer systems. So yeah, I divulged more to her than I probably should have, but she's like a consultant on the case."

"Oh, well, that's okay then, because I haven't had any musical training at *all*," Robyn said, and David noticed a dangerous spark in her eyes.

Nate's face flushed a furious red. "I didn't mean—"

He broke off as the server arrived with their salads. She placed a basket of warm bread in the center of the table and flanked it with four small bowls of olive oil for dipping. It smelled heavenly. David, sensing what was coming and knowing Robyn's love for bread, thought it might be enough to distract her from the topic, but she was not to be deterred.

"Did you hear about the murder of Medora Marcsello out at Sylvan Manor last summer?" she asked. Nate looked relieved at what he perceived as a change of subject. David winced.

"The Hungarian concert pianist?" Nate shook his head. "I remember hearing she was killed at some kind of artist retreat, but that's about it. I'm sorry. I have my hands full just trying to keep up with the crime in my own district."

"David and I were there," Robyn said, raising one eyebrow to highlight the import of her words. "Sequestered as actual suspects. But David picked up on little details the police deemed unimportant. He's the one that solved that case and brought the murderer to justice, and if you don't believe me, ask Detective Chandler. She doesn't like sharing the credit, but she will if you ask her pointblank."

"Wait a minute," Nate said. "Is that the case that started with the cat?"

Robyn beamed. "That's the one."

"I read about that," Riley said. "You were suspects?"

"Oh yes. Confined to the artist's retreat until the killer was caught. By David, I might add. When he lost that little slice of brain tissue, he gained some unique abilities."

David snorted. "That's one way of putting it."

Robyn ignored him. "His sculpting style changed radically. What you saw at the event last week was an example of what he can do. He has the ability to strip away the layers and see what's beneath. You could use his keen eye, Detective. Call him a consultant, like Riley."

Nate held his hands up in surrender. He chewed and swallowed. "If you weren't such a talented pianist, Robyn, you could have been a lawyer. I'm convinced I need you all! I'll divulge certain details of the case, but only if I can rely on your discretion. What we discuss between us, stays between us."

"Deal!" said Robyn. Under the table, she pinched David's leg.

"Deal," he echoed, rubbing the sore spot. He saw Robyn exchange a conspiratorial grin with Riley as they all leaned their heads together to hear Nate's lowered voice.

"It's true that Abraham Gentry is our prime suspect. He's the only one with both means and opportunity, though I admit we haven't uncovered a motive yet."

He looked at Robyn. "Riley tells me the two of you watched him leave, headed for the parking lot. Members of the valet crew say he spent less than ten minutes among the cars before returning to the house. No one else came or went after that until Layla left. And we were right behind her."

David felt the sparks of interest in his head flare to life. "What was he doing in the parking lot?"

"He claims he was looking for a box of headshots, for autographing. Thought they must have been left in the car, but it turns out they were inside all the time, hidden by a stack of books."

"Hmmm. Anyone at the event could have cut the brake line at any time," David said.

"Not according to our auto specialist. Judging by the amount of brake fluid that leaked out onto the ground, he says it was done shortly before Layla started the car and left. Consider this as well—the morning after the murder, a member of my team found a pair of diagonal cutters snagged in a bush several feet down a ravine behind the mansion. There was brake fluid in the blades and the prints we pulled from it are Abraham Gentry's. It looks like he tried to dispose of the murder weapon in the dark and didn't realize it ended up where we could easily find it."

"It looks pretty black for our man of words," said Robyn. "Maybe if he wrote mysteries, instead of literary dramas, he'd have done a better job of it."

"But would he have enough time to cut the brake line and disable the security system in that ten minute time frame?" Riley asked.

A thought occurred to David. "Was the system disabled from the car's interior?"

"Our guy wasn't positive about that. The wreckage was such that he couldn't give us a definitive answer. However, here's something interesting—one of the guests we questioned mentioned that Layla had been looking for her car key earlier in the evening. She thought she'd lost it, but it turned up later, under a wadded Kleenex in her pocket. What if Abraham hid the glossies, giving him an excuse to go to the parking lot? He filches Layla's car key, uses it to get in and disconnect the system, then slips it back into the pocket of her pantsuit along with a tissue to cover it?"

"Right," said David. "If he knew what he was doing it wouldn't take long to accomplish that. He probably could have learned how to do it on YouTube."

The waitress arrived with their meals. Stuffed sole for Riley, Fettucine Alfredo for Robyn and Nate. David barely looked at his plate of manicotti. He'd been so keen for it, but now he found his appetite for the facts of the case overpowering the demands of his stomach. He shoveled in a bite or two, graciously allowing Nate to sample his fettucine before plowing ahead with more questions.

"So, it looks like Abraham really was the only one with means and opportunity," he said. "But why would he do it, Nate? Can you shed any light on that?"

"Maybe. Abraham and Layla had a history. Twenty-six years ago, they were engaged to be married."

Robyn's fork froze, a creamy-sauced noodle dangling from her lips. "What! There's bound to be plenty of room for motive in that. What happened?"

"Three weeks before the wedding, Abraham left a note of apology and disappeared with Tricia, Layla's best friend."

"Holy moly," said Riley, doing the math. "That must have been soon after his first book became a bestseller."

"It was indeed. He had enough money rolling in to support his new lifestyle in a provincial French village. He was joined by his personal assistant, a Mr.—" Nate pulled a notepad from his breast pocket and flipped through a few pages. "Clint Barstow. Abraham continued to produce books, but none of them sold very well after the first. Eventually, both Clint and Tricia must have concluded he was washed up. They deserted ship, and Abraham was left alone."

Robyn stabbed her fork into the air. "Deserved it, the chump."

"I can see why Layla might want to murder *him*," said Riley. "But the other way around?"

"How, and when, did he end up back in the States?" asked David.

"Apparently, his latest book caught the interest of several publishers and there was a bidding war. His agent got him a smashup deal, but the publisher insisted he do a stateside tour. It was too good to pass up, so he got on a plane. Claims it's his first time back since he left, all those years ago, and we haven't found any evidence to the contrary."

Riley finished her sole and pushed the plate to the side. "How did he reconnect with Layla?"

"According to Abraham, she told him she heard about the publicity tour and decided to show up at a book signing. They met for coffee afterwards and she told him she'd long since let go any hard feelings. They exchanged contact info, and a week later she calls up to invite him to the charity event.

"Awfully generous of her," Robyn said, "given his past behavior."

"Seems he's a huge Quinn Owen fan—you know, the jazz saxophonist who went on after Riley's performance." Nate took a bite of pasta before continuing. "It was too big a draw for him to turn down, and Layla sweetened the pot by allotting him a table for book sales. So, even though he thought it might be awkward and his wife was angry about it, he accepted the invitation."

"His wife. What's her story?" asked Robyn

"Her name's Ariel. They met in France. She was an American tourist, he was hungry for a taste of home. They hit it off."

"Could she have a part in this?"

"She could. I just don't see how. Yet."

David watched Riley smooth her napkin on the tablecloth. He felt like snatching it up to wipe his own mouth and looked away before the urge became uncontrollable.

"There are a lot of emotional factors here that could shape up to motives of love, hate, or jealousy," said Riley. "But show me the money. Who benefits financially from Layla's death?"

"That would be Layla's brother, Joel. He lives in Kent."

"Was he at the fundraiser?" Robyn asked.

"No, but he doesn't have an alibi for the time in question. He had an argument with his girlfriend and went for a drive. She says he was gone for three hours. That's enough time for him to drive from Kent to the Mackenzie mansion, do the deed, and return home."

"But no one saw him there," said Robyn.

"It was dark," said Riley.

"Check please," said David.

Now that he had the basic facts of the case, he was impatient to find a quiet place to ponder them. He'd lost a lot under the surgeon's knife—his fiancée, his easy-going personality, the artistic flair he'd cultivated since boyhood. But he was learning to enjoy some of the perks of his new condition.

He did see things differently than he had before, and that was not always a comfortable thing. The way he experienced emotion had changed, and he often didn't recognize what he was feeling or know how to react to emotions in those around him. Formerly a life-of-the-party type, he'd become socially awkward and was flat-out amazed to be with a woman like Robyn.

Especially now, during the holiday season. There was a Christmas not that long ago when his only companion was a shiny black Glock. The two of them had gotten real close.

He still missed the artist he used to be, but his current work was selling well and his early pieces carried a posthumous sort of cachet since the sculptor who created them was dead. Consequently, their value had increased, along with his net worth.

Life was full of trade-offs.

Riley pulled up the collar of her raincoat, expecting to step out into a dripping cold rain. But the sky had emptied, leaving the freshly scrubbed clarity that comes in the wake of scudding gray clouds. She smiled and looked back, waiting for the others. Nate was raiding the toothpick dispenser while Robyn and David helped themselves from a jar of candy canes.

The four of them stood under a flickering streetlamp in the parking lot to say their goodbyes. Night insects bobbed and weaved above their heads, playing chicken with the high-wattage bulb. The occasional *ff-sthht* of a bug body going into the light punctuated their conversation. Riley sensed David's eagerness to get on the road.

"Well, I've got a ferry to catch," she said, allowing their exchange to segue to a smooth conclusion. As she and Nate waved to the disappearing rear bumper of David's Toyota, he said, "What time does the ferry leave?"

"Not for another forty-five minutes, but I feel like walking. Do you mind? It's only a couple blocks, isn't it?"

Nate eyed her shoes. "I suppose you'll make it in those, but the sidewalk's pretty darn steep. You may wish you could fly by the time we get there."

"I always wish I could fly."

Nate laughed and took her arm. They strolled downhill, the air crisp but unstirred by any breeze, as if holding them in a gentle hand. The doorway of an Irish pub stood open as they passed and Riley heard the strains of a band playing "Whiskey in the Jar." She thought about the thieving highwayman and his treacherous Jenny. Heady, romantic stuff.

She recalled Nate was of Irish ancestry. His mother was an O'Malley. Swinging his arm, she held all the tighter to him as the slope of the sidewalk took on a sharper pitch, leading down to the waterfront. As Nate had predicted, it was painful walking with gravity trying to push her entire foot into the toe of her shoe. She decided to ignore the discomfort.

"Did you spill it all, Nate?" she asked. "Or did you hold something back just for me?"

He flashed a smile at her, the one with the dimples that made her swoon. "I might have saved you a tidbit or two. I didn't say anything about what I found when I searched Layla's house."

"Oh goody. Let's hear it."

"At the back of her bedroom closet, Layla kept a box of letters and old photographs. Most of them were grainy and faded, so it's hard to say for sure after twenty-six years, but a lot of the photos were of her and Abraham, and they looked close. Real close. Layla never married, and I'm betting she never got over him. Some of the letters say as much."

A wave of sympathy washed over Riley. She remembered how immobilized her heart had been after Jim died. She couldn't imagine suffering two and a half decades of feelings like that.

"The lady caught some tough breaks," Nate continued. "Her medicine cabinet was full of old prescription drugs. Some people never throw them away, convinced that as soon as they do, the old condition will come creeping back."

"And what 'old condition' was Layla afflicted with?"

"Breast cancer. I called the prescribing physician. She beat it, though. Still cancer free as of her last checkup."

"Only to be killed in her Caddy. How sad."

They fell silent, traffic sounds and the tapping of their shoes filling the gap.

"How are your feet holding up?" Nate asked.

"If wings were to sprout from my shoulder blades, I'd be a happy camper."

"Chin up, dear lady. You're nearly there."

Heart still fluttering a little after a brief snuggle with Nate before he left to walk back to his car, Riley found a window seat on the westbound ferry and stared out the glass. Lights from the cityscape shimmered on the water, creating an image that made her think of those paintings on black velvet, vibrant colors held aloft in a sea of darkness.

The night had turned cold, and a chill radiated from the window. Riley sighed and drew back a few inches. The seat opposite was occupied by a man in a Santa suit, cherry-nosed as the poem dictates. She smiled, and he returned a half-hearted "ho ho ho" before closing his eyes for a long winter's nap.

Weariness tugged at Riley, as well. Her feet no longer hurt, but another pain had taken their place. The ache of guilt. She felt terrible that Nate shared his secrets so fully with her while she kept so much from him.

She couldn't divulge where she really went when her calendar specified a rehearsal with Sara. She couldn't tell him about her clandestine meetings with his former partner. He couldn't know she spent several hours each week training to go undercover.

She hoped someday to be able to tell him, to open herself to him without reservation. For now, she would try to make up for her subterfuge by lending him every help she could.

She prayed it would be enough.

Riley stooped, ducking under the strip of crime scene tape barring the gateway of Layla's house as Nate lifted it for her. A cold drop from the overhanging branches of a scraggly maple tree fell squarely into her left eye and she paused to blot it out, hoping her mascara hadn't spread to give her that prizefighter look. The smell of wood smoke hung in the air and Riley noticed the residences on either side of the Haversham house were pumping out clouds of vapor from red-brick chimneys. The weather had taken a raw turn, yet it was unlikely to be a white Christmas. The forecast was for gray.

"I wish I could take you into the house the Gentrys are renting," Nate said, "but they might kick up a stink. Poor Layla is unlikely to object to having you in her home. Especially since you're helping to solve her murder."

"What happened at the Gentry house?"

"Remember how Abraham and Ariel insisted that Layla had never been in their home? We busted that myth. We found traces of oily footprints on the floor of the garage, made by high-heeled shoes, and we matched them to a pair of pumps taken from Layla's closet.

"When confronted, Abraham got all hot under the collar. Insisted he'd done nothing wrong. He was working on the engine of a used BMW he picked up when Layla pulled into the driveway. He says she came onto him strong, like they could go back twenty-six years as if nothing since had ever happened. She was like a crazy woman. She had him in a clinch when Ariel arrived on the scene, none too happy. The two women had a bit of a scrap and Layla left."

"But that gives Ariel motive," Riley said.

"Perhaps. If she really feared Layla's power to mess up their lives."

"What else did your search turn up?"

"We found a set of tools that should have included a diagonal cutter, except the diagonal cutter was missing. No surprises there—we already had it booked into evidence. But we also found a crumpled handkerchief stained with brake fluid in the pocket of the suit Abraham wore to the benefit."

"That seems careless."

Nate shrugged. "People forget things when they're under a lot of pressure—they don't always think straight. It's what keeps us in business. Without those little slip-ups, we'd have no line to follow."

They'd entered Layla's living room and Riley gasped with pleasure, remembering this was the home of an art museum curator. Framed paintings, tastefully arranged, graced the walls and intriguing *objets d'art* rested on tables and shelves throughout the room. Intricate, filigreed clocks, cleverly crafted boxes fashioned from exotic materials, miniature sculptures, and a single larger one in pride of place between the two oversized windows. Riley wondered what David would think of it all.

The carpet felt very plush beneath her feet. Layla's life had been difficult and painful, but at least she'd had some creature comforts and compensations. Riley passed through into the formal dining room. Running her hands over the satiny polished wood of the beautiful inlaid table, she admired the ornate silver candlesticks and rich brocade of the six straight-backed chairs.

"All these things will fetch a pretty penny if Layla's brother decides to sell. How much did she have in other assets?"

"Enough to kill for. We've still got our eye on brother Joel."

They finished the tour of the house and ended on the rear patio leading down into a lovely rose garden. Riley felt bad that she hadn't picked up on any patterns or discrepancies anywhere in the house. She wanted so much to earn her keep.

"Sorry I wasn't any help."

"Just having you here is a help to me. This time, going through the house, I was seeing it through your eyes. Having that different perspective is useful for a guy like me who wants to think he doesn't miss a trick."

They walked the short flagstone path to the garden. It was small and simple, the perfect grace note for the house. She sank down onto a bench, drinking in a fragrance made up of mulch and the rain-washed rose petals which lay scattered beneath the bushes. The spindly branches were laden with rosehips and a dozen or so dead blooms, their sad heads bowed and windblown.

"This was Layla's work of art," Nate said. "The gardener who cut the grass and attended the rest of the yard told me he was never allowed in here. It was Layla's baby."

Riley's gaze traveled over the drooping deadheads and litter of petals. "She can't have spent much time here lately."

Nate indicated Riley's seat. "Actually, the gardener said she often spent hours on that bench. She cultivated that rose bush herself and named it for Abraham."

He indicated the plant next to Riley, its branches bearing a few curling corpses of former splendor, creamy petals touched by flame-colored accents.

"What did she name it?"

"The gardener said she called it The Burning Bush."

"Isn't that Moses?"

Nate shrugged. "I guess she figured one scriptural reference is as good as the next."

"She was brooding over something," said Riley, "rather than caring for the garden. Something was bothering her."

She stood. The stone bench had been slightly damp and Riley felt the moisture soaking into the seat of her pants. She examined the surface where she'd been sitting. The bench was rough-hewn from a block of granite as if the mason couldn't spare the time to fully articulate its finer points. Riley supposed that lent it a sort of rustic mystique.

"Perhaps we should bring David out here to have a look at this bench," she said. "He might see something in those layers of stone to put us on the right path."

"I think we're on the right path with Abraham. We just need to firm it up a little before we make an arrest."

"Still, as you say, another pair of eyes couldn't hurt," said Riley. "Especially if those eyes are powered by a human microscope."

David opened the refrigerator in the chic modern kitchen of his mid-town apartment and stared at the mostly empty shelves. He hadn't prepared for company.

"Would anyone like a beverage?" He spoke over his shoulder to the group in the living room. "You can choose from a wide selection of water, ketchup, and soy sauce."

"Water's good," shouted Riley. It was her go-to drink. Robyn joined him in his perusal of the forlorn fridge.

"I'd planned on hitting the grocery store on the way home from Layla's," he said. "Like we usually do when you come up. Pick out some things to fix together." He couldn't remember how big a faux pas it was, having nothing to offer your guests.

"It's fine, David." She caught and held his gaze. "Really. Now let's get in there before we miss the juicy stuff."

David grabbed glasses and a large bottle of chilled water, feeling so out of his element. He thought that after Robyn's buildup of his abilities, Nate and the others must be disappointed that he hadn't unearthed any leads. Even the bench, though a lovely piece of granite, was just a bench.

With the damage to his frontal lobe, his ability to interpret social cues had been impaired, along with his capacity for selecting an appropriate emotional response or picking out socks to match his suit. But he was working hard to relearn these skills, and he hadn't noticed anything to suggest his new friends found him lacking. He thought he was pleased about this.

He placed his offering on the coffee table, the clink of glass on glass ringing like a bell, and poured everyone a drink. Settling into the comfort of his favorite armchair, he felt the petal-soft leather embrace him like a caress, accepting his contours from long practice. Before he'd even had time to draw a breath, Robyn pounced on Nate.

"David's here now, and I can't wait any longer. What's the bombshell, Detective?"

Nate leaned forward. "Remember now, this doesn't go beyond the four of us." Three heads nodded. "I've had my team putting out feelers for Abraham's PA, Clint Barstow and Layla's former best friend, Tricia. They've turned up empty."

"You mean there's no trace of them since they came back to the States?" David asked.

I mean there's no hard evidence they ever left the States. No flight, passport control, or customs records that we could find. Sometimes the absence of evidence *is* evidence, but after all this time some of that stuff is pretty patchy. Child's play for a good lawyer to tear it apart in court."

"What are you saying, Nate?" asked Robyn. "Are you suggesting someone killed them twenty-six years ago?"

"I'm suggesting Abraham Gentry did."

"What about their families?" said Riley. "When did they last have contact?"

"Clint was pretty much alone in the world. No brothers or sisters, parents died in a car accident when he was ten. He lucked into the PA job and it seems his life was taking care of Abraham. As for Tricia, her mom got a few postcards from France. Kept them for years, she said, but finally got rid of them in a fit of pique when she downsized to a smaller house after her second husband passed. Regrets it now, but they're gone."

Riley rose from the sofa she shared with Nate and refilled her water glass. "What reason would Abraham have for killing them?"

"You three are the consultants. I've come to you for ideas."

"I'm just brainstorming," David said, "but maybe Abraham caught Clint doing something that made him angry—like stealing, or seducing Layla—and murdered him. Tricia witnessed the deed and had to be silenced."

"Maybe one or both of them was blackmailing Abraham," said Riley.

"What if Abraham was in love with Tricia," said Robyn, "and he found out she was involved with Clint? He killed them both in a jealous rage and hid the bodies, then fled to Europe to provide a cover for their disappearance."

"You're giving me some great theories, but in all of these cases, what happened to the bodies?"

Silence descended, accompanied by the soft spatter of rain on the windows. David thought hard, sensing something beneath his consciousness struggling to get free. He had only to peel back the surface to see what it was, but that uppermost layer stayed firmly in place.

Across from him, Riley uncurled from the sofa and sat forward.

"When was the rose garden planted?" she asked.

That broke it free, surging up from the depths, and he spoke with conviction. "If you dig beneath the roses, you'll find—"

"Two bodies!" Riley finished his sentence.

Nate pulled out his phone. "I'm sending a team now."

Riley tried to concentrate on properly fingering the Polish Christmas Fantasia, but her mind was across the water with Nate, wondering how the excavation of the rose garden was proceeding. She had a week of holiday concert performances coming up and if Nate didn't provide some answers soon, she'd never be prepared in time.

The pleasantly resinous scent of pine drifted over her left shoulder from where the Christmas tree stood behind her in a chipper effort to foster the holiday spirit. Without Jim and Tanner to help decorate, putting up the tree scored as one of the lowest points of her year, but as long as she was in town, she refused to skip it.

She realized she'd muffed the same passage three times in a row and gave up. Practicing the mistake would only perfect her execution of that mistake. Before she could rise from the bench, her phone vibrated, and she snatched it from her pocket, her mind racing with anticipation.

"I'll get right to the point," Nate said. "The diggers found the remains of two bodies."

"I knew it! Do you have enough to charge Abraham now?"

"Hang on, there's a bit more to the story. One of the bodies has been ID'd as Tricia Morton. The other belongs to an unidentified male."

"Well, can't you get Clint's dental records to confirm a match?"

"That's my point, Riley. We did. Whoever's buried alongside Tricia, it's not Clint. We're checking into missing persons, but—"

"Oh my heavens," said Riley, realization hitting her like a thunderclap. "Schedule another dinner party, Nate. And this time, bring those old photos from Layla's closet."

David picked the restaurant this time, a steak house with the tenderest T-bones he'd ever eaten. He and Robyn were first on the scene, and she'd insisted he order for everyone so the food could be on the table when Riley and Nate arrived.

The aroma of grilled beef from the kitchen and cinnamon from the table centerpieces mingled to remind him of his trip to Athens, eating moussaka at a sidewalk café in the Plaka. He and Claire had planned to return there for their honeymoon. That was before the surgery, before everything changed.

He was glad to see the others come in, shucking their raincoats before settling at the table just as the server brought out their meals. Their greetings were brief but cordial and the conversation sparse as they ate. Mouthwatering as it was, David did not linger over his favorite menu option. Like the others, he was anxious to get down to business.

The waiter cleared their plates and brought complimentary glasses of mulled cider with the wish of a Merry Christmas from the manager. As soon as he stepped away from the table, Nate began.

"Riley told me she passed on the information about the excavated bodies. Let me fill you in on what else we've discovered. Layla's brother, Joel, has serious money issues. The business he started two years ago is on the verge of going under. Layla's legacy will just about fix him up if he can hang on through probate. He admits he asked his sister for a loan and was furious when she turned him down. But angry enough to kill? He says not."

"Of course he would," said Robyn. "Don't mean a thing."

"Spoken like a true skeptic," said Nate. "You could get good at this."

She sketched out a mock curtsey and made a rolling motion with her hands, bidding him to continue.

"All right. One of Layla's neighbors intercepted a member of my team during the dig. She had a letter addressed to Layla from Ariel Gentry. There was a slight error in the address, so it had been delivered two doors down and the woman didn't know what to do with it. She forgot about it until she saw my guys on site."

"Let me guess," Riley said. "A death threat."

"Well, not exactly that, but menacing language directed at Layla if she didn't leave Abraham alone. Not explicit, but a jury might interpret it as a death threat. Especially under the circumstances."

"And what did Ariel say about it?"

"She said she'd be stupid to put a threat in the mail one day and kill Layla the next. She has a point. The lady's not stupid. All said and done, Abraham's still the front runner, unless one of you can change my mind."

"Show him the pictures," said Riley.

David realized she meant him. He was in the hot seat, expected to perform a mangled-brain miracle and he had no expectation of succeeding. Nate handed three photos to Robyn, indicating that she should pass them on. She took a long, curious look before doing so. When they came to David, he saw they were aged, the colors mostly faded to a sickly green, and the photographer had not been skilled at his craft.

He stared at a picture of a smiling young couple. Layla as a young woman, her hair tied back with a ribbon, cuddled a puppy in one arm and a handsome dark-haired man in the other. In another photo, the same couple posed next to a sand castle they'd presumably built. The third showed them at a birthday party, wearing silly hats and eating cake.

What was he supposed to be seeing? Robyn believed he'd acquired some sort of extra perception but it seemed clear to him that he'd simply made some lucky guesses in the investigation at Sylvan Manor. As for his sculpting abilities, the Muse had taken pity on him, but how long would she guide his hands? He saw nothing significant in the photos. At last, he passed them back to Nate.

"Who's the man she's with?"

Robyn stared. "What do you mean, David? You know who it is."

He shook his head. "I've never seen him before."

Robyn gave a protesting laugh. "But, it's Abraham."

A little buzz of excitement burned deep inside him and he felt immense relief. He'd seen something in those photos, after all.

"That man," he pointed, "is not Abraham."

Nate and Riley exchanged high fives. "Yes!" Riley said. "That confirms it."

Robyn looked peeved. "Will someone please tell me what's going on?"

Riley shivered and chose a seat close to the roaring fireplace in the Mackenzie living room. The cavernous space would be difficult and expensive to heat now that it was not filled with a hundred warm bodies. But Nate had insisted on this venue, and the Mackenzie's had granted his request.

She watched him as he strode about the room, making sure all was ready for his big moment. She felt a tiny stab of envy, but it quickly faded. The thing about being a covert consultant is that you can't take credit. The collaboration between the four of them had broken this case wide open, but Nate was their front man. She wasn't in it for the credit anyway, and she'd better get used to not getting any. A bit of a switch for a concert pianist.

David and Robyn shared the adjacent love seat. His face was somber and Riley noticed he wore one gray sock and one blue. Robyn's cheeks were flushed with excitement. Abraham, Ariel, and Joel, along with his girlfriend, were scattered among the inner ring of seating around the fireplace. A surrounding fringe of support officers stood back, and Nate took center stage, clearing his throat.

"On behalf of the Bellevue PD, I want to thank you all for your patience and cooperation throughout this investigation. We're here to wrap things up, and you'll be relieved to know we've found our murderer."

He pointed to Abraham. The novelist looked aghast, a rush of blood tinting his face a virulent crimson.

"You've got it wrong. I didn't kill Layla."

"Correct. You did not."

Abraham held up his hands in mute protest, an indignant look on his face.

"But," Nate continued, "you did kill Layla's best friend, Tricia Morton."

The blood in Abraham's face drained away, leaving behind a pale gray. He shook his head, but didn't speak.

"You buried her in Layla's newly planted rose garden where no one would notice the disturbed earth. When we found her, Tricia wasn't alone. You buried someone else beside her, Abraham. Who was it?"

The novelist turned a baleful glare on Nate. "I don't know what you're talking about."

"The game's up, sir," Nate said. "We've matched the dental records."

The man crossed his arms over his chest and pressed his lips together, saying nothing.

"The remains we pulled from the soil belonged to Abraham Gentry."

A ripple of astonishment passed through the ranks. Ariel stared at her husband with dawning comprehension.

"You dirty, stinking wretch." She spit the words out, loathing etched in her face. Riley suspected there'd been trouble in that marriage for a long time. "You killed Abraham and stole his identity." Her eyes grew ever wider as the enormity of the truth sunk home. "You lied to me. I thought I'd married the genuine article. No wonder you could never duplicate the success of that first novel."

"I *have* duplicated it," shouted the man formerly known as Abraham Gentry, his face lit with triumph. "My latest book is a bestseller!"

"Marketing department voodoo," Arial replied. "As soon as the publisher pulls support, the book will spiral into oblivion."

The novelist's face turned crafty. "They won't be pulling support. This will skyrocket my book to the top of the charts for a good, long time. Plus, I can write another bestseller based on my story."

"You'll be doing it from prison," said Nate.

"Excuse me." Joel interrupted, a mystified expression on his face. "If this man isn't Abraham Gentry, who is he?"

"You're looking at Clint Barstow, Abraham's personal assistant. He had access to Abraham's passport, ID, important documents—everything he'd need to take over the writer's identity."

"But he looks just like Gentry," Joel protested. Riley saw the look of incredulous denial on David's face and almost laughed. The sculptor saw things so differently from the rest of them.

"I'll wager he handed over a hefty whack of Abraham's money to a plastic surgeon," said Nate.

"Why'd you do it? Why'd you kill my sister?" Joel asked. The pleading note in his voice struck a chord in Riley's heart.

"I told you, I didn't."

"Why should I believe you? You murdered two people for money and some dream of immortal glory. But why Layla?"

"Abraham was a fool. I guess I thought I could play him better than he played himself. And I did. For twenty-six years. I killed Tricia to sell Abraham's disappearance. I had to get him out of the country with a plausible excuse. So he fled with the best friend and was later joined by the PA. Or such was the story I sold the world."

"So who murdered Layla?"

"No one did," Nate said. "She died by her own hand in an attempt to bring Abraham's killer to justice. We'll never know exactly how the pieces came together, but I think I can take a fair stab at it.

"When she showed up at a book signing for Abraham's latest novel, she realized the man behind the table was an imposter. Putting two and two together, she figured out what Clint had done, and how very much he'd stolen from her. The only man she ever loved. The life they could have had together. The children that might have been theirs."

Riley squeezed her eyelids shut against the prickle that threatened them. The kinship she experienced in that moment for Layla was overwhelming. She'd known such thoughts and feelings herself.

"She started planning how to expose Clint's sins to the world. During that time, she realized the breast cancer she'd conquered years ago was back. She drove to Ellensburg to see a doctor, knowing that if we discovered she was terminal, we might place her death as a suicide. She wanted us to find and follow the trail of clues she left pointing to Abraham. Or Clint, as it turns out.

"She wore a distinctive pair of heels to the Gentry residence, managing to stain them with grease, leaving footprints on the floor of the garage. She also took the opportunity to nick a pair of diagonal cutters covered with Clint's fingerprints. At some point, probably at the charity event, she slipped a handkerchief bearing traces of brake fluid into the pocket of his suit.

"Then, before leaving the event, she cut the brake line on her Cadillac with Clint's cutters and threw them into a bush where we'd be sure to find them. Then she drove off the lot and let the icy, twisting road do the rest."

"That's quite a charade she went through. Why not just go to the police with her suspicions?" asked Joel's girlfriend.

"I doubt they'd have paid her theory much attention," Joel told her.

Nate shrugged with an apologetic expression. "I can't say."

"Layla was a resourceful lady," Riley said. "She achieved justice and revenge in one stroke."

"That she did." Nate turned to the bestselling author. "Clint Barstow, I'm placing you under arrest for the murders of Tricia Morton and Abraham Gentry. You'll be spending Christmas in lockup."

Riley's skin heated under the radiance from the stage lighting, but the glow she felt within brought the real warmth. Waves of applause rippled through the concert hall, echoed by waves of relief flooding through her veins. It was over, and she'd performed well. Her Christmas concert season, though short, was a success.

In the dressing room, she traded her emerald green gown for jeans and a sweater—a goofy holiday one decked with snowflakes and reindeer. The intercom system piped in Bing Crosby singing about olden days, happy golden days of yore.

Riley's heart ached in her chest, and she was surprised to register it as a good ache, one made of gratitude for the love she'd had in her life and for the spirit of Christmas.

A huge bouquet of red roses and bronze chrysanthemums had been delivered and Riley thought they looked like nothing so much as a burning bush. She buried her face in the blossoms, breathing in their fragrance. The surging adrenaline that always coursed through her during a performance was dissipating, bringing in its wake a mellow contentment.

She plucked the card from the flowers and read:

Awesome performance! Now, hurry up and change. We're waiting for you to join us for a late supper.

Your friends—Nate, Robyn, and David

P.S. It's Nate's turn to pick the restaurant. We're eating Greek tonight.

Riley grabbed her purse and headed for the exit, crooning along with Bing, thinking she agreed with his sentiment to the roots of her heart, and willing to sing it out loud.

Have yourself a merry little Christmas now.

*Note: If you enjoyed spending time with Riley, Nate, and David, you'll be happy to know there's more where that came from. In the thriller novel, *Nocturne in Ashes*, Riley and Nate meet for the first time, in dire and explosive circumstances. If you like a gripping, suspenseful tale, grab your copy of *Nocturne in Ashes* today and prepare to burn the midnight oil!

David Peeler made his way into the world in *Death of a Muse*, where he attends an artist's retreat stalked by murder. If you love crime stories with a puzzle to solve, grab *Death of a Muse* today.

Cold Busted

This is a "you-solve-it" minute mystery, kind of like an old Encyclopedia Brown story. The solution is in the next chapter. Have fun!

Sheriff's deputy, Vanessa Hale, set the parking brake on the cruiser and stepped out, one hand securing her hat against the wintry breeze off the Hood Canal. The towering pines whispered and moaned as she and her partner, Scott Adkins, hurried across the frozen pavement of Marjorie Weaver's driveway.

"Hey, Chief," Adkins said, "what nationality is Santa Claus?"

Hale wasn't in the mood for a debate over holiday origins. "I don't know," she said, teeth chattering.

"He's North Polish."

"Ha! A joke. Good one. Maybe you can share it with Mrs. Weaver as they're loading her into the ambulance."

"Come on, Chief! EMTs tell me she's going to be fine. They'll probably take her in for observation."

"Not before we get a chance to question her," Hale replied.

Inside, the temperature jumped a good fifty degrees. Hale's cheeks flushed and she removed her jacket, resisting the temptation to loosen her collar. In a corner of the living room, on the right, Mrs. Weaver lay on a stretcher tended by medical personnel. A distraught young man stood beside her.

On Hale's left, an expanse of hardwood floor stretched along a gallery display of artwork and valuable relics. Scattered across the floor beneath an empty shelf were the shards of a broken vase, splayed out clear to the baseboards on the far left. From her position in the entryway, Hale studied the deep blue and flaking gold of the shattered bits.

She joined Adkins at the stretcher. "What happened here?" she asked.

The young man cleared his throat. "I'm Dewey Weaver," he said. "Marjorie's nephew. We'd gone out for lunch and when we returned, a masked thief was stealing Aunt Marj's vase collection. They're very valuable."

"Did you see anything that could help us identify the thief?"

"I didn't see a thing," Marjorie said in a quavering voice. "As soon as I walked in the door my glasses fogged, as they always do in this kind of cold, and I took them off to clean. Dewey shouted, and I heard a vase fall. Then conk—and that's the last I remember."

Hale turned her gaze on the nephew. "I only got a glimpse as we walked in and surprised him, making him drop that vase. He must have had an accomplice," he added, pointing to a spot beside the front door. "Someone pushed me from behind before hitting Aunt Marj with that bookend. They kicked me and fled, taking four vases with them."

A flurry of cold air fluttered at the back of Hale's neck and she turned to see a girl come through the door and straight to Dewey.

"I got here as soon as I could," she said. "Oh, Aunt Marj!"

"This is my girlfriend, Kathy," Dewey explained.

Hale left them and examined the entryway. A nearby case held a silver filigreed bookend. Its twin lay on the floor, having delivered the blow to Mrs. Weaver's head. Hale noted flecks of silver and gold on the hardwood floor. She returned to the stretcher.

"Bad luck, walking in on a robbery like that," Kathy exclaimed, clasping Marjorie's hand.

"The vases—and the thief—were long gone by the time Marjorie arrived," Hale said. "Deputy Adkins, arrest these two on charges of robbery. They were in it together."

How did Chief Deputy Hale know the robbery scene was staged?

SOLUTION

By the shatter pattern of the broken vase—scattered toward the far baseboard rather than in a concentric pattern as it would be if dropped from above—Hale knew the vase had been thrown from the entryway, rather than dropped inside the gallery.

Also, gold flecks in the entry told her the vase had been there, waiting for Dewey to toss it while his aunt was temporarily blinded.

Hale deduced that Kathy had let herself into the house and taken the vases while Dewey kept his aunt occupied at lunch. On their return, he threw the vase, then hit his aunt hard enough to daze her and keep her from putting her glasses back on. After that, Dewey pretended the thieves had knocked him down as they rushed out the door with the loot.

Bowling in the New Year

*C*lank!

Jerked awake by the squeal and moan of rusty pipes coming to life inside the dingy wall, I sat straighter in the hard-backed chair and strained forward to wipe the blear from my eyes. A scotch-taped fringe of shiny tinsel, forgotten remnant of the recent holiday, fluttered listlessly in the feeble breath of heated air. Neither warmth nor cheer reached me where I sat, hunched and miserable.

Blinking, I looked down at the cold metal cuffs and length of chain tethering my wrists to the table. They made me think of the gaudy, chunky jewelry sported by some of the rough types I'd seen roaming Fremont Street the night before. Hours before the ball came down.

I hadn't been around to gawk at the big screen as the giant scintillating globe in Times Square descended. By that time, I'd been out committing the crime of the century. Apparently. I still didn't understand exactly what I was being charged with.

Clearly, it was serious.

The door opened, letting in the smell of spiced cider and a diminutive woman with mocha-colored skin and the dignified bearing of a queen. She nodded to the uniformed officer at the door who promptly pulled it shut, making me flinch at the resounding clang. It felt like one more nail pounded into my splintery pine-box coffin.

"My name is Lee Branneth, you may call me *Ms.* Branneth." One delicately curved eyebrow rose as she emphasized the Ms. and snapped open the clasps of her briefcase. "I've been appointed by the court to provide counsel."

Her tone suggested displeasure at having her New Year's Day celebrations intruded upon. I resisted the urge to point out that *I* hadn't been the one to call her, that I was just a stupid college kid caught up in some kind of incomprehensible misunderstanding. I bit my lip. There was no need to whine—she'd figure it out soon enough. I hoped.

Extracting a notebook and a gold-trimmed fountain pen, she opened to a fresh page and let her hand hover. "Well, Brenda Marks," she said, piercing me with her gaze. "What's your story?"

Where before I'd been cold—shivering even—I now felt like a pig on a spit. Hot blood rushed to my face. My armpits sweltered, feet roasting inside my woolen socks. Embarrassed by what I had to say but feeling the need to get someone on my side, make someone understand things from my perspective, I let the words spill out too fast.

Ms. Branneth held up a fine-boned hand, graced by a delicate topaz ring. "You're babbling," she said. "Slow down and start over."

I pulled in a rasping breath, dismayed to hear the stuttering hitch as I let it out. I hadn't realized I was that close to losing it. Bracing my palms against the scarred tabletop, I drew another deep breath through my nose and let it out slow. Ms. Branneth watched me, her face impassive. She looked like the bust of Nefertiti, exquisitely sculpted and hard as ancient limestone, her sleek-styled hair suggesting the classic Egyptian headdress.

"You're a college student. University of Nebraska, is that right?" she asked.

I nodded.

"What brings you to Las Vegas?"

I swallowed. "My boyfriend is from here. He brought me home to spend the holidays with his family."

"That sounds innocent enough." Narrowing her eyes, she folded wool-clad arms across her chest and stared at me. "Now tell me what you're really doing here, you and your boyfriend. Are you working in a small group or as part of a larger organization?"

I leaned forward. "We're not *working* at all. We came over for the Christmas break and tomorrow we're headed back to Nebraska."

She gave me a smile, thin as tissue paper. "I'm afraid not. By the looks of your file, you'll be finishing that degree behind bars, or not at all. If I'm to help you, Miss Marks, I need to know all the nasty details. That's the only way I can plan an effective defense." She tossed the pen onto the notepad and leaned back in the chair, crossing her legs. "Tell me everything."

I'd already told everything. Multiple times, to an assortment of law enforcement officials. It sounded worse each time.

I pinched the bridge of my nose to stave off a headache, and sighed. "I suppose I'll start at the Goodwill. That's when I began to suspect something odd in the making."

Ms. Branneth glanced through my file and nodded her approval. "Is that the Goodwill on Sahara Avenue? What happened there?"

"We bought a bowling ball."

She pursed bronze-tinted lips. "Is that all?"

"And some old cups and plates. I asked what everything was for, but Rick and Sharkey just laughed. They said it was a surprise."

"You're suggesting you're an innocent participant? That you didn't know what they were planning?"

"I'm suggesting we were *all* innocent participants. We never planned what happened."

"Hmm. What did you do next?"

"We bought four pairs of goggles at Walmart."

"What were the goggles for?"

"They wouldn't say. Only that it was part of a long-standing New Year's Eve tradition. Next, we picked up Sharkey's girlfriend, Kara, and found a place to park near Fremont Street. We walked around, just feeling the excitement. I wanted to ride the zipline and get my picture taken, but Rick said the wait was too long."

"Okay, so then what?"

"We left about 9:30 and I kept asking why we weren't staying to watch the ball drop. I mean, I thought that was the point of going to Fremont Street on New Year's Eve. They just smiled and ignored my questions. Even Kara."

I burned with indignation at the memory of their superior grins. I'd felt like the unwitting victim of a silly party game, but my curiosity got the better of me. I *had* to know what all those secretive smiles were hiding. I'd climbed back into the car willingly enough and strapped in for the ride.

Ms. Branneth turned her attention to the file folder and skimmed her finger through a printed report, stopping halfway down the second page.

"Miss Marks, you're attempting to paint me a picture of college pranks and schoolyard innocence, but I see here that your hands were tested for gunshot residue and the result came back positive. Did you shoot a firearm at any point during the night?"

The depths of my stomach heaved. "That's what the plates and cups were for," I answered. "We drove out into the desert and set them up for target practice."

"What were you practicing for?"

"What?" I began to see how it would go in the courtroom. Anything I said could be twisted into nefarious intentions. "Nothing! We were just goofing around."

"A gun is not a toy, Miss Marks."

I looked down at my hands, imagining I smelt the whiff of GSR. "Of course not," I answered meekly.

I'd never fired a gun before and this one had belonged to Rick's father, and *his* father before him. It was an old black powder .45. In the empty desert, far from everything, it seemed like harmless fun. Rick loaded each shot for me and warned me about the recoil and the noise. We used earplugs and goggles and I'd shattered four plates and half a dozen cups. Almost as good a shot as Rick.

I'd felt pretty pleased about it until Sharkey cast a sly glance in my direction and cinched shut the munitions bag. "Save some for later," he said, with another one of those knowing grins.

Ms. Branneth made a note on her pad. "What happened after that, Miss Marks?"

What happened after that was that Rick kissed me. Long and hard and sweet. The sky draped over us like darkest blue velvet, spattered with tiny diamonds and a halo of gold from the distant lights of the strip. I saw it still when I closed my eyes, strewn across my mind, and beautiful.

The music of the desert night rose around us, faint peeps and whirs, a world alive beneath our feet. My heart thrummed, and the roughened skin of Rick's fingers brushed the base of my neck, raising goosebumps and making me shiver with pleasure.

When we pulled apart, Rick squeezed my hand and announced, "Now for something you'll *really* like."

I looked at Ms. Branneth. "That's when things got weird," I said.

Somewhere on the other side of the sturdy door, I heard the faint echo of hearty laughter and pictured the unfortunate souls stuck working on New Year's Day. They'd be gathered around a table of goodies, guzzling apple cider and swapping stories, ignoring the stacks of paperwork mounding up on their desks.

This side of the door, the muscles in my backside stiffened and protested. I'd been sitting in this hard, ergonomically-indifferent chair for hours and I needed to get up and stretch. Instead, I powered through, told my own story, and braced myself for the reaction. The finely chiseled face of the woman opposite me registered first confusion and then amused derision.

"I know, right?" I said. "That's why they wouldn't tell me anything. There's no real way to put it into words. It sounds ridiculous." I paused. "The truth is, it was surprisingly fun. Exhilarating, in fact."

"I guess I'm missing the point," Ms. Branneth said, her voice chilly. "Explain it to me again."

Friends since childhood, Rick and Sharkey had developed a unique way to celebrate the New Year, beginning when Sharkey got his first driver's license and growing into an unbreakable tradition. I couldn't fathom every nuance of the ritual, but I gave my counselor a rough outline, as I knew it.

"It starts, every year, at the local Goodwill," I said, "with the selection of the ceremonial bowling ball. Then after dark, but with a few hours to spare before ringing in the New Year, they head out into the open desert. No people, no buildings, just dirt roads and cactus."

"Right, I get it," Ms. Branneth said, making an impatient rolling gesture with her hand, light sparking off the topaz ring like the butt end of a lit cigarette. "You're all responsible citizens, avoiding damage to persons or property. Maybe you'll get a medal."

I ignored her sarcasm. "After a little target practice—for fun—they get to the main event."

"And this is where you lost me."

"I'll try to describe it better," I told her, "but you really have to be there to understand the appeal. The driver finds a straight stretch of road and gets the car going really fast while the passenger holds the bowling ball at the ready, poised outside the open window. When the driver slams on the brakes, the passenger launches the bowling ball."

"Whoopie," Ms. Branneth said. "Is that it?"

"No, that's not it. Then you follow the bouncing ball, and it's *wild*. Who knew a bowling ball could leap so high? It rolls across the desert hills and disappears down into the dips and you think you've lost it and then, all of a sudden, it vaults into the sky half a mile away, in a completely different direction. It goes and goes and *goes!*"

She stared at me, one eyebrow lifted, utterly unimpressed.

"Really," I admitted, "it loses something in translation."

"I won't argue the point." She fluttered the pages of the file in front of her. "You claimed the police pulled you over at some point. When did that happen?"

"I think we'd launched the ball four or five times, so it was probably about eleven o'clock. I guess they'd seen our headlights bobbing around crazily while we chased the bowling ball. They must have figured us for a carful of drunks."

"Did they ticket you?"

"No ma'am."

"*Ms.* Branneth, please."

"No, Ms. Branneth. They separated us and questioned us individually. Of course, we all told the same story and when we finished, the cops were laughing so hard they could barely stand. Said it beat all, and wished us a happy new year."

My counsel, the woman assigned to fight for me in court, closed the file folder and leaned over it, her lips forming a hard, straight line, every sparkle of bronze lip-liner doused within their confines.

"Miss Marks, you do a passable job of presenting your intentions as benign, just a group of friends out for a night of harmless fun. But prosecution will shred you to bits on the witness stand."

"All I'm trying to—" Ms. Branneth slammed a palm against the manila folder, silencing me.

"A man has been hospitalized in serious condition, his political career in tatters. A woman is suffering emotional trauma and the probable end of her career, as well. An automobile has been destroyed, burnt down to the bare metal frame on a patch of scorched earth the size of an Olympic swimming pool."

I opened my mouth, but she made a chopping motion, cutting me off.

"The report I've read beggars belief," she continued, one index finger tensed against the manila cover, pressing down hard enough to turn the skin a pale pink. "Will you please explain how we went from bowling for cactus to a flaming car bomb."

"Well," I said cautiously, dipping a toe in to see if it was really my turn to speak. "It was almost midnight when the cops drove off—about fifteen minutes to the new year. Rick handed me a pair of goggles and told me to put them on, then he and Sharkey opened the munitions bag."

"Now we're getting somewhere."

I squirmed in my chair, feeling a cramp in my left buttock. I really needed a break but we were coming down to the crux of the matter.

"Look, I know it sounds bad," I pleaded, "but it's just part of the whole tradition. The big bang at midnight to bring in the new year and a glorious goodbye to the old bowling ball. It's almost like they're custom-crafted for the occasion, with the pre-drilled finger holes and all. Rick and Sharkey have repeated the same process for six previous years and no harm done."

Ms. Branneth stared. "Are you telling me that when the report comes back from the lab, it will identify the remains of the incendiary device that fried Senator Whitfield's car as a Goodwill bowling ball?"

I crossed my arms and shrugged. Bowling ball, yes. I doubted the report would detail the thrift store provenance of the missile.

Ms. Branneth gave me a sardonic smile and applauded. "What a fantastic story. And by that, I mean verging on fantasy. Can anyone corroborate this desert escapade? Any witnesses to this bizarre ritual?"

I slumped in my chair. If this was the reaction of my own defense attorney, I dreaded to imagine how a jury would respond. The desert that night had been wide open and empty, all sensible people gathered within the city lights, ready to kiss and sip champagne at the stroke of midnight.

But there had been witnesses. Two of them.

"Policemen make good witnesses, don't they? What about the two cops who pulled us over for questioning."

"Those two would make fine witnesses," she agreed with a tight smile. "Do you remember their names, badge numbers, patrol car identifier, anything?"

"No, but surely there's a record of our encounter—"

"If," said Ms. Branneth, stabbing a finger into the air to emphasize the point before lowering her voice to a silky whisper. "*If* the encounter happened, I've found no record of it. I've searched every database that might claim jurisdiction over that patch of sand."

My heart dropped to the bottom of my rib cage, beating sluggishly like a dying fish. I had only one thing left to say.

"My rear end's asleep. I feel like I'm sitting on pins and needles. Can you unlock me, let me walk around a bit?"

She made a moue of disgust. "Do you understand the depth of trouble you're in, young lady?" She rose from the chair. "Your actions—intentionally or otherwise—sent a burning projectile through the windshield of a United States Sen—"

"Good thing they were in the back seat then, wasn't it? Is it our fault the Senator is too cheap to spring for a hotel when he picks up a call girl?" I held up my hands. "Honest, I really need to get off this chair. And can I get some water, please?"

Ms. Branneth pursed her lips, a look of weariness settling over her Egyptian princess features. I was not helping her career. Sighing, she walked to the door and gave a sharp rap. Outside in the corridor, several voices were yukking it up and I wondered how long before I'd feel like laughing again.

After a moment, a uniformed officer poked his head in, visibly trying to wipe a smile off his face. "Yo, Counselor. What can I do for you?"

"Would you bring a cup of water and maybe one of those pastries I saw when I came in earlier."

"Sure thing, only you might want to come get it yourself. There're a couple of cruiser cops out here with a story you don't want to miss. One for the record books."

He let out a hoot as the door shut behind him. Ms. Branneth shot me a look and went after him. I sat, still shackled to the table, and struggled to manage my hopes and expectations. Straining my ears, eager to hear some fragments from the hallway, I shifted from one buttock to the other, trying to work out the numbness.

Ten long minutes ticked by before she returned, leaving the door open and trailing two officers behind her, each with a familiar face.

"Yep, that's her," one of them confirmed, giving me a grin. "The bowling ball girl."

Ms. Branneth skewered the officers with a stern look. "If you had put a stop to their ridiculous shenanigans, Senator Whitfield wouldn't be bedded down at Centennial Hills hospital with third degree burns."

"No, ma'am," said the officer who'd questioned me last night. "But evidence suggests he'd be bedded down somewhere, with *something*."

More guffawing from the corridor. Before the laughter stopped, a tall woman in a navy pantsuit pushed through the doorway. "That's a safe bet," the newcomer agreed. "Besides, the media's been exaggerating the reports. Whitfield has a third-degree burn on *one* finger and minor burns on the rest of the hand. He's hiding in the hospital to dodge the press."

"And his wife, Chief," someone shouted from the hallway.

The chief acknowledged the comment with a wry nod. "I just talked with our crime scene unit," she continued, adjusting the scarf at her neck with unconscious grace, "and they tell me the car wouldn't have exploded and burned so merrily if there hadn't been an open case of vodka in the front seat."

"My firefighter buddy said it burned a nice, clean blue," said one of the policemen. "Pretty as a Christmas tree."

"But he'll lose his senate seat over this," protested Ms. Branneth.

"Hear, hear!" shouted the men in the corridor, toasting each other with mugs of cider.

My diminutive counselor, dwarfed by the swirl of activity around her, retreated to a corner of the interrogation room. No one had taken it upon themselves to release me from the chains that held me bound, but from my position I had a good view of Ms. Branneth's face.

I watched it change from consternation, to resignation, and finally to delight. She turned, graceful as a jewelry-box ballerina, and approached my table, chin up, queenly demeanor in sharp evidence. Dropping back into her chair, she reached across and took my hand.

"I believe I have all the pieces I need to make a winning case, Miss Marks. Congratulations. It looks like you might finish that college degree, after all."

"Great!" I gave her the brightest smile I could muster and jangled my chains. "Now, could someone please let me out of this chair?"

Thank you for reading *Crimes Upon a Midnight Clear.*

If you enjoyed the book, I would love for you to leave a review to help other readers find and enjoy it, too. Thank you so much for taking the time to share your opinion.

If you haven't yet joined my readers' group, you're just a click away from VIP access to bonuses and updates.

Visit https://joslynchase.com or scan the QR code.

I'd love to welcome you aboard!

Scan here for more books by Joslyn Chase

SAMPLE FROM STEADMAN'S BLIND

PROLOGUE

Fifty-eight miles south of Seattle, Mt. Rainier rises to meet the clouds. Reigning queen of the landscape, she symbolizes the pristine beauty of the Pacific Northwest, robed in emerald, and crowned with diamond-sparkling snow, the graceful sweep of her slopes soaring up to draw the eye and gladden the heart.

But the benevolent appearance of the mountain masks a deadly and volatile might.

Within the reach of that power, communities nestle. Secure in the belief that life today will continue as it did yesterday, and the day before, and for so many days before that, people build houses, elect officials, establish commerce, and do all manner of things to create a haven for themselves and their loved ones.

While deep below Rainier's surface, a river of molten rock pushes up against the stratified layers, fracturing the bed of stone into splinters and sending tremors through the mountain and surrounding areas. For thousands of years, torrents of rain and melting snow have mixed with sulphuric acid, seeping into the rock, altering it into a crumbling clay-like substance, unstable and susceptible to landslides.

Fifty-six hundred years ago, Rainier's eastern flank blew sky high in the great Osceola mudslide, covering 212 square miles in a thick, acidic sludge, obliterating every living thing.

Now her western side is primed to go.

Early in the summer, the volcano woke like a fussy baby after a long nap, burping and bawling, grabbing everyone's attention, and mobilizing politicians, the media, and emergency response teams to prepare for a major catastrophe. For months, regal Rainier has entertained her surrounding human subjects like an eccentric hostess at a cocktail party. Trembling, grumbling, puffing smoke—fierce and lively one moment, silent and sulking the next.

In her shadow, life continues. People sleep through the night, get up, and go to work. Families argue, play, walk the dog, and love each other. Like the story of the boy who cried wolf, people find it easier and easier to ignore Rainier's dramatics as everyday life reclaims them. Politicians give in to pressure from loggers and business owners losing revenue due to road closures. Government agencies run out of money for maintaining watches and road blocks. Life in Seattle and surrounding communities returns to business as usual.

Only a handful of scientists and researchers remain vigilant and concerned.

They gauge the tremors beneath her, noticing how her shape is changing, like the burgeoning of a woman preparing to give birth. She is distending under the building pressure within, equalized only by the yards-thick layer of snow pack pressing down from without. They worry that the icy shell is cracking, destabilized by the earthquakes and the heat of the magma as it travels up into the throat of the volcano. They fear that a few degrees more, and the coat of snow will slide down the mountainside like butter off a hotcake, triggering an avalanche of unparalleled proportions.

They know what will happen next. The enormous weight rolling off Rainier's western shoulder will allow the inexorable pressure of gas and hot rock to spurt forth, uncontained, blowing aside the weak, altered rock in a savage eruption with a power 7500 times greater than the atomic blast at Hiroshima.

A poisonous plume of ash and gas will rise into a hideously exaggerated mushroom cloud extending miles into the sky, where the negatively charged ash will clash violently with the positively charged gas to spawn a hellish network of lightning bolts and streaking balls of fire.

It will be the deadliest day in American history—ending lives, changing lives, reminding people how precious life is.

And how precarious.

Chapter 1

Chief Deputy Randall Steadman set his jaw and ground his teeth together. Fear wrestled against frustration somewhere behind his belt buckle, stirring up a queasy tightness in his gut. For miles in front of him, traffic inched forward on streets crammed to capacity, allowing him to experience the full joys of a Portland rush hour, complete with rude hand gestures, honking horns, and blaring car stereos.

He itched to flip on the light bar and clear a path, but he wasn't behind the wheel of his service vehicle and he was out of uniform and out of his jurisdiction. He'd made the three-hour drive south after a frantic phone call from his sister.

A phone call that left him cold.

Nan was a pretty put-together gal. Whatever happened down here in Oregon had spooked her good and that scared Steadman. He'd relied on his big sister for most of his life, and now it was plain she was relying on him. For reasons that went deep—beyond standard sibling solidarity—he could not let her down.

The late summer sun beat down through the windshield of his car, canceling out the efforts of his air conditioner, and the engine temperature gauge was creeping higher than he liked to see. He switched off the AC and powered down the windows, resigned to suffering through until traffic picked up again. According to the GPS, he only had two-and-a-half miles to go before he reached the hospital.

The hospital.

Nan hadn't told him why she'd chosen that as their meeting place and she hadn't left him time to ask, but Steadman knew it couldn't be good. He dreaded what he might find when he got there. A sudden gust of diesel fumes from a truck up ahead permeated the air and Steadman felt like he might suffocate—from the smell, from the heat, from the anxious stone that pressed down inside his chest.

Whatever this was, whatever tragedy Nan faced, it surely couldn't be as bad as his gut was making it out to be.

Could it?

The red light blinked to green and Steadman let off the brake, moving forward enough to get a slight breeze across his sweaty brow. Another ten minutes and the robotic GPS voice let him know he was arriving at his destination. He pulled into the first parking spot he came across, not caring how far he had to walk. He needed that time to decompress and prepare.

Nan had texted him a room number. After checking in at the front desk, he caught the elevator up to the third floor and passed a nurse's station where a solitary head bent over a stack of medical files. The hallway was deserted. Only the smell of rubbing alcohol lingered there, following him as he made his way down the corridor to stop outside room 324.

He took a deep breath and let it trickle out, readying himself to push open that door and be strong for his sister. But before he could reach out a hand, the door swept inward and Steadman was staring at two cops in uniform. They hesitated, looking him over, and Steadman knew what they were thinking. It was all the things he would be thinking, the way you get after years on the job.

Nan pushed between them and folded Steadman in a tight embrace.

"I knew you'd get here quick," she said.

He pulled away enough to look her in the face. A reddened lump swelled beside her right temple, and the eye was shadowed by bruises, black turning purple.

"What happened?" he asked. "Were you in a car accident? Is Hank okay?"

Steadman looked beyond her to the hospital bed, swathed in sheets and shadows. The sleeping form was her husband, Hank, and Steadman got a quick impression of tubes. Lots of tubes.

Nan closed her teeth over her lips in that bulldog way she had and Steadman saw a pleading look in her eyes before her gaze dropped away. He noticed she was shivering.

"This is my brother, Chief Deputy Randall Steadman," she told the policemen. "He drove down from the Seattle area."

Steadman shook their hands, and they exchanged professional courtesies before he turned back to Nan and lifted his fingers to her damaged cheek.

"What happened?" he repeated.

There was a pause before she answered. "It wasn't a car accident," she said. "We were attacked."

"Attacked? What—"

"I'm sorry, Rand." She staggered under his grip and raised a shaky hand to her throat. "I really need some coffee and something to eat." She turned to the officers. "If there's nothing else you need from me, I think I'll go to the cafeteria."

"Of course, Mrs. Meninger. We'll be in touch."

They nodded their goodbyes and left. Nan clutched Steadman's arm as she watched the policemen stride down the corridor. He felt her tremble like a sapling in a windstorm, but she didn't speak until the men stopped at the elevator and punched the call button.

"I'll go get my purse," she whispered. "We need to talk."

Chapter 2

Nan's cup of coffee sat untouched on the table in front of her, the rising tendrils of vapor waning as it grew cold. Steadman watched her face, the leaden lump in his stomach growing with each moment that passed. She was tough, his sister, and the bones of her skull stood out under pallid skin like a Mt. Rushmore monument, solid and unmoving. But there was fear in her eyes, tinged with despair. That alarmed him, and the swelling at her temple and blackened eye sent anger swirling through his growing sense of dread.

"Tell me what happened, Nan," he prompted. "When, where, and—if possible—who."

A wash of color came into her face, and he was relieved to see there was still some spirit left in her.

"Oh, I know who well enough," she said, her voice shot through with acid. "They made no effort to disguise themselves."

"Did you tell the police?"

She pressed her lips together, blanching them white. Her nostrils flared as she drew a breath through her nose. "I did not."

The heavy lump in his gut sank. "What's going on, Nan? I guess you've got a lot to tell me, but first I want to know about Hank. How bad is it?"

She closed her eyes, face twisting as she wrestled her emotions. Steadman covered her shaking hand with his own and waited. Almost a minute passed before she swallowed hard and opened her mouth to speak.

"They kicked him. Two bastards taking turns with their heavy boots." Her voice went squeaky, and she paused, taking a deep breath. "He's got four cracked ribs, a broken arm, a broken nose, and a ruptured spleen. He lost three teeth and his face is unrecognizable. He'll never again be the pretty boy I married."

Steadman squeezed her hand. Bad as it was, he had feared worse. "Well, Nan," he said, hoping to lighten the mood, "that ship sailed a long time ago."

She gave him a weak smile. "Don't I know it. But—" A little sob escaped her lips and she bit down hard, staunching the flow. "I love him so much, Rand."

"I know, Sis. I know."

A loud clatter reverberated through the room as an attendant deposited a load of clean trays into a rack at the head of the cafeteria line. Steadman watched an elderly couple pry one from the top of the stack and begin working their shaky way along the path of options, consulting each other with every choice. Hank and Nan would grow old together like that—sweet to each other, caring, united.

He turned his gaze back to Nan. "Hank will be okay, then. His prognosis is good, right?"

Her lips thinned to a grim line and again he saw that spark of color come into her face.

"He'll survive. Until they come for him again."

"Why would they do that, Nan? Who are these guys?"

"They're sharks."

"You mean, like loan sharks."

She nodded. "Yes, and worse. I'm not sure what all they're into, but they're bad news."

"How on earth did Hank get mixed up with them?"

She sighed. "You know Ronnie's in his second year at MIT."

Steadman stared at her. "Hank borrowed college funds from a loan shark?"

She leveled that big sister glare at him across the table. "He's not stupid, Rand. It didn't happen like you think. Hank got sucked in, little by little, by pros who know just where to put the pressure."

Despite the anxiety that gnawed at his gut, Steadman admired Nan for standing by her man. They might be going down, but they were going down together. He hoped he could find a way to throw them a lifeline.

"Start at the beginning, Nan," he said, trying to keep his voice free from any trace of judgment, "and put me in the picture."

She canted her lower lip and blew out a frustrated sigh that reached her bangs, fluttering them as it passed. "As you know, Hank's a night manager at the Hilton. In the course of his business, he became aware that these guys were running an illegal high-stakes poker game from their hotel suite. Their leader is a man they call Honest Abe, and no one even tries to keep a straight face about it. He offered Hank a thousand dollars to look the other way."

She broke off, swirls of red staining her cheeks. "It sounds terrible, the way I put it," a pleading note crept into her voice, "but you've got to understand there was a lot going on for us. We were squeezed pretty tight with no room to breathe or see our way clear. Car broke down, late on the mortgage, bills coming due, and time to pay another round of tuition. College costs more than a house, these days. Hank thought it would be a onetime deal. He let it slide."

Steadman saw all too clearly where this was going. It was like letting the camel put one foot inside the tent. Pretty soon you've got the whole animal on your lap and you're drowning in sand.

"I can see the wheels churning inside your head, Rand, and whatever you're thinking, it's probably not far off the mark. The games continued, the payouts got bigger, and by the time Hank realized how deep he was in, he couldn't get out. He was complicit. So when they stopped paying him there was nothing he could do about it. They had him by the balls."

Steadman grimaced. "Ouch. So why'd they beat him up? Did he end up ratting them out?"

Nan clenched her fists on the table in front of her, nearly spilling the cup of congealing coffee.

"I only wish he had. No, we'd come to count on that extra money, and when they stopped paying for Hank's silence, it hurt. But Abe wasn't finished with Hank. He brought him into his fancy suite, buttered him up, told him the hush money had stopped because he was one of them now, part of the team, and he was welcome at the table. They'd even stake him the first game."

Steadman groaned. "You've got to be kidding. What the hell was he thinking, Nan?"

She scowled at him, her teeth going up over her lip in that classic Nan expression of stubborn annoyance.

"You don't know these guys. They're urbane and charismatic. Car salesman types that can convince you they're your best pal while they're sizing you up for a coffin. Hank figured it wouldn't hurt to play that first game, with their money. He cleaned up, too. Brought home a pile, that night."

Steadman snorted. "Naturally, Nan. That's how it's done. He was hooked, right?"

She sighed. "By the nose. They sucked him dry, and then some." She rubbed at a spot on her forehead with two shaking fingers. "We're putting the house on the market and hoping it sells before they come back to break Hank's legs."

"Oh heavens, Nan," Steadman felt a vein of cold misery spreading through him. "Why didn't you tell the police?"

She gave him a pointed look. "That's the first thing they warned us about. Told us they had police protection, key officers on the payroll, and it would only go harder on us if we squealed."

Steadman swallowed and tossed through his mental inventory for some way to bring her comfort.

"They're not going to hurt you so bad you can't cough up the money. They want you operational, Nan. It sounds like they're giving you some sort of deadline?"

"Six weeks. They said if we didn't pay up in six weeks, Hank's a dead man."

He patted her hand. "They're not going to kill him, Sis. That's just to scare you."

Her face crumpled, and she bit her lip, silent tears spilling from her reddened eyes. She brushed them off and stared across the table at Steadman, her jaw hardening.

"Jeb Openshaw, the man Hank replaced at the hotel—he died in a hit-and-run accident. A newspaper clipping about the incident was left in an envelope on Hank's desk. If they don't get their money, they cut their losses and make an example."

Steadman saw the shudder that ran through her. He moved his chair next to hers and wrapped his arms around her, rocking her, wondering what the hell his next move should be. After a few moments, she pulled away and smoothed the hair back from her face, sitting taller in her chair, chin lifted.

"I spent a lot of time thinking," she said. "While Hank was in surgery, while I waited beside his broken body for you to arrive." She speared Steadman with her big sister gaze.

"And I came up with a plan."

Chapter 3

Newly christened Detective Cory Frost tried balancing his breakfast in one hand while pulling open the door to the training room with the other. The two slabs of peanut butter toast were no problem, held firmly together, face to face, and wrapped in a paper towel. And the pint of chocolate milk rested firmly against his wrist. It was the orange that defeated him.

He lost his grip on the soft-ball-sized fruit and it bounced, then rolled into the path of a sergeant in a hurry who kicked it back in Frost's direction.

"Sorry about that," Frost mumbled, bending down to retrieve the orange.

The notebook tucked beneath his elbow slid down the side of his uniform trousers and splayed open on the floor. He sighed. Picking it up, he used it as a tray and arranged the breakfast items on top, except for the orange, which he tried to cram into the pocket of his jacket. Again, it escaped him, but he managed to scoop it from the air before it hit the floor, bringing him into a crouching position like a catcher at home plate.

Before he could rise, a shapely pair of ankles appeared in front of his face.

"That's some impressive juggling, Detective. Do you do birthday parties?"

He stood, feeling his face go hot. The uniformed woman regarding him with an expression half scorn, half amusement, was a heart-stopper. Glowing, cocoa complexion, glossy dark hair cascading in a smooth sweep over a perfect brow, lips a cover girl would kill for. Frost stared.

The woman raised an eyebrow. "I'll hold the door for you," she said, reaching for the handle, "but I get half the orange."

Frost froze like a deer in the headlights. Not a single clever response came to him, but he was saved from saying something stupid when the door burst open, nearly knocking them down, and Sheriff Polander glared at the both of them.

"Hurry it up, people. We're about to start."

Frost waggled his eyebrows, getting a grin in return. He held tight to his breakfast and stepped into the room after the woman, getting another glimpse of her stunning figure. His heart sank when he saw the crowded tables with no two seats together. He'd started to imagine sharing his day—as well as his orange—with his captivating colleague, but they were forced apart, to opposite sides of the room. He took a seat at the front table to the left of the podium and laid out his items, noticing that the woman was across the aisle and well behind him.

He hadn't seen her before, but he was brand new in the detective division and still had a lot of people to meet. In the brief moment he'd been with her, he noticed she wore no ring on her left hand and the name on her tag was longish and started with a J. And she was gorgeous and witty and...

He crushed a mental boot down on these thoughts. He needed to reclaim his focus, get his head in the right place or he'd end up back in Patrol for another rotation. He'd worked hard for this promotion and it jazzed him to be part of Investigations. He opened his notebook and wrote the date at the top of the page, ready to record the salient points of the training.

"Jamieson!"

The sheriff bellowed the name to the back rows. "Did Chief Deputy Steadman come over with you?"

"No, sir." Frost recognized her voice and turned in his seat. Jamieson.

"He's on emergency leave," she continued. "Had a family issue down in Portland."

"Why am I just hearing about this now? He's supposed to give the potential hazard report."

"Yes sir, I know. He asked me to apologize, and he prepped me to do it."

"Is that right?" The sheriff took a sip of coffee. "I want you here up front, then. Dooley," he gestured to Frost's table mate. "Trade places with Jamieson, if you would."

"Sure thing, Sheriff."

And just like that, Frost was sitting next to the most beautiful girl in the room, trying to listen and stay focused on the subject at hand. His peanut butter toast went untouched, cold and forgotten.

But he peeled the orange, keeping the skin intact, and laid a perfect half on top, sliding it in her direction like a supplicant's offering to his goddess.

Chapter 4

Steadman choked on a mouthful of lukewarm coffee, getting half of it down, spewing half of it back into the cup. He coughed, working to clear his throat so he could spit some words out, though he had no idea what he might say. The suggestion his sister had just made was the most ridiculous thing he'd ever heard.

"There's no need to be so dramatic about it, Rand," she chided, handing him a napkin. "It's a pragmatic plan that has a good chance of working."

"In what universe?" Steadman asked, his head reeling. "I don't play poker, Nan."

"Yes, but how hard can it be?" she countered. "For you, I mean. You're trained to observe and interpret body language. You know when people are lying, all the little things they do to give themselves away. Nobody can bluff you."

He stared at her. "Nan, this isn't television. Poker is a whole different thing and—listen carefully because here's the important part—I don't play it. I barely know a full house from a straight flush."

"But you can learn. You live right around the corner from that big casino. You can do some research on the internet and practice the skills at your friendly neighborhood poker tables."

"For Pete's sake, woman—have you gone insane?"

Steadman felt a pressure building inside his chest. He took a deep breath and let it roll out of him, rubbing the muscles at the back of his neck in an effort to relax.

"Nan, I understand you're upset and worried, and you have every right to be. You're looking for solutions to what feels like an insurmountable problem. I get that. But this plan sounds like a recipe for even more trouble. I can't believe—"

"Rand, just shut up for a minute. I told myself all these same things while I sat in a cold, hard hospital chair waiting for my husband to come out of surgery after being beaten within an inch of his life. These are very bad men, playing a whole lot of angles, and the only way to escape this is to beat them at their own game—and that's poker."

Steadman sighed and dropped his head to rest in the palm of his hand. How did she still have this ability to reduce him to younger brother status, reminding him she was in charge?

"It takes money, Nan, to win at poker," he pointed out. "And we don't have any."

She was nodding. "I know. I had mom's jewelry appraised when this whole mess started. I hoped I wouldn't have to sell, but I can get close to six thousand dollars for it. You can take that to the local casino and parlay it into a bigger stake. Hank said the buy-in at Bernie's table is ten thousand."

She really had been thinking about this, scrambling to cover all the bases.

"This'll be second nature to you, Rand," she continued. "I know it will. I heard you telling Hank about that non-verbal communication seminar you attended in San Diego. Four days, Rand. Four days of intensive training so you can read the unintentional signals people give off. If anyone can do this, it's you, little brother." She dropped her hand over his and squeezed. "And you're the only one who cares about me enough to even try."

And there it was, Nan going for the heart string, twanging away on familial duty, love, and the ever-powerful chord of guilt. They both knew she still held an ace up her sleeve, a card she could play with perfect assurance he'd comply. A card with Thad's name on it.

He wouldn't make her do that. Reaching that deep into a painful memory would leave a gash in both of them that might never heal. He dug the palms of his hands into his eyes and rubbed, hardly believing the sentence that was forming on his lips.

"You sell mom's jewels, Nan, and I'll see what I can do about learning some poker."

As he spoke the words, he made a promise to himself as well. He'd do some digging behind the scenes. There had to be another way around this problem.

If you enjoyed this sample, you'll love where *Steadman* goes from here. Grab the book and enjoy the ride!

ABOUT THE AUTHOR

Joslyn Chase is a prize-winning author of mysteries and thrillers. Any day where she can send readers to the edge of their seats, chewing their fingernails to the nub and prickling with suspense, is a good day in her book.

Joslyn's story, "Cold Hands, Warm Heart," was chosen by Amor Towles as one of the *Best Mystery Stories of the Year 2023* and "A Band of Scheming Women" was a finalist for the Derringer Award in 2025. The second book in the Riley Forte Suspense Thriller series, *Staccato Passage,* was chosen as a semi-finalist for the Adventure Writer's Grandmaster Award in 2025, as well.

Her short stories have appeared in *Alfred Hitchcock's Mystery Magazine, Malice Domestic's Mystery Most Devious, Thrill Ride Magazine, Fiction River, Mystery, Crime, and Mayhem, Mystery Magazine,* and *Pulphouse Fiction,* among others.

Known for her fast-paced suspense fiction, Joslyn's books are full of surprising twists and delectable turns. You will find her riveting novels most anywhere books are sold.

Her love for travel has led Joslyn to ride camels through the Nubian desert, fend off monkeys on the Rock of Gibraltar, and hike the Bavarian Alps. But she still believes that sometimes the best adventures come in getting the words on the page and in the thrill of reading a great story.

Join the growing group of readers who've discovered the thrill of Chase! Sign up for Joslyn's readers' group and get VIP access to great bonuses—like your free copy of *No Rest: 14 Tales of Chilling Suspense*—as well as updates and first crack at new releases.

Visit joslynchase.com to get started now!

bookbub.com/authors/joslyn-chase

facebook.com/joslynchasewriter

goodreads.com/author/show/16850235.Joslyn_Chase

linkedin.com/in/joslynchase/

pinterest.com/joslynchase/

youtube.com/@joslynchase5955/videos

www.ingramcontent.com/pod-product-compliance
Lightning Source LLC
Chambersburg PA
CBHW010642190726
48289CB00009B/2812